Love and Other Wild Things

Love and Other Wild Things

Alyson Root

SAPPHIRE BOOKS

SALINAS, CALIFORNIA

Editor - Tara Young
Book Design - LJ Reynolds
Cover Design - Fineline Cover Design

Sapphire Books Publishing, LLC
P.O. Box 8142
Salinas, CA 93912
www.sapphirebooks.com

Printed in the United States of America
First Edition – February 2024

This and other Sapphire Books titles can be found at
www.sapphirebooks.com

Dedication

FOR ANGELIQUE, MA RAISON D'ÊTRE. JE T'AIME.

FOR ANGELIQUE, MA RAISON D'ÊTRE. JE T'AIME.

Acknowledgments

As always, the first person I have to thank is my wife. No one in my life has supported me the way she does. Effortlessly and unconditionally. It is no lie to say without her guidance and helping hand, I would not be in the position I am today, doing the thing I love for a living.

To Monna Herring, my superstar, as I like to call her. Thank you for always taking the time to listen to my ideas, proof my work, and boost my confidence. You have been with me from my second book, and I'll know you will be with me down the road. I promise to keep the books flowing!

Gloria Umali, thank you for reading my books and giving me the honest feedback I need. I appreciate the time you take out of your busy life to help me deliver the best stories possible.

Last but by no means least, I would like to thank Chris Svendsen (publisher), Tara Young (editor), and everyone else at Sapphire Books Publishing for taking a chance on my manuscript. I can't tell you how grateful I am to work with you. Thank you.

Chapter One

Ellie

"I don't want to do this, Gabe. Not one bit. Do you understand that?" I practically shout into the phone. Gabe Bishop is an asshole of the highest magnitude. I don't care if he's my brother.

"Ellie, come on, this is guaranteed gold." As if that's a valid reason for me to do what he wants. As if disregarding what I want is a valid reason to force me into something I vehemently do not want to do.

"Gabe, I'm the last person on this planet that needs money. I'm thirty-seven and could retire. Actually, I could have retired when I was twenty-five."

"It'll be fun. Come on, your career is in a slump. You need this." Son of a bitch.

"My career is in a slump because you only put me up for the same tired roles. The girl next door should have been shelved ten years ago. I've begged you for grittier roles, but you keep peddling the same crap." As well as being my asshole brother, Gabe is my asshole agent.

"But your face says girl next door. You need to play to your strengths. Your looks won't last forever, you know."

What a fucking tool. Sorry for all the cussing, but this ass drives me to distraction. "My face is going to be saying, 'you're fired,' if you carry on." I will never fire him because the backlash I would get from my mom isn't worth it. Maybe a severe pay cut will do the trick. I might not have full control, but I have some, and I'm not afraid to use it.

"I kind of already sealed the deal, El. Look, it's a month, that's it. You do this show, then afterward, I swear, I'll get you all the dark and arty roles your heart could ever desire."

Breathe, Ellie, breathe. "You made a deal before talking to me." Forewarning, the next part of the conversation is going to get very explicit. "You fucking prick, how fucking dare you do this? The next time I see you, I'm going to take my trusty baseball bat to your nuts, do you hear me? You'll be lucky if you can—"

"Okay, okay, I get you're angry, but that doesn't change anything. You start filming in two weeks. I'll send you over all the details."

"Gabe, I'm from New York. I was raised in a fucking mansion that overlooked Central Park, as were you. I love comfort and nice things. In what world do you think I'm capable of spending a month in the motherfucking jungle?" Let's be honest, he hasn't thought about it at all. He saw the dollar signs and signed on the dotted line.

"New York is called the concrete jungle, and you do pretty well in that." Oh, he's got jokes, brilliant.

"The concrete jungle has a Starbucks on every corner. Restaurants open twenty-four-seven. Is that what I'll get on this show? I don't think so." My life revolves around those kinds of things. That might sound shallow, but it's true. I love and need coffee in my life. I love going to restaurants whenever I want. I do it frequently. What I don't want is to be in the goddamn jungle. I'm a star, for fuck sakes.

"This is the most popular show on TV. Please calm down and see what an opportunity this is. The world wants to see the real Ellie Bishop."

"Then send a camera crew to my house, and I'll happily show the people who I am from the comfort of my own home."

"Ellie, it's done. Get on board."

If I grip this phone any tighter, it's going to explode in my hand. How I wish I could reach through the phone and strangle him. "Send the details over. And FYI, your salary has just taken a fifty percent dip, you dick." Having the last word hasn't even made me feel better, which is a first.

Well, crap! What the hell am I going to do now? I cannot survive for one month in the jungle. Ellie Bishop—that's me—is known for glamour. I'm the actress people want to debut their designs on the red carpet. I'm the actress everyone wants to wear their perfume or designer shoes. I'm a box office wonder. I'm not the actress who bumbles around the jungle in khaki pants—that have a thousand pockets—and chunky walking boots. Dear Lord. This can't be happening.

My phone rings again, and I'm ready to tear whoever it is a new one. Thankfully, I see the name before I answer. "Toni, thank God."

"Hey, honey, what's up?" Toni Fresh—yes, that is her birth name—is my best friend. We met on the set of my very first show when I was ten and she was fifteen. We bonded over long days, early call times, and the very attractive coffee cart woman. I was in awe of her when she came out a few years later and proceeded to ask out that very cute coffee cart woman.

"Gabe." I don't need to say any more. Toni gets it.

"What did that douche do now? Will you please just fire him?"

"Do you know the torrent of shit I would get if I did that?" I'm not exaggerating. Even from three thousand miles away, my mom can make me feel… Ugh, no, no, no. I can't start that train of thought now. My therapist is in the Bahamas, and I don't have enough medication in the house to dose myself numb.

"Well, tell Toni what he's done."

"I hate it when you talk in the third person, T, it's weird." It is, right?

"Ellie, spit it out."

"He's signed me up for the next season of *Wild Celebrities*. I start filming in two weeks. In the jungle. In the jungle, Toni!" The line is silent. Did she hang up? I check the screen. Nope, she's still there. Then the hysterical laughter starts. And it doesn't stop for a good five minutes. I put the phone on the side and leave her to calm down while I pour a large glass of wine. I down that and pour another.

"Oh, damn." She finally gasps. I'm a third of the way into my second glass by now.

"Yeah, oh, damn, indeed." My original boiling anger is now a simmering rage. Is that better or worse?

"He can't be serious. You! In the jungle? Ellie Bishop who needs a caramel frap with skimmed milk three times a day and weekly pedicures?"

"Yup, me." I pour myself a third glass and wait for the second round of raucous laughter to die down. I'm pleased she finds it so funny. When I'm not seething, maybe I'll find the funny side. Maybe not.

"Ellie, you can't, honey."

"I have zero choice. The sneaky toad has sealed the deal. I wouldn't like to imagine how much it would cost me to buy myself out of the contract." Honestly, it's not the money, it's the optics. If Gabe signed, I guarantee he's already hot on the marketing. Which means that too many people know I'm committed. It'll look so bad if I back out now, and the last thing I want is to be known as a troublesome person to work with or a flake. I've sculpted my reputation for years. I work hard, and I try to be easy. It doesn't take very much in this industry to wreck all that and become known as a diva.

"Which jungle?" Toni laughs. She's going to get something really shitty for Christmas. She's enjoying this way too much.

"No clue. I presume it'll be on the paperwork."

"Will you need shots?"

"What for?"

"You know, diseases and stuff. Don't jungle mosquitoes kill or something?" Wonderful, just to add to the nightmare that is this show, I now need to worry about dying from a bug bite.

"I can't do this, Toni, I can't." Panic and anxiety are now coursing through my body. I put the wine down and stick my head between my legs. I can feel the room closing in on me.

"Hey, hey, hey. Breathe, Ellie, just breathe. I'm on my way over." Toni puts the phone down before I have the chance to answer. *Deep breaths, come on, El, you can do this, calm down.* It's been a long time since I've had a panic attack. I don't want to start now. I sit up and take in my surroundings. Focusing on the items I can see dotted around my living room helps me calm down. It's the familiarity. It's also the thing my therapist told me to do.

"El?" Toni shouts from downstairs. Harold, my housekeeper, must have let her in. Seconds later, she strides into the room in all her six-foot glory. There was a time when I had a major crush on Toni, back when I was a baby gay and was struggling with hormones. Toni was—and still is—one of the most beautiful women I have ever met. Think Nordic Viking goddess, and you're close to figuring out how gorgeous she is. It's no wonder she has half of Hollywood clamoring after her.

"T, I'm good, really. You didn't need to rush over."

"I live three houses down, honey." She sits next to me and strokes my back. "Buy your way out of the contract, Ellie. Seriously, it's not worth it."

"I can't." Toni knows I can't. Damn it, Gabe.

"Who's the host this season?" As if that matters.

"I don't know. Look, Gabe literally told me about this like twenty minutes ago."

"All right, but you should have received the details through email. Maybe if you have Colin Berk or Richard Bell, you'll be okay. They're like ex-military or something. They wouldn't let anything happen to you."

"Do you watch it?" Her face grows red. I've caught her. She watches *Wild Celebrities*, Jesus.

"Fine, guilty. I, Toni Fresh, am addicted to *Wild Celebrities*. If you liked penis, you would be too." Toni is bisexual, whereas I am only about the ladies.

"Right, so Richard and—"

"Colin."

"Yeah, Richard and Colin are hot. That's why you watch it?"

"Too fucking right. They spend half the time with no shirts on." Toni fans herself with her hand.

"Fabulous," I deadpan because now, not only do I have to deal with the jungle and killer bugs, I also have to be in close quarters with a sweaty, shirtless man. Toni has opened my laptop and my emails. As promised, Gabe has sent over the paperwork. Toni scans down the documents on the screen.

"Hmm."

"Hmm? What does hmm mean?" I crane my neck to see what she's reading.

"It's not going to be Richard or Colin. The host is named Robin Stuart. Never heard of him."

"Great, I'm getting a newbie." This just gets better.

"Oh, damn, they're sending you to South America. The Amazon, to be specific."

"The Amazon?" My voice has reached the pitch where only dogs can hear me now.

"Yup, and they've listed the shots you have to get. Hep A, typhoid, and yellow fever. Oh, and they recommend you get a malaria one, too." I think I might vomit. I hate needles. I hate all of this. I hate Gabe!

"T, this is too much."

"All right, I know what you need. Come on." Toni stands and drags me to my feet. I'm pulled along to my room and practically shoved in my walk-in closet. "Pick something hot and get dressed. We're going out."

Alcohol, yes! That's what I need: copious amounts of booze so I can forget all about this horror show. "Where are we going?"

"Love P, obviously. Let's get you a lady to dance

with. Between that and a shit ton of alcohol, I think we can get you in a different headspace."

"Temporary headspace, Toni. I still have to do this thing. Robin what's-his-name better be the toughest man alive. He also better know how to build a cabin because I am not sleeping in a tent." Toni laughs at me again, then starts rooting through my clothes. I'm not sure what she's looking for.

"This, wear this." It's my blood-red party dress. It only just covers my ass. "With these," she says, handing me my best pair of Jimmy Choo black patent heels.

"Is this a slutty night out?"

"Yes, Ellie, it is. Get your slut on, honey. I will. God, I could do with a good servicing. Brad just didn't do it for me." Brad Clarence aka Hollywood's "it man" is—or should I say was if that statement is anything to go by—dating Toni for a few months.

"You guys split?" God, I hope so. Brad is a douche. I've never wanted to slap someone so much, and that was after only ten seconds of meeting him. Slimy cockroach. Thinks he's God's gift to women. You know the type.

"Hell, we split two months ago, honey. I was sick of having to finish myself off in the shower. He was a two-pump wonder and then fell asleep." It's my turn to laugh now.

"Life is too short for bad sex," I state.

"Amen, honey." Toni laughs and fist bumps me.

"Hey, sorry I didn't know about you guys splitting." Toni and I haven't had the chance to hang in a while. Thankfully, we've both had projects, but being that busy does eat into close relationships. Honestly, Toni is about the only true friend I have.

It's difficult finding genuine people around here.

"No worries, I get it. You're a boss bitch." Toni continues to rummage through my closet. I'm not sure what she's looking for. I'm a good few inches shorter than she is. Any dress of mine is going to show off her ass and…well, you get the picture.

"So are you, T."

"Yeah, I am. Now shower, shave, and get ready. We are hitting it hard tonight."

⁂

The club is thumping when we arrive. Pulling up in a limo means we don't have to wait in line. Well, my name alone means that, too. Love P is one of my favorite lesbian clubs in L.A. In my late twenties, I went a little crazy and spent nearly every weekend there, savoring all the delicious sapphic delights on offer. Eventually, Toni told me to chill out. I was on the verge of making a name for myself that would have seriously damaged my reputation among the higher-ups in Hollywood. You know, the people who give me jobs.

Now I come here maybe every three months if I'm lucky. The good thing about Love P is the crowd is huge. Plenty of choice. Saying that, though, it's not so easy for me to have a one-night stand. Every woman wants the Ellie Bishop experience, and some of them aren't afraid to sell it to the first paper that offers them a bit of cash.

My dipshit brother did one thing right. He set up a non-disclosure agreement that women have to sign electronically on my phone before they get to sample my goods. Not the most romantic thing in the world to present to a woman, but nine times out of ten, romance isn't on the agenda. I think the NDAs have saved me a few times from getting screwed and not in the way I like.

Toni is already dancing as we walk through the door. The room is a sea of bodies dancing and grinding. The music is deafening, and I love it. We head over to the VIP section. We get a little more privacy there. The section is guarded by security women who honestly scare the shit out of me but also turn me the hell on. I do love a strong woman, especially if she can throw me around a bedroom.

A bottle of champagne is already waiting in a bucket of ice. I waste no time pouring us both a glass and downing the entire thing. I want to be so drunk I don't remember my name. Not the best way to deal with what's going on, but I need it, and so does T. That woman needs to get laid. Hell, I need to get laid.

Three glasses of bubbly later, and we brave the main dance floor. The women here are gorgeous. Sun-kissed beauties as far as the eye can see. So far, no one has caught my attention. Toni has only been dancing for a minute, and already she's got a target. *Go get 'em, T.*

My plan to get wasted and dance with a lovely lady is failing. We've been here for two hours now, and my mind is too fixed on the Amazon-goddamn-jungle! I'm sweaty and gross, and I want to go home. Toni is playing tonsil hockey with a beautiful redhead, so I'll be going home alone. That's fine. The booze is working against me now. It's just upping my anxiety levels, which is fucking worse.

I send Toni a message and tell her I've left. The limo is waiting by the curb. I go to get in, but I'm distracted by a stunning woman waiting in line to get into the club. She's tall, maybe a few inches taller than me. She's toned, as in she has visible muscles. That tank top is great. Her black jeans are tight. I bet her ass is firm. She has long black hair and very blue eyes. Wowzer! I consider going back inside. I'm sure she could distract me for a few hours. No. As much as I would love to get to know that fine specimen of a woman, I need sleep.

Because you know I have to prepare to go to the Amazon-fucking-jungle!

Chapter Two

Robin

"No."

"What do you mean, no? I haven't asked you anything yet."

"But you're going to, and the answer is no."

"Come on, Robin, don't be like that."

The cheek of this guy. He knows damn well why I'm being like this. Every time he asks me for something, I always end up with a shit deal. The last time he asked for a small favour, I ended up in the Arctic for six months. The Arctic is not a fun place to go. Ever!

"No." He won't wear me down, not this time.

"Just hear me out, please." Ugh, he's using his whining little boy voice. I hate it when he does that because nine times out of ten, it works.

"Fine, you have one minute to tell me what you want, and then I'll tell you no for the last time."

"Okay, so you know I signed on to do *Wild Celebrities*."

"Yes." I can see where this is going, and I don't like it one bit.

"Well, I've had a tiny accident, and I can't do it. The problem is we were due to start shooting next month. I need you to fill in for me."

"Nope." I really emphasised the "p" just for

effect.

"Robin, please, I wouldn't ask if I had any other choice."

"What about Dick?"

"You mean Richard?"

"Yeah, but Dick suits his personality better." Richard Bell is an idiot. I can't stand the man. He's one of those guys who thinks he can pull any woman regardless of her sexual orientation. After he came on to me for the millionth time, I introduced my knee to his balls. No one grabs my arse without permission, not even Richard Bell, beloved TV star.

"Okay, I'll give you that. He's a tool. But anyway, he's in the Himalayas on another job. You're my last hope. Please, please, please."

"What accident did you have?"

"Oh, er, it's nothing, really, but I'm out of action for a while." Now my interest is piqued.

"Now, now, Colin. You want my help, don't you? Come on, spill."

"It's just a fracture, nothing to worry about."

"If it's just a fracture, then why are you being weird about it?"

"Jesus, Robin, it's my penis, okay? I fractured my penis." Please hold on whilst I laugh for the next half an hour. "Will you stop laughing, you arsehole?" That makes me laugh harder.

"Okay, okay, sorry. Pray tell how you fractured your penis?" Who knew that was a thing?

"You're the worst, do you know that?" He's trying to sound pissy, but I can hear the chuckle in his voice.

"Yes, I do, but I also know you want me to do this stupid show, so get talking, mate."

"Fine. You know Jill and I have been trying to get pregnant."

"Yup." Bless them. They've been trying for a while. I hate to see the look on Jill's face every time she tells me that another test came back negative.

"Well, with no luck, Jill decided to do some internet research."

"Because everything on the net is one hundred percent accurate."

"Right?" He laughs. I can understand their desperation, though. All they've ever wanted was to become parents. Jill was born to be a mother. When they do have a kid, and I'm positive they will, even if that's through adoption or surrogacy, that baby is going to be the luckiest human alive.

"So she found this article that said trying a few unique positions could help with conceiving. We tried a couple. I can't see how they help, but whatever, Jill wanted to try. Anyway, the last one was complicated. I didn't know my wife was so bendy, to be fair."

"Colin!" Not an image I want in my mind. I certainly don't want to think of Colin's hairy arse in the throes of passion. Gross.

"Sorry. Anyway, we were in position, and Jill started moving. Well, she got a tad enthusiastic at one point, and she moved in the wrong direction. The next thing I know, I have searing pain in my knob. Jill called the ambulance because I thought I was dying. Turns out, I broke my penis. A little operation later, and it's all good, but I can't do anything strenuous for a few weeks."

I'm trying my level best not to burst out in hysterics again. "Wow, that sounds bloody awful. I'm a little sorry I laughed now." I'm not. "I mean, I don't have a todger, and even I just crossed my legs." I really did cross my legs. Ouch!

"Does that mean you'll do the show for me? Please."

"Colin—"

"Rob, you're more qualified than me to do this gig. And what else have you got to do? I know the private security work is done with."

Crap, he's right, I haven't got anything on right now. "Yeah, permanently, I think. The last client was just ridiculous." Rich people suck! Why does money make some people believe they can treat others like dirt?

"Exactly. If you do this, it's just one month with one person and some camera crew. You'll get paid wads of money, giving you time to decide what you want to do next."

The money would be nice. I got paid handsomely for my last security job. It wasn't enough for me to take an extended period of time out, though. If I did the show, I could probably take a break from work for a few months. I have no idea what I want to do with myself. Hell, I don't even know where I want to live. I'm old enough now that I should probably have a house or something. But here I am, still living out of a bag. Jumping from apartment to apartment.

Damn it, he's convinced me. "Fine, I'll help, but I'm not signing anything until I've spoken to the show runners and read through the contract."

"Absolutely, no probs. Can you be in L.A. by tomorrow lunch?"

"Yeah, I'll get packed and fly out. I'm staying with you, so get the spare room ready."

"Jill would kill me if I let you stay anywhere

else."

"Okay, see you tomorrow." *Well, that's that then. Once again, Rob, you did a tremendous job sticking to your guns.* I roll my eyes at myself.

I look around my sparse apartment. I've never lived a life of materialism. All I need is my duffel bag and I'm ready. There's a red eye out of Washington that has availability, so I book myself a seat.

L.A., here I come.

❧ ❧ ❧ ❧

Colin meets me at the arrivals gate. I didn't need to check in my luggage, so I'm one of the first out of the terminal. I last saw Colin Berk three years ago in the UK. He was doing a survival documentary close to where I was working. Colin was in the same regiment as me in the UK until he retired. Once he'd done his duty, he moved to America to be with Jill. They'd met when she was on holiday in Cornwall and Colin was on leave. It was love at first sight for them. Jesus, the amount of times I had to sit there listening to him pine over her was insane. Considering he was a big burly soldier, he didn't half sound soft when he spoke of Jill.

I spent another two years as a Royal Marine Commando before retiring my beret. It was probably the best experience of my life, but it takes a toll. I'd done my bit.

"There she is." His British accent has an American lilt to it now. I'll make a mental note to take the piss out of that later.

"Ah, limp dick, how ya doing?" I couldn't help making the joke. Come on, you would've, too. It's not every day you get to see a man with a knob cast on.

"Low blow, Stuart, low blow."

"Hey, it's the only blow you're going to be getting for a while." I'm hilarious!

"You're an arsehole, Stuart." When we regroup after not seeing each other for a while, it's customary for us to call each other by our last names. Just like we did in the Marines.

"Where's Jill?"

"Cooking. She's bought enough food for half the bloody regiment." I laugh because Jill is a feeder. She loves cooking for the masses, which winds Colin up to no end. Once she threw a block party without telling him beforehand. It was only when he got home to find half the street in his living room that he caught on to what his wife had done.

"Please tell me she's made lasagne?" Her lasagne is to die for.

"Obviously. Come on, let's go. It's gonna take us an hour to get home." Jill and Colin live in Manhattan Beach. I've only visited a handful of times, but it's a beautiful area. Colin only had one stipulation when they were looking for a house, and that was it had to be near the water. We are born water babies, so I get why he needed to be close to the ocean. I can see life here is treating him well. Apart from the broken twig and berries, he looks in good shape.

We roll up to his house twenty minutes later. Colin just likes to make out that L.A. traffic affects him. It doesn't—like at all. Friggin' drama queen. Their home is a stunning three-bedroom made of brick and glass. It's a modern delight, and yes, I'm jealous. Maybe that's why I've never committed to buying a place. I want what they have but can't afford it. One day maybe.

"I'll get your bag. You go in and see Jill." I have no problem with that. I've missed her. I walk in the door, and I'm instantly salivating. The smell of Jill's cooking is out of this world good.

"Jilly Bean, where are you, woman?" I hear her laugh as I walk into the kitchen. Jill stands there in all her five-foot glory. Colin and I are near six feet, so she's used to craning her neck to look at us. Jill has beautiful gold hair that hangs down her back. Being a native to the West Coast means she has a permanent tan. I'm pasty as fuck compared to her. Casper is a favourite nickname Jill likes to roll out now and then.

"Get your ass over here, Robin." We hug, and I pick her up as usual. She squeals and then bats me to put her down. I stand there looking her up and down for a second. There's something different about her, but I'm not sure what. Is she glowing?

"You look good, Jilly Bean." I gave her that nickname when I was sloshed. We'd been celebrating the Fourth of July, and I was two sheets to the wind. I called her Jilly Bean, and it's stuck ever since.

"How did Washington treat you, Rob?"

"Not my favourite place, if I'm honest. Way too many politicians for my liking."

"Wasn't your last client a politician?" She laughs.

"Daughter of a politician, and that was bad enough. I'm just glad it's done. I think a change is in order." It was a nightmare job. The girl I was protecting had a stick up her arse about me being there. I lost count of the number of times she tried to ditch me.

"Robin, move here, please. Colin and I want you close." Jill wanted me to move to California when I decided to live in the U.S. My dad is British, but my mum is American, so I have dual citizenship. After the military, I was ready for something new. My parents left the UK when I was sixteen. Mum missed her family, and my dad was happy to move overseas. They live in Florida now.

"The rent here is stupid. And I am not getting a roommate."

"The pool house is free. It's like a mini house in there. Imagine waking up to the beautiful sun every day. The smell of the ocean. You could surf. Jog along the boardwalk." Wow, she's really selling it. It sounds idyllic.

"I'd just do what she says if I were you, Stuart. We know she's the boss of us both." I laugh because he's not wrong. I would do anything for Jill and Colin.

"I tell you what, let's table it until I come back from…shit, where am I going?" It's just occurred to me that Colin left out the location where this stupid show is going to take place.

"The Amazon!"

"The Amazon?"

"Yup, you know the place with loads of trees." Real comedian, this guy.

"Yeah, you've got jokes. How's the baby maker feeling there, bud?" This time, Jill bursts out laughing. Colin huffs but grins. Our friendship is built on gibes.

"Did you set up a meeting with the studio? I'm not completely sold until I talk to them." Maybe I can still get out of doing it.

"Tomorrow at ten. I'll take you there and introduce you to the relevant people. Tonight, though, I thought we could just chill. I think Della might stop by." Ah, Della, Jill's younger sister. We had a couple of fun nights together, but neither of us wanted it to go any further, but true to the lesbian code, we remained friends. She's the wild child of the family.

"Cool, it'll be good to catch up."

"Don't sleep with her," Jill calls from inside the pantry.

"I don't plan to." The thought had crossed my mind. It's still lingering, if I'm honest. Della is fire between the sheets, and it's been a while for me.

We chat for a good couple of hours catching up. I notice Jill hasn't touched her beer, which I find strange. Colin, being the unobservant neanderthal he is sometimes, sets another bottle on the table for his wife. I catch her eye and quirk my eyebrow. She smiles sweetly and winks. That's all the confirmation I need.

Della turns up at nine; she's dressed for a night out. "Robin, looking good, honey." As smooth as ever. It's no wonder I fell into bed with her. She's the spitting image of Jill. The only difference is she's much taller. Almost as tall as me.

"Della, good to see you, too. You're looking nice. Going out?"

"Yes, and you should come. Love P is going to be wild tonight." I've only been there once, and it was fun, although I'm thirty-five now and can't party like I used to. I'll never admit that to any of my regiment buddies.

"Not tonight, Del, I only just got in."

"Fuck that. When was the last time you let off some steam?" My silence says it all. "Come on. Jill and Colin will be in bed soon because you know they're old and married."

"Hey," Jill protests, laughing. Della grins.

"Please?" Della has the same ability as her sister to get me to do things I don't want to. What is it with this family?

"Fine, but I can leave when I want. You party until the sun comes up if you want, but I've got a meeting tomorrow, so for once, I have to be sensible."

"Deal." She sticks out her hand, and I shake it, laughing.

I throw on a clean tank top with my black skinny jeans. Thankfully, I washed my hair before travelling, so all I need to do is let it down. Since being in the forces, I automatically put it up every day. A bit of makeup and I'm ready.

I kiss Jill good night and punch Colin in the arm because that's what we do. The cab is waiting outside. Della hops in and asks the driver to put on something hip-hop. It only takes us fifteen minutes to get there, and I curse under my breath because the queue is stupid long.

"Can't you go all commando on their asses and get us closer to the door?" Della jokes.

"What do you think the commandos do exactly?"

"No clue, really, but I presume you're all tough and shit. I glaze over when Colin harps on about his commando days." Colin *does* enjoy reminiscing.

Two women join us in the line. I've never met them before. Turns out they have both slept with Della but are just friends. The lesbian community guidelines need to be updated. Amendment One: You do not have to stay friends with all your exes.

In the distance, I see a limo pull up. No one gets out, so I presume they're picking up. A few seconds later, a blonde in a sexy-as-hell dress steps out of the club and heads for the car. It's a shame she's leaving. I wouldn't have minded tracking her down for a dance. Oh, well, plenty more lesbians in the sea.

The club is insane. I instantly feel old. Every person in here looks way too young and way too pretty. That's Cali for you, though. I grab us all a drink and settle against the bar. Della and her friends are on the dance floor immediately, but I can't get myself in the right frame of mind. I keep thinking about the meeting tomorrow.

I've been to the Amazon before, and I didn't like it that much. We were there training, so it wasn't exactly a holiday. I'm curious to find out who the celebrity is. I pray they have some outdoor bones in their body. The last thing I need is some prima donna in the friggin' rainforest. I down my beer and head to the dance floor. Tomorrow is going to suck, I can feel it. So tonight, I'll dance and drink.

Chapter Three

Ellie

My day got off to a pretty shitty start. Having a kajillion needles stabbed in my arm was just the beginning. I tried to reassure myself that it was unlikely I was going to get some hideous disease in the jungle, but still. The thoughts lingered. I am too young and pretty to die that way!

Those thoughts lead to the second reason today started out bad. After getting home from Love P, I tried to get some rest, but it was a futile effort. I was just so angry that I'd been railroaded into this project. It's not the first time Gabe has crossed the line. Those thoughts had then led to me spiraling about my brother and my mother, which is never a good thing.

The doctor, or Doctor Dan as I like to call him, prescribed me sleeping pills years ago, but they leave me feeling groggy in the morning. So instead of medicating myself last night, I tried to meditate my way to rest. It didn't work. I tossed and turned for hours until I eventually gave up and lounged in front of the TV until the wee hours. Maybe I should have hit my home gym to work off some of the stress. I laugh at the thought. I haven't used the gym once because I hate working out.

Of course, it wasn't just the bullshit that is my family that stopped me from sleeping. Obviously, the fact I will be going to the goddamn Amazon was a major contributor. There isn't one person on this planet who would think sending me there is a good idea. No, scratch that, no one who didn't want to make money off me.

At the end of the day, that's what it comes down to. Gabe can spout off all he wants about "the world wanting to see the real Ellie Bishop," but it's garbage, and he knows it. My brother is a money-grubbing weasel. He has no problem selling me out if it lines his pockets. Toni despairs that I won't fire him. She's right, of course. That lowlife should have been cut off years ago, but I can't. I send a message to Caroline, my therapist. I need to vent soon. Preferably before I go to South America.

So here I am, exhausted and with a sore arm sitting in the window of my favorite restaurant, waiting for Gabe and the studio execs.

I might be powerless to stop this from happening, but that doesn't mean I have no power at all. If I'm going to do this, the least the studio can do is meet me on my terms. It's petty, but it's all I have. A minor victory getting them to come to me instead of me sitting in their offices. Plus, I can drink on their dime. Nothing like ordering top-shelf champagne to help take the sting out of my current predicament.

The meeting is supposed to highlight what's expected of me and give me the chance to ask questions. The problem is, I only have one question, and that's how can I get out of doing this without ruining my reputation?

Gabe saunters in like he owns the place. God, he's hateful. I don't know how we can be related. He takes after my mother entirely whereas I inherited all my father's genes. The universe is a cruel mistress. She took away a good man and left that pair of snakes unscathed. It might sound heartless, but I swear, they are the worst.

Snapping his fingers at the waitress, he barks an order for a scotch. I hope she spits in it. "Ready?" he asks. Like he cares.

"I suppose." I don't want to look at him.

"Just let me do the talking, okay?" Not likely.

Two men approach the table. They're dressed in nice suits. I bet they cost a small fortune. "Gabe, hi," one man says before turning his attention to me. His face lights up. "And, Ms. Bishop." He takes my hand and kisses it. I want to sanitize my arm, but I have to play nice. Why do men think it's okay to do things like that? I don't know him from Adam. Gabe gets a handshake, but I have to put up with a stranger's lips on my hand.

"Hello." I don't know if this is Craig or Billy.

"Billy and I are so pleased to have you for this season of *Wild Celebrities*." Right, so he's Craig, the money man. That tracks, he looks oily.

"I'm excited to do it." Wow, I am an excellent actress if he's buying that crock of shit.

"So, gentlemen, let's talk details." Gabe has his scotch and is inhaling it.

"Hi, Ms. Bishop, I'm Billy, the director."

"Hi, Billy. And please, call me Ellie."

"Great, okay, Ellie. This season is going to differ slightly from the last." I don't like where this is going, and he just started talking.

"In what way?" Does my voice sound calm and collected? It should. I'm putting every bit of skill I have to make out like I'm as carefree as a fucking summer breeze.

"So, normally, the show is scripted." I'd read that last night. Before I'd binge watched Netflix, I did a bit of research on the show and shows like it. What I read was pleasing. Apparently, most of the shows are completely scripted. What the audience sees is fiction. The celebrities *seem* to stay in some remote location, but behind the camera is a four-star hotel. It's the same with the food. On camera, it's gross shit like bugs, but off camera, the celebs are eating chef-prepared meals.

"Okay, so what's going to change?"

"All of it," Billy says, and my heart sinks. "We want to be the first show to really give the audience a genuine survival show."

Of course they do. Of course!

"Meaning?" I wish this guy would spit it out already. I signal the waitress with a giant smile indicating that I need more expensive champagne. I'm going to take a bottle home with me. Screw these guys.

"You'll be sent into the Amazon with a survival expert as normal, but there will only be two crew members going with you. We'll give you GoPros and leave you to record the show yourselves essentially. The two crew members will be there to get the professional shots, but we really want to lean on you and Robin to do the rest."

"Right." I think my throat is closing up. I can feel my breakfast trying to reintroduce itself.

"You guys will be completely alone. Obviously, we'll have an extraction plan and all relevant emergency services ready, should anything go wrong. Not that anything will, of course."

This restaurant is one of my favorites because

it has the best duck in L.A. I've been looking forward to ordering it all day, but now I have no appetite whatsoever. Surely, they can't expect me to do this. It's insane.

"Gentlemen, I'm not sure this is something I can do. I understand you want to make this show unforgettable, but I think I'm the wrong person to do it with. I am *not* outdoorsy in the least."

"But that's why it's going to be so good. People want to see you struggle and work hard. I guarantee you this is going to be huge. Hell, that's why we agreed to Gabe's outrageous demands." What demands? I didn't read the paperwork after I got back. All I know is this Robin dude is going to be my *survival expert.*

"I need to think about this."

"Nothing to think about," Craig says stiffly. "Gabe signed the paperwork. It's a done deal. He's already received the payout." My insides are boiling with rage. I can't look at my brother. I will get him back once this meal is done.

"What's the next step?" There's no point blathering on, the contract is done. I have to suck it up and figure out how to get through this.

"Right. We have a guy coming tomorrow that we'd like you to meet. He's going to give you the rundown on the native wildlife. I've asked him to make up flashcards, as well, so you can take them with you."

"Shouldn't the survival person know all that?" They better have given me someone capable of actually keeping us both alive. If my survival hinges on a few flashcards, I'm fucked.

"Yes, of course, but we feel it's necessary for you to be as prepared as possible. Can we say nine tomorrow morning at the studio offices?" I nod.

Sure, why not? I can't wait to learn about everything that's going to want to kill and eat me.

"Good, now let's order," Gabe says. He's been about as useful as a fart in the wind.

I sit listening to Billy talk about the show and the different celebrities who have been on before me. Craig spends most of the time conversing with Gabe. I try not to vomit with anxiety. Overall, a pretty crappy lunch, really.

"When will I meet Robin?" I want to see for myself if this man is going to be able to keep me safe.

"Not until the day you fly out. It's all part of the surprise." Wonderful. It keeps getting better.

I get the hell out of there as fast as possible once the check has been paid. My first bit of business is to call my lawyer. Gabe needs bringing down a peg or two. "Sandra, darling, hey."

"Ellie, you're not in jail, are you?" I laugh because she asks me the same thing every time. I have never been in trouble. In fact, Sandra tells me I could do with a little trouble in my life. She thinks it would justify the amount I pay her. I'm an easy client.

"No, of course not. I need you to go over Gabe's contract of employment—"

"Oh, fabulous, are you finally firing him?" See, even my lawyer knows I should get rid of him. I hate myself a little, knowing how easily I let my mother manipulate me. She is the master at it, though. God, I wish my dad was still here.

"Not firing, but I do want to cut his salary in half. I need to make sure I can do it without him having any recourse." Let's see how smug he is after I gut his paycheck.

"I don't need to look. I know you can. I had it

written in that you could adjust the amount at your pleasure. The greedy asshole was too quick to get your money. He didn't read it properly." See, this is why I love Sandra.

"Great, I'll call Pam." Pam is my manager. For once, I wasn't bluffing when I told Gabe I would reduce his salary by fifty percent. "One more thing. Do I have life insurance?"

"Of course, why?" I fill her in on the show. She assures me I have life insurance but tells me to go home and read the contract carefully. If anything happens to me, Sandra will destroy them in court. To do that, she needs to know what insurance and safety measures they have in place.

We chat for a few minutes longer before we say our goodbyes, and I call Pam. She's another person who is delighted that I'm giving Gabe a little hell. I feel a bit better after that, so I call in to Starbucks and get an iced latte. The cap and sunglasses do nothing to stop me from getting recognized, but that's fine. I spend some time signing autographs and getting selfies with random fans.

The drive home is relatively quick. I pull into my driveway and sigh in relief. Yes, I'm one of those actors who bought an obnoxiously large house in the Hollywood Hills. At the time, I thought it was fabulous, but now I just feel lonely. Toni is the only one who really visits. The pool boy pops by every few days, but that's it.

At thirty-seven, I thought I would be further along in life. You know, wife, kids, etc., but it never happened. I was being naïve to think I could have such normality. Women want the actress, not the real Ellie Bishop. They want the glitz and glamour. I know

I portray that, and honestly, I love it, but I kind of thought I would find a partner who wanted me for... well, me.

My high heels echo through the house as I head to the kitchen. I finished my iced latte in the car. I'm ready to get on to the harder stuff. The bottle of white in my fridge will do. Hell, I'll drink mouthwash if it helps me get buzzed.

My phone vibrates. I know exactly who it is, and I can't stop the grin. I swipe the screen and hold it away from my ear. Hearing Gabe's screaming is all I needed to turn my shitty day around. I put the phone on the kitchen island and proceed to cut up some fruit. I think a nice dip in the pool, then a steak dinner is in order. Finally, the screaming stops.

"Ellie, are you there? Ellie!" I can almost see him pacing in his house. That makes me smile. I bet his face is red and his neck vein is popping out.

"I'm here." Oh, I sound so calm and collected.

"Explain what the fuck is going on." Ugh. I bet he just spit everywhere when he shouted. Nasty.

"Oh, you thought I was joking about the pay cut, huh?"

"How dare you—" My turn to get pissed!

"How dare I what? Hmm? Carry on, Gabe, and you'll see another reduction. You may have Mother to stop me from firing you, but that's all she can do. Without me, you are nothing. If you were, you'd have other clients. You'd make a name for yourself without riding my coattails. Shut your mouth and do your job. That means you do what I say. And before you argue. Every time you go behind my back, I will drop your pay by ten percent." I press the red button before he can reply. Damn, that felt good.

My laptop is still in the living room with the contracts for the show on the screen. I look at the money that was agreed, and I almost choke. Shit, Gabe *did* squeeze them. I also notice he's earmarked a very generous amount of that money for himself. That's going to change. I find a list of items they expect me to take. I want to cry again. There's only one person who can help.

"Paris, I need you." Paris is my stylist. She's been with me for over ten years, and I trust her implicitly. I haven't done my own clothes shopping since the day I hired her.

"What for? You have no upcoming events." She knows my schedule better than I do.

"I'm going to the jungle." Silence. "Paris?" Still silence. I check the phone to make sure I haven't hung up with my face. "Paris?"

"Who the hell is this? Do you know impersonating someone is a criminal offense!"

"Paris, it's me, for god's sake."

"The Ellie Bishop I know would never step foot in a jungle. Nice try. I'm calling the police."

"Paris, you have a tattoo of a man mowing your pubes."

"Ellie, why the fuck are you going to the jungle?" I sigh and tell her the tragic story.

"I'll be over in an hour. Email me the list of items, and we'll discuss what we can do. You might have to be in a sweaty jungle, but that doesn't mean you can't be the most stylish woman ever to step foot in the place." I love her with all my Versace-loving heart.

As I wait for Paris, I Google this Robin fella. Nothing. I find absolutely nothing, which does not bode well, right? Everyone has an online presence. Honestly, all I want is confirmation he's a strapping six-foot beast who could kill a tiger if needed. Shit, are there tigers in the Amazon?

I am definitely going to die.

Paris saunters in with her arms laden with clothes. The list I was given is quite precise. None of the things Paris has brought are on that list. Will I need a dress in the jungle? Or wedged heels? No, but they are lovely.

"I'm thinking jean shorts, halter top, and wedged sandals for the journey," she says, laying everything out.

"I love what you've brought."

"Of course you do. I'm brilliant at my job, El."

Toni's voice echoes downstairs. I shout my location and wait for her. Toni loves to play dress-up. She's also very jealous that I snagged Paris all those years ago and won't share her. "Hello, lovely ladies. I come bearing gifts." Toni stands in my doorway with a bottle of tequila in one hand and a DVD in the other. I didn't know they still made DVDs.

"Hey, T, you planning a party?" Paris asks from inside my closet.

"We're having a *Wild Celebrities* marathon, and I thought it would be better to do that with some good tequila."

"I don't know, Toni." I sigh.

"Listen, it's better to get an idea of what you're going to be doing, right? Plus, you can see the survival experts in action. I brought the first three seasons."

"None of those are my survival expert, though," I protest.

"No, but they'll have the same skills as Colin

and Richard."

"She has a point, El." Paris walks back into the bedroom. "What do you think about sequins in the jungle?"

"I'm thinking I don't want to attract anything, so maybe not."

"Maybe pack something practical, too," Toni suggests.

I look at all the clothes Paris has picked out for me. If I die, at least I'll look good, I suppose.

Chapter Four

Robin

Oh, yeah, my head hurts. Like, wow, this is not fun at all. At least the bed feels comfy. It's not the bed I'm supposed to be in, but that's fine. I didn't get so drunk that I can't remember what happened or who I went home with. Jill might have something to say about it.

The painful groan next to me signals Della's awakening. She drank more than me but was still able to give me a good time when we got back to her place. Actually, she gave me several good times if I remember well. "Oh, shit, my head hurts." She's stating the obvious, considering she's clutching her temples.

"We should've had water." I grumble. Such a rookie move. Everyone knows you down several pints of the clear stuff to ward off feeling like death. We were a bit preoccupied, though.

"And when do you think we should have done that? When we were in the kitchen and you were on your knees or in the bathroom when I had you bent over?"

"All right, point taken. Coffee?" It's not my apartment, but I feel comfortable enough to make myself at home.

"Yes, and that breakfast you do." She's referring to a full English. It's greasy and calorific. Perfect for a hangover. "Everything's in the kitchen. Call me when it's done. I need to close my eyes again."

I laugh and make my way to the kitchen. Once I grab some painkillers, I'll be right as rain. Della will be feeling this until tomorrow, I'm guessing.

The sausages go under the grill whilst I prepare the bacon, eggs, and baked beans. Della is probably the only Californian bar Jill that stocks proper English baked beans. Hash browns are a staple in a full English, but I think they're the devil's food, so Della will have to do without. Everything is cooking nicely. The smell takes me back to the mess hall in our barracks.

Grant Bird, aka Budgie, was our resident cook back then. He made the best breakfast outside of a greasy spoon. I'm sure we all have blocked arteries due to the amount we consumed over the years. Anytime we went out on the piss—and that was a lot—good old Grant would suffer through his hangover to cook for us all.

Snapping back to the present, I get the coffee machine going for Della the heathen. I find it sacrilegious that Della will drink coffee with her food. It's a cup of strong tea or nothing at all in my book. I plate up and call Della. She shuffles into the room, looking like she was dragged through a hedge backwards.

"Still feeling rough?" The painkillers I took have kicked in now, and I feel fine.

"What, you mean since the twenty minutes ago when I woke up? Yeah, I still feel fucking awful."

Laughing, I slide a plate to her and tuck into my food. Della nibbles her sausage. I can tell she's forcing it down.

"Can I borrow some running shorts?" My energy levels are high. Seems all the fun with Della last night didn't do what I wanted it to. I was hoping I could shag my feelings away. You know, the healthy way to deal with a problem.

"You're going to run back to Colin and Jill's, aren't you?"

"Yeah, it's a beautiful day, and I need to get in a workout." I can't wait to feel the sun on my skin.

"I hate you."

I laugh harder. Della will hide in bed for most of the day, cursing the world. I'm feeling energised. I needed last night for sure, and now I need this run. The past few months have been hard. I didn't tell Colin and Jill just how bad my last client was. This break is a welcomed one.

We finish our food, and I stack everything in the dishwasher. Della collapses on the couch, mumbling to herself. Probably telling herself off for doing those tequila shots. I nip back to her room and grab some shorts and a T-shirt. We're the same size shoe, so I take her trainers, as well. I pack my clothes from the night before in a small rucksack.

"I'm off, Del. Drink water and take some pain-killers."

"Mmm." Della has wrapped herself in a blanket, making herself into a human burrito.

I jog over and place a kiss on her head. We don't need to have a talk about last night. It was what it was. Two friends having a good time. I just hope Jill sees it that way. Actually, no reason to tell her anything. Della will probably let it slip at some point, but hopefully, I'll be thousands of miles away in the Amazon when that happens.

The sun is beating down already when I hit the street. The run back to Jill and Colin's can be done on the beach. I've missed being by the water. I get myself into a nice rhythm. It'll take me about thirty minutes to get back, a perfect workout. As I run, I let my mind wander.

Later today, I'll be meeting the director of the show. I'm not sure what to expect. Colin tells me the job is going to be easy money, but my gut says otherwise. For once, I wish Dick was here, not in the Himalayas, doing God knows what.

I crash through the front door, sweaty and out of breath. I really pushed myself on the last stretch. "Jesus, Rob." Colin is sitting at the kitchen table reading a paper. He is so far from the young playboy Marine I remember.

"Sorry," I pant. Sweat is dripping down my face, back, and arse.

"So which lucky lady got you as an overnight guest then?"

Instinctively, I look around. I don't want Jill to hear. "Della."

"What a shock. Don't panic, Jill doesn't care. Della's a big girl."

"Where is Jilly Bean?"

"Says she's not feeling too well. I think she threw up this morning." I look at Colin, willing him to stop being a dumbass and realise his wife is pregnant. Maybe his broken penis is taking all his focus.

"Grab a shower, and we'll get going to the studio. Traffic will be shit." I shake my head and go in search of Jill. She's lying in bed looking a little green. "Hey, mama," I say. "Morning sickness?"

"Mmm, it's a bitch."

"Why havven't you told Colin?"

"I just wanted to make sure it would stick. We've

been waiting for so long. Plus, I knew I was pregnant before the penis-breaking incident. He might get mad."

I chuckle quietly. "Bullshit. He's going to be delighted. Broken penis or not, he would think it's worth it." I give her a quick kiss and tell her I'm hitting the shower.

I'm not a woman who spends hours getting ready. In the Marines, you had to be fast and efficient. I've never been able to let that go since becoming a civvy. What women do for hours on end in a shower is mystifying. I mean, you literally have to shove some shampoo in your hair, wash your body, and boom. Done.

"Ready to go, Col." He's already waiting in the hall with his car keys. For once, Colin wasn't being dramatic. The traffic sucks. I will keep this in my mind when deciding if I should move here. We arrive, and I have to stop myself from laughing at Colin as he waddles to the office where we're meeting the director.

I look around and discreetly take out my phone to record him. Before you judge, he would totally do the same. I can't wait to send it to the squad. I laugh as I follow him. I can see on my screen that his trousers are tight because of the padding. It's just too good.

Many people probably get starstruck when visiting a studio like this. I'm not one of them. None of it impresses me, really. I find the studio fascinating, though, from a technical point of view.

Colin introduces me to Billy, the director. He seems very excited to meet me. "Robin, what a pleasure. Colin has said great things about you." I know he's blowing smoke up my arse. Colin is not a gusher, he would present my credentials, and that would be it.

"Good to meet you, Billy." Only a small lie.

"Sit, sit. Coffee?" We're in a big conference room. Why, I'm not sure, there are only three of us.

"Black, no sugar, please." I settle in and wait for Billy to finish putting our coffee orders in to his assistant, I presume.

"Okay, let's get straight to it. Colin has told me you have some reservations."

"Not reservations. I just want clarification. What is it you're expecting?"

"Okay, I take it you're familiar with the show." Of course I am, one of my closest friends usually stars in it.

"Yes, I know it. Am I to assume it will be filmed in the same way as usual?" By that, I mean I'll pretend like I'm really showing some entitled celebrity how to survive in the wild when really we'll eat nice food and stay in lodgings behind the camera.

"No, not this time." I see Colin shift in his seat. He's looking concerned. He wasn't aware of the changes, obviously. That or his nappy is chafing.

"And what exactly does that mean?" I sit up a little straighter. The young assistant interrupts us to distribute the coffees, which I'm not in the least bit inclined to drink now.

A moment after the door shuts behind the assistant, Billy launches into his sales pitch of the new and improved *Wild Celebrities*. I sit with the information for a second. "So let me clarify. You want me to take an untrained civilian into the Amazon rainforest with no crew bar two other people for a month?"

"Exactly."

"Have you lost your mind?" Sorry, but this fella is bonkers. "Do you know the risks? Even trained professionals would struggle in those conditions."

"You'll have backup if needed." I look to Colin for help, but he looks down at his lap.

"No, sorry, it's a no from me." There's no way I'm putting myself through that nightmare.

"Ah, that's a problem." I don't like the look on Billy's face.

"A problem for you," I say.

"No, a problem for Colin, actually." I look at my friend, who's red and a little sweaty.

"Why?" This Billy is getting on my tits now.

"Colin signed the contract before his little accident. If he breaks it, he'll owe the studio a significant amount of money." What the...

"Colin?" Why the hell didn't he tell me this?

"Yeah, Rob, it's true. I didn't want that to colour your decision is all." Oh, how chivalrous.

"Well, actually, Col, you've just bent me over a barrel, mate. How can I say no now?" Fuck, I'm pissed at him. "Fine, I'll do it." Colin is like a brother to me. We've stuck together through some really messed-up situations. I'm not going to abandon him now.

"Excellent," Billy chirps, and I want to punch him in the throat. "You fly out in ten days. Until then, I'll set you up with everything you need. Your celebrity is meeting a nature expert today to give her an idea of the creatures you might come across."

"Who is my celebrity?" Please let it be some douchebag actor who has at least had *some* training in martial arts or something. Anything.

"Ellie Bishop."

"Ellie Bishop?"

"Yes, you must know her. She's the biggest name in Hollywood." Oh, I've heard of her, all right. She spends her days being pampered and preened.

Her movies are okay, if you like that sort of thing. The news outlets always report on her when she's on the red carpet showing off her designer dresses and shoes. What are they thinking sending *her* into the rainforest?

"Please tell me you're kidding." Billy has a smile etched across his face. I really, *really* dislike this man.

"Not at all. It's going to be great. Imagine the ratings when you take a hopeless city slicker and turn her into a survival expert. The audience is going to love it."

"I…I really am lost for words." I am, genuinely. This has to be the stupidest idea I have ever heard, and that's coming from someone who once dressed in an inflatable cow costume to…never mind. It's just a really dumb idea.

"You won't meet Ellie until the day you fly out."

"Why the hell not? I'm going to be spending a month with her. It's pretty important we have some time to prepare ourselves."

"The surprise factor, it's gold." This is the last favour I'm ever doing for Colin in my life.

Billy slides the new contract over to me. Once I sign, Colin is let off the hook, and I'm firmly on it. I take a second. Surely, it can't be as bad as I'm thinking. Ellie Bishop is a megastar. No studio would risk her life. Yeah, I'll keep thinking that. Maybe I can actually get myself to believe it.

I sign the paper, shake twat face Billy's hand, and leave with Colin waddling behind me, trying to keep up. I'm definitely putting that video on YouTube now. Colin deserves his broken penis to go viral.

The assistant who got the coffee runs over with a bunch of papers. She gives me a kit list and a schedule.

I also have a badge to gain access to the studio. I fold the papers and shove them in my back pocket. I have to shout at Colin for a while before I can focus on them.

The entire ride back to Manhattan Beach is me yelling at Colin. By the time we enter his house, I'm a little calmer. Jill has managed to get out of bed and is making lunch. I don't want her to get stressed out, so I act as normal as possible. Once we've eaten, I excuse myself. I need a little time to process.

The beach is quiet when I sit down. The ocean has always calmed me, even before I joined the Marines. I take out the kit list and browse the items. I have everything in storage already. I add a few items of my own that they should have thought of. Next, I check the schedule. Tomorrow I get my vaccinations, and then I have refresher courses on plants and wildlife.

If I wasn't taking a civilian with me, I'd probably be getting quite excited. Months of walking round in a suit guarding one rich arsehole after another has me craving an adventure. Sometimes I think I made a mistake leaving the military. But then again, living life in a war zone is *no* adventure.

Stupidly, I Google Ellie Bishop. I'll ignore the fact that she is stunning. Long blond hair, excellent body. I shake away the tingle I feel and focus on the reality of her. The fact that she is gorgeous doesn't mean a thing, not when she's going to be utterly useless in an emergency. Fuck, I think she's going to be useless full stop.

I wonder why she signed up in the first place. Is she trying to prove something? It can't be about the money. Ellie Bishop must be one of the highest paid actors in Hollywood. I watch a couple of interviews she did last year. She seems pleasant enough. If she listens to me and comes prepared, we might just get through this unscathed. Why is my Spidey-Sense telling me that's not going to be the case?

I set myself a plan on my phone. As well as everything the studio has set up for me, I add on my own refresher courses. I'll hit the gym. My knife work is pretty good still, but I'll ask Colin to spar with me. I know his crown jewels are damaged, but he owes me.

I don't relish the idea that I'm going to have to eat ration packs and foliage. I hope Ellie is ready for that. There will be no fine dining for either of us for a while. I note all the things I need to teach her first. Making a fire, building a shelter, cooking food. It's going to be interesting. I'd bet my left nipple she's never stepped foot outside a city before.

The day is getting hotter, and I'm suddenly feeling fatigued. I strip off my top and bottoms and head for the water. It's colder than I thought it would be, but it revitalises me. I think as I swim. I don't like the idea of not meeting Ellie until we ship out.

Maybe I could arrange a meeting with her without the studio knowing. Hmm, would that get me in the shit, though? I'm very much aware that *I'm* the one with an iron-clad contract now. I cannot afford to owe the studio money. Not if I want to move here and rent a place.

Back on the beach, I stretch out, letting the sun dry me off. I could get used to living here, that's if I make it back. It has to mean something when I'm more nervous about this job than I ever was shipping off on a mission.

What the hell has Colin gotten me into?

Chapter Five

Ellie

According to the wildlife man sitting in front of me, I have several things to shit myself about. Let me recount those for you. One: leopards. Two: poison dart frogs. Three: cougars and not the kind I like in my bed! No, these fuckers have bigger teeth and claws. Sorry, let me continue. Four: anaconda snakes. Five: armed spiders! What does that mean? Six: piranhas. So basically, every creature from every movie that depicts a blonde like me getting eaten!

Mitch—said wildlife man—looks positively giddy as he spouts off all the things that will try to kill me. I'm super glad he's enjoying himself. One of us should, I guess. Why the studio thought this was a good idea escapes me. There is no way I'm going to remember everything he's saying. Even if I did, what the hell would I do if I came across a leopard, for shit's sake?

"Are you ready to move on to poisonous plants?" Mitch asks me. Am I ready? Yeah, sure, why the hell not? Please note that I'm thinking those words with as much sarcasm as I can muster! My brain hurts, and I have a headache building.

"Could you just write them down and I'll study them? I'm still trying to wrap my head around the animals." Even though I'm screaming internally, I still have to be polite and kind. It's not Mitch's fault I'm being forced into this.

"Oh, sure, but the studio wanted me to take you through it all." Yeah, that's because they're covering their asses. If I'm injured, they want to keep me from suing.

"Right, okay, go on then."

I lose track of time. Mitch is more than happy to jabber on about plants. I can't fit anything else into my brain. Billy interrupts us, and I could kiss him. "How's it going, Ellie?" He's just as upbeat as Mitch. I kind of hate them both.

"Great, Billy, did you know there are two big cats that could potentially disembowel me? Oh, and trees that can melt my face off." I want to laugh because Billy looks afraid *for* me. I doubt he was thinking about all the potential but real dangers when planning this show. Oh, no, he was only counting dollars and thinking about audience ratings.

"Now I'm sure that's an exaggeration." He laughs, but it's a nervous laugh.

"No, she's right," Mitch chimes in, and I suddenly like him again.

"Don't worry, you won't be in any danger. Now I just wanted to grab Mitch. He's due to speak to Robin soon, and I wanted to catch up with him first."

"Robin is here, like the Robin who's going to keep me safe?" Here's my chance to scope the guy out.

"Yes, but you're not meeting. It's a surprise, re-member?" Billy laughs again. He's back to his jolly ways. I tell him it's fine because I'm so done with this conversation and learning about the dangers of the Amazon.

Ralph, my driver, is waiting to take me home.

I settle in the back of my SUV. It's only been forty-eight hours since I learned I was signed up for this godforsaken show, but in reality, it feels like a lifetime. My anxiety has never been this bad.

My phone rings as we approach the house. It's Sandra. "Hey you, everything okay? I'm not in jail." I laugh.

"I know that." Sandra chuckles. "I just wanted to let you know I called the studio and put the fear of God into them. I said that if they willingly put you in harm's way, I'm going to take them for everything they're worth, then I'll go after them personally." I fucking love Sandra. She has ovaries the size of watermelons. There isn't a lawyer in this town who hasn't heard of her and isn't scared shitless of her, either.

"And how did that speech go over, I wonder." I laugh.

"Wonderfully! I was able to clear a few things up. Basically, they're feeding you shit. All this crap about you being left to 'really' survive is bull. They just wanted to get you worked up, so you're more believable on camera. I have it in writing that you'll be dropped off in a guarded area of the Amazon. There will be a perimeter surrounded by guards. Yes, they want you to survive on the food you find and build a shelter, yada, yada, but that will be up to this Robin Stuart."

"Really, it's fake? I'm not going to get eaten?" Sandra laughs out loud at that question. I wish she understood I'm being deadly serious. The thought of getting hurt for a show I don't even like that much has kept me up.

"Parts of it are real. The food, the shelter, and the GoPros. But, and this is a massive but, you will not be alone. It's all for appearance's sake. I trust what they say because they know full well I will destroy them."

"Oh, Sandra, I could kiss you, really, thank you!"

"That's my job, El. Although it has got me thinking."

"About?"

"Your will."

"Jesus, you just said I wasn't going to die!"

"Calm down, Ellie, this isn't a movie, less of the dramatics." I should point out that Sandra is one of the very few people I allow to talk to me like that.

"Okay, I'm calm. What about my will?"

"In the event anything happens to you, all your assets and money go to your mother."

"Like fuck it does." That can't be right. Not a chance in hell I would have set that up.

"It's true. I dug out your will after you called me. Honey, you signed it when you were seventeen. Do you remember doing it?" I don't remember at all. Back then, my mom was way more involved; she took care of nearly everything. I just went along to the auditions and played the parts needed.

"No, I don't remember, but that needs to be updated immediately. Especially before I fly out to do this thing."

"I thought you might say that. So, who do you want to leave everything to?" Ah, let me think. I have no significant other, no kids, no nieces or nephews. I don't even have a dog. So who gets my millions?

"Sell all my shit and donate the proceeds, plus all the money I have in my accounts to an LGBTQ+ charity. You pick one. Write it up and I'll sign it."

"You sure?"

"Yeah, I mean if in the future my life changes

and I have someone, I can always amend it, right?" I'm still hoping for that life.

"Of course. I'll get it written up, and I'll bring it over tomorrow. Fancy having dinner?"

"Yes, perfect. I'll see if Toni is free, oh, and Paris."

"Oh, Christ, Paris, really?"

I laugh. The history between Sandra and Paris is that of drunk fuck buddies. They always claim they don't really like each other, but they get a drink in them, and they screw like rabbits for a few days. Usually in my house. I really need to stop inviting them over at the same time.

"Yes, Paris. Just don't drink if you don't want to get in her pants!"

"Why should I give up a night of wine?" I laugh again because she's so transparent it's unbelievable. I guarantee as soon as this conversation is over, she'll call to make an appointment for a wax.

"Sure, okay, drink. You're a grown-ass woman."

"I'll bring pizza."

"Yes, Papa J's only, remember!"

"You insult me sometimes, Ellie Bishop. See you at eight."

We hang up, and I feel a thousand times calmer. Those sneaky bastards got me riled up for no goddamn reason. They are soulless, the lot of them. Why do I still work in Hollywood? *The money, Ellie, the money.* That's a depressing reason, isn't it?

❧ ❧ ❧ ❧

Paris is the first to arrive. The promise of Papa J's is too much for her to withstand. The promise of Sandra is also probably hard to resist, too. As she approaches my front door, I see two burly men carrying boxes bringing up the rear.

"Ellie, I come bearing gifts."

"And what gifts are those?"

"I've been out all day scouring this city for fashionable clothes for you to take to the sweatbox. I've decided the ones we picked out the other day are no good. You can still wear the jean shorts and halter top with the sandals to travel, but everything else needs to go."

"Sweatbox?"

"That's the word you focused on after everything I just said?" She rolls her eyes. "Yes, it's going to be a sweatbox, a nightmare for your luscious locks. For the love of Prada, only wear your hair in a bun or ponytail. America does not need to see you looking like a cavewoman."

"Duly noted."

"Good. Now let's have a look at why you pay me the big bucks!"

Paris begins ripping open boxes. We spend the next hour perusing my new jungle wardrobe, and I'm quite happy about it. I'm going to look hot as hell.

The door opens, and Toni marches in. "Hello, ladies, what's happening here?" She eyes the clothes and starts picking her way through them. Now and then, she holds something up against herself and makes an approving sound.

"None of this will fit you, T." I know her too well. Half my gear will be stashed in her overly large purse by the end of the night.

"We'll see." She laughs. Sandra struts in next, looking great in her skirt suit. I notice Paris give her a once-over, and I have to smother a grin. Yeah, I'm gonna find them hooking up in my bathroom later.

"Evening all. Ellie, can I borrow you?" Sandra is holding a file that I presume has my new will in it. Better to get any business out of the way first. We head into the kitchen, and Sandra walks me through it all. I sign and instantly smile. My mother obviously believed I'd never check my will or have someone looking out for me who would check.

Knowing that neither my mother nor my brother will get any of my money should I keel over, I'm ready for a good night in with the girls.

The pizza is demolished quickly, and we start on the wine. "So have you figured out who this Robin guy is yet?" Toni asks.

"Nope, the studio is being super tight-lipped about him."

"I bet he's ripped. I'm jealous, Ellie. I would love to have a jungle man look after me for a month."

"Gross, T. He better learn to keep his shirt on."

"Hear, hear," Sandra calls. She's a lifelong carrier of the Lesbian Card, just like me.

"Oh, I don't know, a sweaty hunk isn't something to scoff at," Paris chimes in. And the games begin. This is like Paris and Sandra's foreplay. They like to wind each other up and get under each other's skin. Then they'll excuse themselves within thirty seconds of each other to fuck. It's a bit messed up, but it works for them.

"There's nothing a man can do that a woman can't do better!"

"Stop. All right, I'm cutting this off before it begins. You're both two wines in, therefore the drink threshold for your fuck buddy rules have been reached. Please spare me and Toni the foreplay. Take yourselves to the pool house and get on with it."

Paris looks at me and bursts out laughing. "Fair enough. Come on, Sandra, time to make me scream." With that, she strolls off toward the double doors that lead to the pool house. Sandra grins, shrugs, and follows. Am I jealous? Maybe. It's not because I want to be with either of them. It's just been a while since I've had a good screw and even longer since it was with someone worth caring about.

"Let's get silly." Toni laughs, pouring us more wine. "So are you really okay with everything now?"

"I'm better than I was. Sandra had words with the studio." I calmed down a lot after talking to Sandra. Don't get me wrong; I'm still nervous, but now I know I won't die, I can start to enjoy the experience.

"Oh, shit, I bet some poor person had to change their underwear after that phone call." Toni is laughing into her wine. She knows Sandra's ability to make grown men wet themselves as much as I do.

"Yes, I would bet my house on it. Anyway, she's reassured me, so I feel so much better about it. I still think the entire experience is going to be fucking awful. I'm a city girl. The jungle is going to suck."

"You never know, it could be life-altering." She looks at me strangely, and I don't know why.

"Okay, what's the look about?"

"Let's be honest, Ellie, you haven't been happy for a while. A lot of that is because you won't get rid of Gabe, and before you protest, you know I'm right, but you also know I understand your reasons for keeping him, too." I was totally going to protest, FYI. "Maybe this is what you need, a shakeup. Something so out of your comfort zone it wiggles something loose for you."

I truly wish that were going to be the case, but I highly doubt it. This isn't going to be an *Eat, Pray, Love* kind of situation. "Maybe," I answer because I don't want to keep talking about it.

My phone buzzes. It's an email from the studio. "What the fuck?" I blurt because that's the only response appropriate.

"What?" Toni asks, worried.

"They've moved the departure date up by a week. They're expecting me in three days. I haven't done half the stuff on their timetable. I can't go in three days."

❧❧❧❧

Shockingly, yet unsurprisingly, I end up at LAX three days later. Even though I protested the early departure date, I got nowhere, and of course, Gabe did nothing. So here I am waiting for a flight to Brazil. At least that part will be first class. I plan to drink copious amounts of bubbly onboard.

Apparently, Robin flew down yesterday. That brings me a bit of comfort. At least I'll get to meet him. I get through security with ease and wait in the first-class lounge. There are a few people looking at me, but thankfully, they have the decency to leave me alone. I love meeting fans, but right now, I'm just trying to keep my breakfast smoothie from making an appearance.

The flight attendants are lovely in every sense of the word. Maybe I could join the mile-high club with one of them. I'm not getting any for at least a month, so it would be a good send-off. The redhead has been giving me eyes since I sat down.

First class isn't full, and most people are asleep. Fuck it, if she'll sign the NDA on my phone, I'll take her in the restroom. It's strange because I'm quite an introverted person. When it comes to women, however, I have no problem taking the lead.

I press the call sign and look at her directly. She gets the hint and walks over with a sway in her hips. She knows exactly what she's doing, and I like it.

Because I don't want anyone else to hear, I whisper my proposal in her ear, and what do ya know, I'm about to get laid before I go to the jungle.

We do an admirable job considering the space we have. I come quickly, which should embarrass me, but, hell, like I said, it's been a long time. I return the favor on my knees. The dopamine rush only lasts for a few minutes because as soon as I sit back in my seat, the captain announces we'll soon land in Brazil.

This is it.

Chapter Six

Robin

Having the departure date brought forward isn't a big deal for me. I lost count of the times a mission was cancelled last minute or moved up. I got used to being flexible and being ready to go on a moment's notice. So when Billy called to say I was needed in Brazil in two days' time, I was chill.

In fact, I was chill about the whole thing. Colin felt so bad that he'd gotten me involved, he took me to one side and told me the studio was laying everything on thick to get me worked up. Apparently, Billy thought it would feel more authentic if I believed we were really being left to survive. I should have known they would never put someone as famous as Ellie Bishop in danger.

According to Colin, we would still have to look after ourselves as far as food and shelter were concerned, but there was a strict perimeter around the place we would be dropped, and it would be guarded. It also meant that we would have emergency responders just a radio call away. I can't believe I was gullible enough to believe Billy in the first place.

Never mind, I was able to relax after that. I still overprepared because that's what I was trained to do. The flight to Brazil was nice, especially because they'd put me in first class. I half expected to see Ellie, but I didn't. When we touched down, I was whisked away to a nice hotel for the night. The next day, I was taken to a smaller airport. I was told that I would finally meet Ellie then.

The show had begun.

The sun is brutal as I wait around like a bloody lemon for Ms. Bishop to show up. Looking around at the small hangar—I wouldn't call this place an airport at all, it's an airfield with like three planes—I take in my surroundings. I meet the pilot who will fly us into the rainforest. He's a lovely man named José. He has two young daughters and a wife he is clearly over the moon in love with. It feels good to chat with him while I wait.

Finally, a big black SUV pulls up. I'm leaning against the wing of a small aircraft. Billy and his assistant move like their arses are on fire to get to the car. I'm going to hang back and just observe. The back door opens and out steps the one and only Ellie Bishop. My first reaction is to gasp because she really is stunning. My second reaction is to cringe. I let my head flop to my chest and curse Colin, Billy, and any other fucker who is involved in this ridiculous show.

I knew she was going to be hard work, but seriously? In less than two hours, we'll head to the rainforest. Looking at Ellie Bishop, she clearly thinks we're going to a poolside party in Miami. A pink sequined halter neck top, denim hot pants, and wedged sandals. How does any of that equal clothing appropriate for the fucking rainforest?

Oh, but it gets better. From the back of the SUV, three large suitcases are hauled out and dropped to the floor. I'm watching this shitshow unfold. Billy and Ellie do the whole fake "I'm so happy to see you" bollocks whilst air kissing each other's cheeks. I just want to have a shot of whiskey and call it a day.

Billy looks over his shoulder and tilts his head, beckoning me over. This is the big moment. I sigh and push myself off the wing. Ellie is talking to Billy's assistant about something as I approach. Billy guides me by the shoulder, which I hate, to stand in front of her. As if Ellie realises there's more than just her in the hangar, she finally notices me standing there.

"Ellie, my dear, meet Robin Stuart. Robin, this is Ellie Bishop." I'm super aware that there's a camera on us.

"Ms. Bishop," I say, holding out my hand. She looks at me, looks at my hand, and then she looks at Billy. Confusion is written all over her face, and I instantly know this is about to go downhill fast.

"You're the survival expert?" Ah, the tone. One I'm all too familiar with. Yes, Ms. Bishop, believe it or not, women can be survival experts! I don't say that, I just nod. "No, this isn't right!" she says, her voice climbing in pitch. I think I can hear dogs howling.

"Robin here is the best of the best, Ellie," Billy says. Nice try, dude, I appreciate the effort.

"I don't give two fucks. Where's the big burly man that can actually stop me from getting eaten? We're going to the jungle, not on a trip to the supermarket. I need someone who can—"

"It's the rainforest actually, not the jungle. And I assure you, Ms. Bishop, I'm more than capable of keeping you safe."

"How? You're my size. What the hell could you do if we get attacked by something?"

"Well, first, let's hope that doesn't happen, and second, I would defend us. You'll be safe with me."

"No way, no fucking way, Billy. Get me a man that can keep me safe."

Yeah, I lose my cool. "Wow, way to set feminism back a hundred years there, princess."

"I beg your pardon!" She's glaring at me with the heat of a thousand suns, but it just spurs me on.

"You heard me. I knew you were going to be difficult, but, shit, lady, you take the biscuit right from the get-go." I laugh incredulously. She's getting angrier by the second. "I'll fucking tell you why I'm better than any 'big burly man,' princess. I am an ex-Royal Marine, I've been to places on this Earth that you could only imagine in your worst nightmares. I've dragged men twice my size across landscapes so harsh and desolate that none of us were supposed to survive. For weeks! I've earned more military commendations than you have awards. And I did all that in the face of misogynistic arseholes like you!" Okay, I may have gone a *tiny bit* too far, but this woman is fucking unbelievable. I turn to Billy. "Sort this out." I point at Ellie. "I'm going to load up. With that, I walk away from a very stunned Ellie Bishop.

Half an hour later, Billy catches up to me. I took myself away to calm down. I could honestly walk away from this regardless of the money I would lose. "Robin, everything's fine. Ellie was just a bit surprised, that's all."

"That's one way to describe it, I suppose."

"Look, we need to get this show on the road, so to speak. Can you come back over and get on with the job? We need more footage of you two meeting." It's amusing watching Billy try to placate us and order us about at the same time. The military woman in me will always put duty first, and whether I like it or not, this show is my duty now.

I follow Billy back to the hangar. The SUV is gone. Ellie is sitting on a chair next to her three suitcases. That's the first thing I need to address. Trying to befriend Ellie is not on my list of priorities anymore. "Are you expecting to take those with you?" Ellie snaps her head up from her phone and narrows her eyes. She's about as intimidating as a tea bag.

"It's my luggage," she snaps.

"Nope, it's too much." I walk over to my kit and take the empty spare pack I brought with me. "This is your allotted luggage." I drop the pack to her feet. "We don't have much time, so I suggest you get a move on." She looks at the pack and then back up at me. I roll my eyes. "Take what you need from your suitcases and repack it into that bag."

"But I need all of it!" she shrieks. Is this what I'm going to get every time I issue an order? My gut says yes. I internally sigh again. Colin will be doing my laundry for a year, I swear to God.

"No, you don't. None of that will fit on the plane. Even if it did, you're telling me you're prepared to lug all of that through the rainforest?" I raise my eyebrows, daring her to argue. "I'll dispel any misguided belief you have that I'm going to be your pack donkey. Your kit is yours to transport." She looks like she's going to explode.

"Fine!" she spits, ripping open her first suitcase. I'm stunned at all the shit she has brought.

"You were given a pack list, right?"

"Of course," she hisses.

"Well, I don't recall stilettos being on it." My voice is calm, and I know it's pissing her off. "Ms. Bishop, I strongly suggest you stick to the list. Anything else is just added weight." She ignores me, so I leave her to it.

I walk over to the two guys organising camera equipment. I know they're the two crew members who will be with us at all times. "Hey, I'm Robin." I shake both their hands.

"I'm Cody C and that's Cody F." That's not going to work for me. I need to communicate easily with them, and that's not possible when you're trying to talk to two people with the same name.

"Cool, so can I call you Mic"—I point to Cody C—"and you Cam?"—I point to Cody F. Cody C is the sound man. So Mic as in microphone is easy. Cody F is the cameraman, so…you get the point with the names. "No risk of confusion then," I say. Both guys agree, and we chat for a bit. They've been in the industry for a while and have worked together for a few years. There's a bond there that I like. We'll get on great.

When Mic and Cam have finished taking me through their equipment and the small GoPros Ellie and I will use, I thank them and wander back to the hangar. To my surprise, Ellie has packed the bag I gave her. She looks like a bulldog chewing a wasp, so I know she's still pissed about it, but tough tits.

"Okay, everyone, let's get loaded and head out," Billy shouts. He's not actually going anywhere, so why he's acting like he's about to hop aboard the plane and do this with us is a mystery. I grab my pack and head to the aircraft. I take a breath and turn to wait for Ellie. She's walking in the opposite direction, which is odd.

"Ms. Bishop, where are you going?" I shout. She stops and turns on her heel. Ice, that's what she's shooting at me, daggers of ice.

"To the plane, obviously." I look past her and see that she's heading to a very nice private jet. Oh, she's going to blow a gasket.

"Then you're heading in the wrong direction. I'm not sure the owner of that fine aircraft will appreciate you climbing aboard." She scrunches her eyebrows. I hook my thumb over to the much smaller and much older plane we're taking. Her eyes go wide with understanding. "This is us," I say cheerfully. She closes her eyes tight, and I'm getting worried she might be about to have a full meltdown.

Seconds pass, and she hasn't moved. I have no clue what to do. Everyone else is just ignoring her and getting on with their jobs. Is she known to be a diva? Should I just leave her to it? Fuck. I walk over to her and place my hand on her forearm. Her eyes open wide, and I snatch back my hand.

"It's a good aircraft. Not as comfy as that one, but it'll get us where we need to go." Did that sound reassuring? I couldn't give two monkeys about the plane. Shit, I've flown in worse. She breezes past me without a word. Well, fuck you very much! It's my turn to close my eyes and breathe. At this rate, if the rainforest doesn't kill her, I might.

Mic and Cam will be the only ones travelling with me and Ellie, and José, of course. There is no room to move in the plane once we and all our gear are loaded. It's going to be an uncomfortable ride. It's cool, though, I can sleep anywhere. With the doors locked and our harnesses tight, José taxis down the runway. I lay my head back and close my eyes.

The plane takes off and I bunk down. I have no intention of trying to make small talk with Ellie. I should probably stick to Ms. Bishop. Formal is better.

We haven't been given the exact location for the drop-off, only José knows that. He said we wouldn't be in the air too long, but that doesn't really help. What's too long?

I look at my watch when I wake up. Two hours have gone by. Mic and Cam are asleep. Ms. Bishop is staring at the ceiling with earbuds in. Maybe she's not a fan of flying. I unclip and head to the cockpit. I want an update and a location. This is my show now. Fuck what Billy wants. As I stand, the plane jolts. I sit back down and strap back in. The plan jolts again but harder this time. Ellie takes out her earbuds, looking concerned. Mic and Cam have also woken up.

The noise I can hear isn't making me feel very good. I try to keep my face as neutral as possible, but my heart is racing. Something isn't right. Suddenly, the plane drops and banks left. I hang on and close my eyes for a second. I'm going to be so fucking pissed if I die in a plane crash. I open my eyes and look at Ms. Bishop, who is as a white as a ghost.

"Just keep calm, everyone," I say in a soothing voice.

"Oh, my God, oh, my God, oh, my God," Ms. Bishop chants.

"Okay, Ms. Bishop, that is the opposite of calm."

"Fuck you, we're going to die!" She wails, and I roll my eyes, but then the plane goes into a steep dive, and I think she's actually right. I need to do something. I fight to unlatch my harness. With the gradient of the fall, I'm propelled to the cockpit by gravity. It takes all my strength to open the door.

José is slumped over the controls. He looks unconscious. I fall into the co-pilot chair and pull back as hard as I can. The problem is that José has all his weight on the controls, making it difficult to pull them up. I scream for Cam. The noise is horrendous, but by a miracle, Cam hears me and comes to my aid. Mic is behind him, and together, they wrestle José into a seated position. I give it everything I have and pull on the controls. We aren't going to hit the ground nose first, because we are coming in hard. I scream at the boys to buckle up. It's been a while since I've piloted a plane, let alone done an emergency landing.

I'm not a woman of God, but right now, I'm praying my arse off to anyone who will listen. As the ground screams closer, I put all my years of training to use. I will land this fucking plane.

Chapter Seven

Ellie

Everything hurts, even my hair, and I don't know why. It's pitch black. Are my eyes open or closed? Shit, I can't tell. My head is fuzzy. It feels way too heavy for my body. What happened? It's bad, I know that, but my brain won't cooperate. *Think, Ellie!*

What can I remember? I recall pulling up to the world's smallest airport after a long flight from L.A. It was boiling, and I was sweating, even though the air conditioning in the car was on. We parked next to a hangar, and I was greeted by Billy and his assistant. She was hot. What then?

Oh, I saw Robin Stuart for the first time. I was shocked because she most definitely wasn't a big burly man. Then I felt incredibly horny because she was *really* hot. I was being sent into the Amazon with someone who looked like a cross between G.I. Jane and Lara Croft. She even had the Angelina Jolie boobs. Um, next. Right, she is a cold, rude bitch. Yep, I remember that. She shouted at me because I dared to question her suitability. I think it was my right, but whatever.

Ugh, my head is pounding. What next? I had to repack my bag, I think. Robin was being an asshole again. There was a plane. It was small. I was seated near Robin the Hun and two other people. Is that right? Who were they? Crew, possibly. I remember feeling anxious because the plane looked as old as me. Robin fell asleep. I watched her for a little while because when she wasn't talking, she looked fine as hell. Those legs. Damn!

Screaming, I was screaming. God, the plane was falling. We were diving so fast. Robin disappeared to the front. The two guys, shit, what were their names? They followed her and then…nothing. I can't remember after that. I must be alive, though, if I can remember all that. Fuck, does my body work? I can feel my hand move to touch my face. There's something warm running into my eye. I think I'm bleeding from my head.

Just get one eye open, Ellie, just one! Yes, okay, I can see a sliver of light. My left eye is welded shut by the blood. I'm still sitting in my seat, the harness kept me in place. Something must have hit me in the head as we crashed. Holy fucking shit, we crashed! We crashed in a plane! Oh, God, oh, God. Yep, I'm hyperventilating. Shit, shit, shit, shit, shit.

"Hey, breathe, deep breaths, Ms. Bishop." There's someone in front of me. Who is it? *Come on, eyeball, focus, you son of a bitch!* Lara Croft, she's alive! Oh, thank you, thank you. I take several deep breaths. She's wiping my left eye. I think I can open it now. The plane and Robin swim into view. I definitely have a concussion.

"What happened?"

"We crash landed." Well, no shit, Sherlock.

"Got that part, thanks. How did we crash land?"

"I see the knock to your head didn't affect your higher-than-mighty attitude." Is she sassing me?

Really? "José collapsed. I think he had a heart attack. I was able to land us without too much damage."

"Who the hell is José?" Do I know a José? Oh, God, have I lost my memories?

"Jesus. José is the pilot, Ms Bishop." Why is she giving me attitude right now? "Look, the plane is stable. We only suffered damage to the nose section."

"I feel like I'm hanging."

"One of the plane's landing wheels burst, so the plane is tilted slightly."

"I take it you've radioed for help."

"No can do. The radio is damaged."

"So what exactly *have* you done to help us?" I can sass right back, lady.

"I, *Ms. Bishop*, have safely landed a falling plane, administered first aid, and gathered supplies. What have you done?" God, this bitch is just too much.

"Can you just get me the fuck down from here?" I wait for her to unbuckle me. I can see, but everything is still blurry. Maybe if I wasn't lopsided, I could focus.

I feel the harness being removed, and suddenly, my weight drops. The plane isn't tilted a lot, so I don't fall far. My knees hit the ground first. I take several deep breaths with my eyes closed. If I can't see what's going on around me, I don't have to admit it's really happening. Robin moves away from me and begins talking to someone.

Feeling my heart rate fall slightly, I finally open my eyes and look around. To my right is José, I presume. He's lying on his back, eyes closed. On my left are the two crew members. What are their names? Mic and Cam, is that what Robin called them? Never mind, they both seem okay. Then there's Robin. Her arm is bleeding. It looks like a deep gash. God, I want to hurl.

I hate blood. Apart from the wound on her arm, she seems all right. Still frustratingly gorgeous. *Damn it.*

"Right, guys, listen up." That English accent is doing it for me! *Stop it, Ellie!* "Here's where we're at. The radio is buggered. I have no idea if the transponder is working. Let's hope it is."

"What's a transponder?" Cam or Mic asks.

"It's the thing that will allow people to find us."

"And if it's not working?" I ask.

"Then they don't find us," she says matter-of-factly. I'm stunned into silence. It's possible my brain is going to explode.

"What the fuck does that mean?" I practically screech. How is she being so calm right now?

"It means that we have to look after ourselves and find a way out of here."

"So you know where we are?" Mic or Cam ask. I should find out which one is which.

"Not really. Like you guys, I wasn't given our location. All part of the surprise, right?" She rolls her eyes, and for once, I can sympathize with her. "I can't ask José because, well..." She points to the man lying near me.

"Will he be okay?" I ask.

"No, he's dead." I catapult myself from where I am to the seat next to Mic (or Cam). We have a dead body on the plane. A. Dead. Body!

"We're going to die here," I exclaim because in my mind that's what's going to happen.

"All right, take it down a notch, will ya?" Robin huffs. "Getting hysterical isn't going to help. Being calm will. Yes, he's dead, and it's horrible, but we can't change it. We need to move him, though. Animals will be attracted to the smell, and that's the last thing we need."

"This can't be happening," I cry. My body starts convulsing. I'm probably going into shock. Suddenly, two powerful arms engulf me and squeeze me tight. I hold on for dear life because right now those arms are the only thing anchoring me to reality.

"I know it's a lot, Ms Bishop. Please try to calm down." At least she said please. A thought suddenly occurs to me, and I laugh.

"What if this is all part of it, huh?" Three sets of eyes look at me like I'm losing my mind. "Think about it. Billy was adamant that he wanted a show that was like no other. Well, this would be that show. Can you imagine viewers watching us crash land and having to survive? Shit, I bet it's a setup. I bet there are hidden cameras recording as we speak." Yes, I'm convinced this is all part of Billy's fucked-up idea of the "new" *Wild Celebrities.*

"Ms. Bishop, I highly doubt that."

"Are you in on it?" I gasp. She must be. That's how she knew to land the plane. "You are, aren't you? Well, listen here, bitch, I'm going to sue you for everything you own. By the time my lawyer is finished, you'll be eating beans in a cardboard box under a bridge." That told her!

"Are you finished?" she asks me calmly. God, she is frustrating. She doesn't wait for me to answer. "I'm not 'in on' anything. I wasn't even supposed to be on this show. Colin Berk was supposed to be the specialist. I got roped in at the last minute. Believe me, I never wanted to be anywhere near this godforsaken show, but here I am trying to keep your arse alive, so please, enough of the theatrics and drama. If you can't help, just shut up."

I'm stunned into silence. No one speaks to me that way. Robin turns away from me and addresses Mic and Cam. "Look, we need to organize ourselves. First, we need to take care of José. Are you guys okay to help me dig a pit?"

"Yeah, I'm okay, but Cam says his shoulder is hurting." Excellent. I now know which one is Mic and which one is Cam. I just hope I can remember. I'm useless with names.

"No problem. Cam, collect all our gear together. We need to take an inventory of our supplies. I'll go outside with Mic and start digging. I have one foldable shovel in my pack." Robin moves and starts rooting around her bag.

"What do I do?" Honestly, I'm not sure there's much for me to do. Maybe I could try to meditate for an hour. That usually calms me down.

"You can help dig, too."

"Dig? I don't think so." Is this woman for real?

"Oh, is that below your station?" Robin arches her very nice eyebrow at me, and I actually blush. It's not below me to dig a hole. I'm sure I could do it, but I mean, really, I'm the least athletic person you could meet. Lifting my latte is a strain sometimes. I'm blessed with good genetics, therefore I don't have to slog away in a gym to keep my body the right size for Hollywood. How do I explain that to Robin? She already thinks I'm a spoiled bitch.

"Fine." I growl. I know this isn't the best time to be acting like an ass, but Robin just rubs me the wrong way. Even more when she rolls her fucking eyes at me, like she's doing now.

"Let's get moving folks." Robin jumps into action, yanking the door open. Sunlight spills into the cabin area. The heat is stifling. It's even worse with the humidity. Jesus, my hair is going to frizz like crazy. Paris won't be happy.

I want to help, really I do, but I just can't move past the fact that I shouldn't be here. This shouldn't be happening to me. I don't want to leave the plane and dig a hole for José, the dead pilot. I want to be at home drinking champagne by the pool with Toni, complaining about Gabe. Hell, I'd prefer to listen to Sandra and Paris doing it in my downstairs bathroom than being here. The moment I step foot out of the cabin, all this becomes real.

I think my ass is fused to the spot I'm currently sitting in. I can hear Robin and Mic outside discussing where they should start digging. How are they acting so normal? Cam has shifted to the back of the plane, where all our gear is stowed. The last thing I want is for some random man to be rooting around my belongings. "Excuse me," I say as politely as possible. Robin may have already made her mind up about me, but that doesn't mean Cam and Mic have to see me that way, too. I'm America's movie sweetheart, for God's sake. "Excuse me," I say again because Cam hasn't acknowledged that I've spoken. "Hey," I shout. Patience isn't a virtue I possess. Cam spins around wide-eyed. It's almost as if he forgot I was there. Not surprising, really, I've been sitting here as quiet as possible hoping all this is a dream. It's not!

"Sorry, Ms. Bishop, I didn't hear you."

"It's fine, and please call me Ellie. Can I ask that you don't go through my things?"

"But Robin told me to do an inventory—"

"Yes, well, Robin isn't in charge," I spit. "Those are my belongings, and it's up to me who sees them.

Am I understood?" Yup, I've gone full diva. Cam looks like he's going to pee his khakis. This is all kinds of awkward now. "I'm going outside to help dig. Do not touch my things," I reiterate.

My legs are shaky when I stand. I don't want Cam to see me looking weak, so I stiffen my back and hold myself up high. I want to portray strength and confidence, just like when I'm on the red carpet. Edging toward the open door, I send a silent prayer that I don't immediately trip and injure myself when I step out of the plane. Why did I wear wedge sandals?

The sun is blinding when I step through the door. There is a cacophony of sound that is so alien to me it takes my breath away. I couldn't tell you what it is I'm hearing. Birds obviously, but also probably a lot of bugs. Gross. Oh, Jesus, I'm going to get bitten to death. It's like I can already feel the creepy crawlies on my body. This is why I don't do jungles—sorry, rainforests!

I summon the courage to hop from the plane to the forest floor. I can hear Robin and Mic, but I can't see them. The area is dense with trees and other plants. My mind tries desperately to conjure the list of flora that the wildlife guy told me was dangerous. God, I wished I'd paid more attention.

Tentatively, I move away from the plane. The crash site is harrowing. How the hell we didn't die is beyond me. There's a wake of fallen trees and broken plants behind the wreckage. The plane is tilted but looks okay. I move to the front and gasp. The nose is crumpled against an enormous tree trunk. Robin should be dead! All she got was a cut on her arm. How did she get out of the cockpit before it slammed into the tree? I want to ask her, but then I remember

I don't like her one bit and have no desire to converse with her at all.

The sound of voices pulls my attention from the plane. All I want to do is run and hide in the cabin, but I know I can't do that. I don't want to give Robin the satisfaction of knowing how terrified I am. I also won't let on that I was wrong to wear these shoes. I feel like Bambi walking toward where Robin and Mic are working on the pit. My shorts are riding up my ass, as well! This is such a shitty day for me.

Only a few minutes pass until I locate Robin and Mic. I tuck myself behind a tree for a few minutes and watch. Yes, I am very much ogling Robin. She's flexing her arms as she digs. I bet her body is amazing under those clothes. Shame her personality is so shitty. Ugh, I suppose I should go and help. It's not like I have anything better to do. Well, unless freaking out and crying in the fetal position classifies as helping.

Chapter Eight

Robin

All I have to do is keep moving. If I do, I won't stop and think about how fucked we are! I suppose things could have been worse. I mean, we landed with no casualties. Obviously, I'm not counting José. Poor man, my heart breaks for his family. After the Commandos, I thought I'd seen the last of death and destruction. What I wouldn't give to be sitting on the beach with Colin and Jill. Oh, God, I hope I see them again and their little one. *No, stop!* Those kinds of thoughts aren't helpful. I need to get myself in the right frame of mind. Focus on the positives.

First positive: We landed intact, mostly. I must admit, it was a close call when the plane hit the forest floor. I had a split second to vacate the co-pilot seat before getting smashed up against the tree we hit. I know I hurt myself. I can feel the gash on the back of my upper arm. I'll tend to that later.

Second positive: The cabin is secure. We can bunker down without worrying about animals getting to us. That leads me to my first problem, though. Poor José. As much as I don't want to do it, I have to get his body out of the plane. It won't take long before we attract all kinds of unsavoury critters that will hurt us to get to their dinner. I feel a little queasy. I've lost my steel since being out of the forces.

Focus, Robin! Once we've dug José's last resting place, I can relax a little. Jesus, I'm going to have to deal with Ellie Bishop. No one needs her attitude, not now. I get she's in shock, but seriously, so are Cam and Mic, but they're still able to be decent people. *Ugh, dig, Robin, dig.*

I found a pleasant spot a few hundred metres from the crash site. We could hit a bunch of tree roots, but hopefully not. I only have one shovel on me, and if I'm being honest, my arm is hurting more than I want to admit. I bet it needs stitching up. That's going to be a barrel of laughs.

The breaking of sticks grabs my attention. Bloody hell, Ellie Bishop has deigned to grace us with her presence. Not sure why she's hiding behind a tree, though! Actually, she probably feels awkward as shit after the way she spoke to me when she woke up. I won't hold it against her, well, not much. She's a vapid celebrity. My expectations for her are pretty low. If she stays out of the way and doesn't cause problems that will suit me perfectly.

"Hey, Mic, can you take over for a few minutes?"

"Yeah, of course."

I need to address this thing, whatever it is, with Ellie. Maybe if I stop addressing her so formally, she might relax. We definitely didn't get off on the right foot. I can hold my hands up and admit that I was partly to blame, but now, in the situation we're in, we have to move past it.

I had plenty of arseholes to deal with in the Marines. If I can put up with a six-foot bear of a man screaming at me for eight hours a day, I can deal with Ellie Bishop, movie diva. I want to laugh a little when she realises I've spotted her behind the tree. *She's adorable.* Whoa, nope! Those thoughts need to bugger off right now! Ellie Bishop is the furthest thing from my type. Okay, that's horseshit. Looks-wise, she's exactly my type. It's the attitude and diva crap I can't gel with. Bloody hell, this is the last thing I need to be entertaining, not when we have a guy to bury.

"Hi, Ellie," I say kindly. Her eyebrows scrunch together. I wonder if she's trying to work out my sudden change of attitude. I would be if I were her.

"Oh, um, hi." she says nervously, although I can see she's trying to come across as confident and in control. Well, that's better than her screaming and shouting at me, I suppose.

"How are you feeling? How is your head?" I'll have to clean it before the day is over.

"Oh, it's fine. Okay, it's a little sore. Um, I came to help dig like you wanted."

"Great. Mic will be good for a few more minutes, then you can take over."

"Right."

Holy shit, it's like prying blood from a stone. We stand there in awkward silence. Christ almighty, this is painful. "Okay, so maybe you could take over for Mic now. See how you get on. We don't need to dig it to six feet, but deep enough animals won't dig him up.

"Jesus," she whispers under her breath. I understand. I'm someone who has been—unfortunately—in these kinds of situations before, and even I'm struggling with the thought of putting that sweet man in the ground thousands of miles away from his family. I can't imagine how tough this is on the others.

"Take a beat, Ellie. I know it's easy for me to say. I'm sure you just feel like raging, but right now, we have to work as a team to get this done. Once José is sorted, you can scream and shout all you want. Fuck, I might just join you." Wow, I think I just got a little smile out of her.

"I'll, just…" she says, pointing to Mic, who has done a great job. With Ellie talking to Mic, I grab a second to calm myself. It's really quite irritating that Ellie is so pretty because it's extremely distracting. My gaze wanders over to the duo discreetly. From what I can see, Ellie is being rather pleasant to Mic. Why *I'm* the one getting shit from her is a mystery.

"Hey, Robin, is it cool if I check on Cam? You might need to look at his shoulder later."

"Yeah, sure. I'll call when we need a hand." And now I'm alone with Ellie. Fan-fucking-tastic! Should I try to talk to her again? Probably. Do I want to? Nope! Ugh, this day really sucks arse! "You only need to do a few minutes and I'll take over again." There, that was a good attempt at easy conversation, right?

"Okay." Sheesh, that's all she's going to give me. I have to bite my lip as I watch her dig. No, I can't in good conscience say that what she's doing is digging. Has this woman ever seen, let alone held, a shovel before? I'm not sure how to explain what it is she's doing.

"If you shove it in the ground with your foot first, you'll pick up more dirt." I shouldn't have said anything because now she's glaring at me. Jesus, those daggers she's shooting are lethal.

"You wanted me to dig, and that's what I'm doing." She practically growls at me.

"No, what you're doing is shifting leaves around."

"Feel free to do it yourself then, *Ms. Stuart*."

"Fine." The niceties didn't last long, did they?

I march over and take the shovel. "Watch and learn. You can try again once you grasp what you need to do." I don't wait for the snarky comment that I know she wants to lob at me. I ram the head of the shovel into the hole that Mic and I created. Using my foot, I push it deeper before breaking off a chunk of dirt. Throwing it over my shoulder, I look directly at Ellie. "That's what I need from you."

"Fine," she grinds out before snatching the shovel out of my hands. I take a step back and wait. I can see her trying to calm herself down, which makes me feel a little embarrassed for my behaviour. Why have I just humiliated the woman? That's what I've done. She came out here to help me, even though I know she didn't want to, and instead of guiding her gently, I mocked her for not digging correctly. Great, now I feel like a right dick!

"You're doing great," I say enthusiastically. To be fair, she is giving it some welly. She's definitely shifted more dirt than her first attempt. My encouragement is not well received. Already I can see sweat staining the back of her top. The hair at the nape of her neck darkens as it gets damp. I chide myself for thinking about licking that sweat from her neck. It's gross and inappropriate, but it seems my mind is off on its own sexy tangent. I'm helpless to stop it. Ellie is sexy as hell.

"Can I take a break?" She huffs. I was so lost in my head I missed the fact that she'd stopped digging and is bent over breathing heavily. It surprises me because I presumed she would be accustomed to working out in the gym or something. That's what these Hollywood types do, isn't it? But looking at how out of breath she is, there is no way she does regular exercise. I'd wager she does very little at all.

"I'll finish up. You go back to the plane. Have some water." Unsurprisingly, she doesn't protest. In fact, I've never seen her so motivated. I watch her for a few moments as she stumbles through the plants in those stupid wedged sandals. The eye roll is unavoidable. Why did no one help her pack appropriate clothing and footwear?

Roughly thirty minutes later and the hole is done. Ideally, I would like it to be a little deeper, but my arm is on fire, and I'm dehydrated. Dropping the shovel to the floor, I make my way back to the plane. Mic and Cam are sitting outside. All the bags are laid at their feet. Ellie is standing in front of them with her hands on her hips looking like she's about to castrate them.

"Hey, guys, is everything okay?" Obviously, everything is *not* okay. Cam's eyes are the size of saucers. Mic is shielding his crotch, looking terrified. If it were any other situation, I would probably laugh at their behaviour. I get Ellie is fiery and imposing, but she isn't that bloody scary. "Guys, what's going on?"

"We...we were going through the bags...like you asked," Cam stammered.

"And I had already made it clear that he was not to touch my bag." Ellie growled.

"We just moved them out here so we could get a better idea of what we had. I didn't open your bag, I swear," Cam stutters. The poor guy is a mess.

"I don't give a fuck!" she yells, causing us all to jump. Christ, this woman is something else.

"Hey, I get that you're upset, but can you stop the shouting?" I keep eye contact with her, hoping she understands that I'm not trying to be combative.

Everyone just needs to take a step back and calm the fuck down.

"No one touches my stuff," she huffs out. At least she seems to be a tad bit calmer. Mic is still protecting his crown jewels, which makes me grin.

"Look, we can deal with the bags later. We need to move José." Well, that sentence certainly got their attention. Ellie looks like she wants to puke. "Mic, will you help me get him out of the cabin? Ellie, can you look for something we can use to carry him? A blanket, something like that." She visibly relaxes, and I pat myself on the back for averting another Ellie Bishop meltdown.

Mic takes José's legs, so I grab under his armpits. José is literally dead weight. My back and arm muscles are wailing at me as I take his weight. With some effort, we get him outside and onto a blanket that Ellie found. Bending over, I take a few deep lungfuls of air. It's going to be a fucking ball ache carrying him to the burial site. *Stop complaining, Marine, get moving!*

"On three," I say to Mic. It's a herculean job, but we get José to his grave. Earlier it made me sad to think this hole would be his final resting place, but I won't let that happen. I'll make sure he gets back to his family for a proper service.

"Should we say something?" Mic asks as we stand there looking down at José, wrapped up in the blanket at the bottom of the pit. I bow my head and say the Lord's Prayer. I have no idea what, if any, religion José followed, but at least he had something said for him.

"Come on, let's get back," I say quietly. All my energy is gone. I've been on an adrenaline rush since the plane crashed, but now it's like a plug has been pulled, and I'm drained. Fuck me, I still have to deal with Ellie.

Mic heads over to Cam when we arrive back. Cam has seemingly decided it's better to stay out of Ellie's way. Can't blame the fella. I go in search of our resident movie star. She's crouched down by her pack. Christ, she looks like she's an animal protecting its kill. What the hell has she got in that bag? "Hey, how are you?"

"Fine," she snaps. I huff out a breath. I'm way too tired for her attitude right now.

"Listen, can *you* at least go through your bag and take out anything that could be of use? I get you don't want strangers rifling through your knickers, but we still need to band together, and there could be something in your pack that helps us." See, I can be a reasonable pers

"There is nothing that will help in my pack, I assure you."

"Are you being fucking serious right now?" All right, not so reasonable after all. "Ellie, take a look around. We need all the fucking help we can get. Saving your fucking Gucci clothes isn't a priority. Keeping us alive and healthy is. Get your head out of your arse and stop causing more problems. We have enough to worry about." Oh, boy. I just dropped a lot of F bombs. My chest is rising and falling rapidly. Crap, I just went off on America's most beloved actress. Ah, whatever! We might die, and she needs to hear a few home truths. I'm guessing she's surrounded by sycophants twenty-four-seven. Maybe it's time she had someone who has the balls to tell her how it is. How her selfish behaviour affects those around her.

"Don't touch my shit," she seethes before

pushing past me to go outside. I drop to one of the seats. There's still so much to do to make sure we're safe. Well, as safe as can be in the middle of the Amazon rainforest in a wrecked plane. I desperately want to shut my eyes and sleep for a year, but I can't.

I haul myself off the chair and shuffle outside. It's the first time I've really looked around. When we first arrived, I was so focused on getting José buried, I didn't stop to take in our environment. The trees are dense apart from the area immediately around us. I wince at the destruction I caused when landing the plane. The sun is streaming through the tree canopy. The heat is all consuming, but it's so far from the heat I'm used to in California. This is a wet, stifling heat. My clothes are already saturated with sweat.

"Cam, how are our supplies looking?"

"I'm no expert, but I think we only have a few days of water, and that's if we drink sparingly. Food-wise, well, it's slim pickings. Out of all of us, you were the only one to bring food." I close my eyes, willing myself not to scream at them all. I told the producers to make sure each of them had at least four days' worth of dehydrated food packs in their bags. Clearly, the message didn't get passed on or they ignored it. I can imagine Ellie not paying a blind bit of attention to what anyone said, but Cam and Mic? That grates me.

"Were you told to add food packs to your gear?" As soon as the words leave my mouth, I can see that they ignored the instruction. Cam and Mic both go red and dip their heads. Ellie—who is sitting twenty metres away—ignores me. I drop my head to my chest. "Can I ask why you didn't do as you were asked?"

"We...I..." Mic splutters.

"Sorry, Robin," Cam mumbles.

"Ellie, what about you?" Frustration is bubbling at the surface of my skin. Ellie is turned away from me. Is she really going to ignore me, even when I'm talking directly to her? God, the gall of this woman. "Ellie?" I bark. That gets her attention. She swings around to face me, her face marred with anger. In a flash, she's on her feet and stomping away. I watch her bypass the wreckage and head into the forest. That seems like a monumentally bad idea.

I'm so fed up with her bullshit that all I want to do is let her stalk off into the forest and get lost, but alas, I can't do that. At the end of the day, she's my responsibility. I turn on my heel and jog after her. I know she's still reeling after I chewed her out earlier, so I'm going to have to swallow my pride and apologise. It's the easiest thing to do to get her to come back and hopefully stop causing more problems.

Laughing at the absurdity of it all, I follow the sound of Ellie tumbling through the undergrowth. She's certainly not stealthy. In all her ire, I wonder if she realised how vulnerable she's making herself by going off alone. I catch sight of her leaning against a tree. I stop and observe. Her shoulders are moving and slouched. Damn it, she's crying.

Chapter Nine

Ellie

I hate that I can't get control of myself. Yes, I'm not made for the jungle, but I know how to survive. I have lived and thrived in Hollywood for years. I can do this. Tell that to my emotions, though. My face feels tight now that the tears are drying on my cheeks. It's not just that I'm *here*, it's that I'm here with no one who knows me. Not the real me. Toni would be able to talk me through this. She's the closest thing I have to a sister. Gabe is fucking useless. I really drew the short straw in the sibling pool.

Why have I let Robin's little outburst upset me so much? Is it because I'm simply not used to people talking to me like that? Maybe. Is it because I know Robin has such a low opinion of me? Also possible. God, I'm so pissed at myself. I don't let anyone make me feel like this. Toni would laugh at that statement. I let my mother and Gabe make me feel like shit all the time. It feels different with Robin, though. She's infuriating and far too full of herself, but it upsets me that she sees me as a useless airhead.

The voice in my head is asking all the questions that I wish it wouldn't. For example: Why have I behaved the way I have since meeting Robin? Hand to heart, I've given her a really shitty first impression of myself. It's automatic. My mother's voice whispers in my ear that I must always hold myself above others. I'm Hollywood royalty. It's fucked up, I know it is, but years of indoctrination are hard to undo. That's why I behaved like a spoiled brat when I first met Robin, Mic, and Cam. Because at *that* moment, I saw myself as better than them.

Since then, I've made it all worse by snapping and bitching at the one person who can actually get us out of this hellhole. On top of that, I won't let them go through my bags, and well, no wonder they all think I'm an asshole diva. The reality is, I have no problem with them using any clothes. I just don't want them finding the add-ons. I don't want to explain my personal business to them. Fuck! I've handled this all so badly. What I wouldn't give for a bottle of vodka right now.

My heart rate is finally settling, and the tears have stopped. I've had a mild panic attack. That's why I stupidly ran off from Robin and the boys. No way on Earth will I let them see me have an attack. They've already seen me freak out after we landed. Now I have to get a goddamn grip on myself. I am Ellie Bishop. "I am Ellie Bishop," I say, a little louder to no one. "I am Ellie Bishop." This time, I say it with conviction.

"Well, Ellie Bishop, can you come back to the plane where it's safe?" The blood rushes to my head before I can school my reaction to Robin's presence. She clearly heard me saying my own name. Great, that's just wonderful. I close my eyes and will the universe to strike me down. I'm tired of the humiliation that is my life right now. "Seriously, Ellie, I don't want you this far away from the plane."

I push off the tree and walk with my head held high past Robin. Conversing isn't an option for me at the moment. Leaves and sticks crunch behind me as I do my level best not to go ass over tits on these godforsaken heels. *Please, please, please, tell me there are some walking type shoes in my bag.*

"Um, not to be that person," Robin says, meaning she is definitely going to be that person, "but you're going the wrong way. The plane is to the left." My eyes brim with unshed tears. I can't get anything right. I couldn't even pack dried food like I was told to, and now we could starve to death.

Once I've rid myself of tears, I turn to Robin and gesture for her to lead. I still can't talk. Thankfully, Robin stays silent and slowly walks in the direction of the wreck. I follow behind, trying to figure out where I go from here. Robin was right when she shouted at me. I *do* need to get my head out of my ass.

We reach the plane. Cam and Mic are still in the same spot they were when I left. Three packs lay spread across the floor. Unsurprisingly, Robin came very well prepared. A wave of guilt washes through me as I think of my unopened pack stored back on the plane. Shaking my head to dislodge the thought, I peer over at Robin. She's slumped on the ground, eyes closed, holding her arm that has the gash on it.

"You need to deal with your arm," I say. I do a happy dance in my head that my voice is clear and confident.

"I'll get it sorted. Just need five minutes," Robin says without opening her eyes again. I take a second to look at her. She still looks like Lara Croft but now a tired version. I can see dark circles under her eyes. All her clothes are saturated with sweat. I was so focused on my own shit that I didn't notice our fearless leader is looking a little off.

"When was the last time you ate? Had some water?" I'm no medic, but I know those things are pretty important. We're all suffering from dehydration, and we've only been here for a few hours. But in those hours, it's Robin who has been working the hardest. She needs to rest and drink water.

"I'll get some in a second," she answers.

"Right." Anger sizzles in my veins. Robin has chewed me out about being part of a team to help us get through this, yet here she is, not looking after herself. How the fuck does that help "The Team"? None of us will know what to do if she collapses, and honestly, the way she's looking, that could happen any time. "Drink some water," I snap. I didn't mean it to come out so harshly. The tone obviously caught her attention because her eyes are definitely open now and staring at me. Wow, she has a really intense stare. Did she learn that in the military?

"Fine." She growls. That's our thing now. Snapping, growling, and seething at each other. She shuffles, trying to stand up. It's a bad idea. I put my hand firmly on her shoulder, keeping her on the ground. Without a word, I stalk off and grab a bottle of water from the pile of rations next to Mic and Cam. They're watching us like we're about to go off on each other. It's possible that could happen. "Thanks," she mumbles when I pass her the water.

"Please get your arm fixed. It's still bleeding. And like you said, we don't want to be attracting anything. Surely, blood will attract *things*." I can't help but look around me as I say those words. Jesus, I feel like there are eyes on me. It's like a slasher movie, but instead of the hills having eyes, it's the trees.

"You're right." Robin wipes a hand over her

face. I wonder if admitting I was right has just caused her physical pain. "Could you ask the boys to grab my first aid kit?" Now that is something I can do. See, not totally useless.

Mic throws me the first aid kit. I want to laugh because he's still unconsciously protecting his man bits when he comes near me. All right, so threatening to turn him into a eunuch was maybe a little extreme, but when I saw that he and Cam were hovering near my bag earlier, I saw red.

Robin struggles to unzip the kit. Lord knows how she's going to fix up her arm. "I can help," I say. Why did I say it? No clue. I have zero experience with cuts and blood. Actually, the sight of blood makes me want to puke.

"I can do it." She really can't. I stand in front of her for a good five minutes before she finally loses her shit and shouts at nothing.

"Would you like my help now?" I ask a little too smugly. Robin squeezes her eyes shut and takes a few deep breaths. Why am I antagonizing a woman who could probably snap my neck with one hand? And why does that thought turn me the hell on?

"Yes, could you help?"

I tell her to shuffle forward so I can sit behind her. The cut is deep and long. Crap, it needs stitches, you don't need to be a doctor to see that. "Robin, this needs a doctor," I say stupidly.

"Well, it looks like you've just earned a medical degree, Ms. Bishop."

"What the hell do you think I can do? It's an open wound," I almost shriek. I really need to get a handle on my reactions.

"I need you to clean it and stitch it. Surely you

know how to sew."

"Why? Because I'm a woman?" I shoot back hotly.

"Yes, and I'm a nineteen fifties man who thinks that you should also know how to cook." Sarcasm. Right, how I love that characteristic in a woman.

"Then why do you think I can sew?"

"I presumed, like most people, you were taught in school. That's how it is in the UK. If you can't sew, that's fine. You will just have to cauterize it instead."

"Cauterize it."

"Yes, take my knife, heat it up, and press it to the cut. That will seal it."

So Robin is a psychopath? You agree, right? In what universe does she think that's something to throw out in general conversation? Okay, not general conversation, but shit, it's not something I ever thought would be said to me, let alone asked of me.

"I'm not doing that. I can sew," I say through gritted teeth because the thought of seared human flesh is making my gag reflex work double time.

"Use the wipes and alcohol to clean it. Thoroughly. Then grab the needle, douse it in alcohol, and get to stitching. It doesn't need to be perfect." Robin grabs a stick from the ground close to her. She picks off some bark and then shoves it between her teeth. I can see her jaw muscles tensing.

I swallow the bile that's trying its hardest to creep up my throat. I follow Robin's instructions and start cleaning the wound. My body tenses with every swipe of the cotton across her skin. I see Robin shaking in pain, but she never utters a word. Jesus, she's probably the toughest person I've ever met.

Discarding the blood-soaked rags, I then set

about sterilizing the needle. My hands are shaking so violently that I have to stop and take a breath. My gaze meets Robin's. Her face is marred with pain, but she's nodding at me, encouraging me to go on.

With the needle threaded, I make the first stitch. Robin has dropped her head to her chest. Her hands are in tight fists, both of them clenching hard enough to make her skin turn white. Every time I pierce her skin with the needle, I want to cry out an apology. I can't fathom how she's remaining so calm and quiet.

Finally, *finally*, I make the last stitch. I tie it off and cut away the thread from the needle. My handiwork won't win any awards, and I'm sure it's going to leave Robin with a scar, but the bleeding has stopped, and the stitches are holding firm. I wipe the area one last time with alcohol before wrapping a bandage around it.

It's then that I notice Cam and Mic staring at me. They give me a slight nod. What does that mean? Robin lifts her head, the stick gone from between her teeth. Her breathing is labored. Understandably so. I pass her the bottle of water, which she reluctantly takes. My mind is whirring. Robin has to be okay. For us all to get home in one piece, Robin has to be okay. Those words are on a loop in my brain.

Mic comes over with a protein bar. "Eat this. You need to keep your strength up," he says to Robin. Robin is still breathing hard. She isn't looking at any of us. I take the bar from Mic. What I think I can achieve is beyond me. Let's be honest, I'm the last person Robin will listen to. Mic eyes Robin for another moment before retreating to Cam. Shuffling forward, I take Robin's hand and place the protein bar in it.

"Thanks," she whispers. I say nothing because I'm likely to ruin the moment if I open my mouth. It's a flaw. Her hand shakes as she tries to unwrap it. Stupid Ellie. I take the bar back again and open it for her. I forgo giving it back to her; instead, I feed her slowly. It was the right call. Robin has no energy at all. Maybe twenty minutes pass, and I'm still on the ground feeding her. I'm worried she's going into shock or something.

"Let's get you to the plane. I think you need to sleep a little," I say, like I have a clue what I'm talking about. "Mic, can you help me?" There's no way Robin will make it on her own. Together, we haul her up, careful not to bang her arm. Robin's head is streaming with sweat. I don't know if it's from the heat, the stitching, or something worse. What if it's infected already? What if she hurt herself worse than we can see? I can feel another panic attack coming on. I can't just drop Robin and run off. Goddamn this place. I take in some really big breaths. I focus on what my therapist told me to do. Five things I can see. The plane, Robin, trees, Cam, Mic. Four things I can feel. Robin, water bottle, my shorts (still up my ass), and sweat on my skin. Three things I can hear. Birds, Robin breathing, Mic humming the *Thunderbirds* theme song. I'll dissect that later! Two things I can smell. Robin, moss. One thing I can taste. Blood.

By the time I have gotten to one, I'm grounded, and we're at the plane. Robin is practically asleep standing. With some difficulty, we get her inside. Cam comes bounding in with blankets and sleeping bags. He makes a bed for Robin. We lie her down and take a second to catch our breaths. Robin is out for the count.

"I'll stay with her for now. I don't think she

should be on her own," I say because that seems like a logical thing to do, right? She could develop a fever or something.

"I'll take the next watch," Cam says through winces. He's still cradling his shoulder.

"We need to deal with your arm, too," I say.

"I think it's popped out." Cam groans. He's obviously in pain. Jesus H. Christ, this day just gets better.

"Any idea what we're supposed to do?" I don't have a clue, well, nothing past what I've seen on *Grey's Anatomy*.

"I've read how to put it back into place," Cam says. He's read it? How and when and why was that a subject he needed to learn? "Robin has a 'how-to guide' in her pack. It's full of shit like that," Cam says wide-eyed. Of course, Robin has a guide of how to put a body back together. Of course!

"Can you do it?" Mic asks me.

"Me?" I blurt.

"You stitched Robin's arm. I couldn't have done it, Ellie. Seriously, that is some gruesome shit. I'll pass out before Cam if I have to attempt it." Dear Lord, I now have to put a shoulder back in its socket. And there goes my gag reflex again.

"Get me the guide," I say a little curtly. I can't be polite and keep vomit in my body at the same time. Mic is back in a flash brandishing the guide like it's a bible. Well, in some ways it is, I suppose. Cam sits patiently as I read and reread Robin's manual about dislocated joints. Ew, it's so gross. I look helplessly at Robin, willing her to wake up and be magically better. No doubt she would have that joint popped back in quicker than I can sink a flute of champagne. FYI, that's really quick.

No luck, she's still out of it. *All right, Ellie, you got this!* "Cam, let's do this outside." Mic is next to me, ready to take instructions. I've told him he can keep his eyes shut, but he has to help. One last glance at the guide, and I get to it. I can honestly say hearing a joint pop back into place will haunt my dreams for the rest of my life. That or Cam's scream as I lifted his arm. Oh, or maybe Mic projectile vomiting. Pick one, and I can assure you I will relive the horror whenever my eyes close.

With Cam passed out on the chair behind Robin and Mic propped up next to him, I have little choice but to lie down next to Robin. The sun is still out, but we decided as a group to retire to the safety of the cabin. Without Robin, we're just three useless Hollywood assholes who will more than likely get eaten on the first night. So we play it safe and secure ourselves away for the rest of the day and night.

The sound of animals and insects seems to reverberate around the plane. I want to sleep so badly, but my mind is refusing to let it happen. Mic and Cam are snoring. I have no idea how long we've been in the plane, but the light is considerably darker. I do my grounding technique repeatedly, but my head won't stop panicking. Then I feel an arm snake around my stomach. My first reaction is to tense. I'm not used to intimate touches like this. Turning my head, I look over my shoulder. Robin is still fast asleep, but she's spooning the shit out of me. I close my eyes and lean into her body. Well, what do you know, my mind is going quiet! Only the birds are singing, and that's something I can deal with. Closing my eyes, I concentrate on the songs of the forest. Robin pulls me closer.

Chapter Ten

Robin

Either I'm having the best dream of my life or my face is somewhere it definitely should not be! Shit, I really don't want to open my eyes and find out. In all fairness, I'm not even sure where I am.

The last thing I remember was blinding pain in my arm as Ellie sewed me up. It's a black hole after that. If I had to guess, I would say I'm in the plane's cabin. There are blankets below me. I can feel them on my skin. The noise from the rainforest is audible but not very loud, so I must be inside. Hopefully, the others are in here, too. Surely, they wouldn't have been stupid enough to stay outside.

So I'm in the plane, lying on blankets. The mystery part is why I can feel soft skin beneath my lips. Now I'm not much of a betting woman, but I'll hazard a guess that whoever slept next to me now has my body wrapped round them and my lips on their neck. Probably should have warned them all that I'm a cuddler in my sleep. I don't discriminate. If you're next to me and I'm sleeping, you will be held. Obviously, I hope that it's either Cam or Mic because that will be infinitely less mortifying than if I've snuggled up to Ellie bloody Bishop.

Time to find out. I crack my eyes open, and my heart sinks. Fine blond hair is in my line of sight. Ellie has blond hair. *Please, please, please, don't be awake!* I very carefully lift my face from her neck. Turning, I see Cam and Mic still snoring. Phew. Next, I lean over to see if Ellie is awake. She's not, or she's faking because she's feeling really fucking uncomfortable.

Like the stealthy Marine I am, I gently extract myself from her body. Rolling over is an epic bastard mistake because now I'm crushing my arm. You know, the one with a goddamn wound on the back of it. Biting my lip, I shift to a sitting position. My head feels woozy. I can't have had much to eat or drink yesterday, and my body is telling me I need to rectify that immediately. The last thing we all need is for me to take a turn for the worse. My arm is already a concern, I have to keep it clean and infection-free.

The light shining through the little windows shows that dawn is arriving rapidly. Ideally, I want to get outside and check out the surrounding area. We need to set up a camp and discuss what our next move should be. With it being so early, though, I could risk bumping into something that's still on the hunt. Best I stay inside for a little while longer. That doesn't mean I should stay next to Ellie. My lips are still tingling from the feel of her supple skin, and frankly, I'm horny as hell. Her body fit mine so well. I could feel every curve. Did I mention that Ellie Bishop is super hot?

Shaking myself out of my lusty haze, I get to my feet. There isn't a lot of room in the cabin, the plane is small. I head towards the cockpit to assess the damage again. Maybe the radio has magically decided to work. It hasn't. No way we're getting through to anyone. Looking at the state of the co-pilot seat, a wave of nausea rolls through me, and it has nothing to do with the fact that I need food. It's suddenly clear how close I came to dying in that chair. I need to get in a better headspace. I know this isn't a war zone, but I think that's how I need to treat it. My mind knows how to compartmentalise in those conditions. I have to be the Marine I was all those years ago.

The sun is much higher now. My trusty watch that I've had since serving is missing from my wrist. Did I take it off yesterday? Jesus, I wish it weren't all such a blur. Now I've drunk some water and snacked on a protein bar, I'm feeling a little more with it. I crank open the door and let the sunlight and heat flood in. Movement from the two lads snatches my attention. Cam is awake, stretching. He smiles at me and nods to signal we should go outside so as not to wake the others. They'll have to get up soon, though. We have a lot to do.

"How you feeling, boss?" Cam asks me. Not sure why he's calling me boss but whatever.

"Better. I guess I passed out, huh?"

"Oh, yeah. As soon as Ellie had finished stitching, you were out of it."

"Any problems?" I'm basically asking if Ellie was a pain in the arse after I passed out.

"None. Ellie popped my arm back in." I stare at him, a little dumbfounded. Did he just say Ellie Bishop, diva of the rainforest, helped him? "She read the manual that you brought. Honestly, she was a badass."

"Wow, okay. Can I look at your arm?" Impressive, she even put it in a sling. I need to check for my own reassurance, though. If she got it wrong, Cam could end up with a lot of problems down the line. Cam slips off the sling and his shirt. On first glance, his shoulder looks like it's where it should be. Carefully, I exam it. Ellie has done a great job.

"Whaddya think, Doc?" Cam grins.

"Looking good. Keep the sling on for another few days. You'll have to limit yourself. No lifting."

"No problem. I can be in charge of admin." He laughs.

"Morning, all." Mic yawns, stepping down from the plane. "Christ, I slept like a baby."

"Me too, buddy. You're comfy. I'm sleeping on your shoulder tonight, as well." Cam chuckles. I like these two. Their easy rapport is uplifting. That thought brings me back to the other person in our stranded group. How much trouble will Ellie cause me today?

"Let's get some food, and then we need to talk. Decide what we want to do." The boys nod. Cam volunteers to grab some of our meagre supplies. Ellie trails behind him when he returns from the cabin. I'm impressed again. Not only did these guys sort me out, they made sure our food was stored inside for the night, too. Not so useless after all.

Ellie looks tired as hell, although she's obviously spent a few minutes on her hair because it's immaculate. Not sure who she's trying to impress. She knows there are no paparazzi in the Amazon, right?

"Morning," she says to us all. Her gaze lingers on me for a second, and I swallow hard.

"Morning," I reply. "Thanks for sorting my arm out and Cam's shoulder." It's the least I can say.

"Sure." That's it. No more words. Great, I'm still on her shit list by the looks of it.

After a delightful breakfast of another protein bar, I gather the squad. That's what I'm going to call them. Hopefully, I can get them to act like one. "Okay, folks, let's get down to business," I say as upbeat as possible. Cam and Mic seem to perk up, but Ellie is looking like someone pissed in her cornflakes. "I think we should set up camp here."

"I'm cool with that. What do you want us to do?" Mic asks.

"First, let's get us some shade. The plane has done a number on the trees, as you can see, so we're going to be exposed to the sun. The plane will be like an oven during the day. Mic, can you fish around the cabin and look for a parachute? We can use it as a canopy. Cam, you can sit with the gear for now. You need to rest that arm." He nods but doesn't look too happy about it. I think he's feeling shitty that we're having to do the heavy lifting. "Ellie, can you help me create a firepit just over there?" I point to a clearing a few metres away from the plane. Ellie nods but doesn't speak.

Within an hour, we have a canopy over the door of the plane. We tied it to a couple of trees, so we have a decent shelter. It will do bugger all if the heavens open, but it will stop us all getting burnt to a crisp under the sun. Ellie was silent throughout the entire process. Honestly, I'm a tad worried. She isn't looking too well at all. Her face is sweaty, but it's not because of the heat. "Hey, you okay?" I ask.

"Fine."

"You sure? You look ill."

"I said I'm fine." Okay, snappy much? I hold my palms up in surrender. That's the last time I will try with her. She's exhausting. I mean seriously, we're all in this mess, not just her. Argh, she's infuriating.

To dispel my bad mood caused by Queen Ellie, I set up the firepit. It'll come in handy if we're able to catch something that needs cooking. I'll set up a few traps and hope for the best. For now, I need everyone to forage. The dehydrated food I brought won't last long at all.

To make sure no one gets poisoned, I hand the group a list of plants that are edible. I only have one copy, so they'll need to take turns collecting the foliage. I studied the list before we came and am confident I can accurately identify the plants and berries we can eat. Mic and Cam volunteer to head out first. I make sure they know to mark their path as they go. Last thing I want is to be going out looking for them. I also make it clear not to go too far away.

Ellie has been sitting by the firepit for a good half an hour now. Her body looks like it's shivering, which is odd. The rainforest is not cold. Her behaviour has me worried. Could she be reacting to the procedures she had to perform yesterday? I could understand that. I doubt she's had to do anything like that in her life. She's certainly never played a doctor or nurse in any of her movies.

There's not much point in me trying to start a conversation with her again, so I head inside to arrange the plane better. If we're going to be sleeping all together, we need to be a little more organised. No way in hell can there be a repeat of this morning. Although, my body would like there to be. God, I can still smell Ellie's fresh scent. *Creep, get a grip!*

Happy that we have a decent sleeping area, I slip back outside. The cabin is like a sauna. Unfortunately, we need to keep the door closed to stop bugs getting inside. Peering over to Ellie, I stop in my tracks. Littered around her feet are at least three protein bar wrappers.

"Have you just eaten all those?" I ask.

"I had to eat," she says. Well, no shit, Sherlock,

we all have to eat.

"So you thought helping yourself to our limited supply was the answer?" I am pissed!

"We still have plenty," she snaps, but she isn't looking at me.

"We will have fuck all if you keep dipping in when you feel like it. Goddamn it, Ellie. We're all hungry, but do you see the rest of us being selfish arseholes? You really take the fucking cake! Understand something, you are not the only one here trying to survive. I can't believe you have been so bloody self-centred." My voice is at shouting level, and I can't seem to rein it in. I am so over this woman. I'm making a vow. If I make it out of this alive, I will never, *ever* work with anyone remotely linked to Hollywood. Utter bastards. Selfish fuckers, the lot of them.

My anger is getting the better of me, and I know I need to be away from her pronto. Storming in the other direction, I head into the forest. I'm not worried about finding my way back. In fact, never seeing Ellie Bishop again seems like a fantastic idea. Maybe I should lose myself! I walk and walk until I'm out of breath. Then I scream like a banshee into the trees. Pretty sure I've scared half the animals to death. No worries about me getting eaten. Every critter within a mile is probably running for its life after that performance. It feels good to scream my frustration away.

What am I going to do? I'd like to gather my pack and leave them all to it. That's not an option, though. It's not Cam and Mic's fault Ellie is so awful and selfish. With my body calming down, I walk back to the wreck site. Avoiding Ellie is going to be my number one goal. I'm done playing nice.

Mic and Cam are back when I round the plane.

They have a nice collection of plants and berries. We spend a few minutes going over them, double-checking we won't shit ourselves to death if we ingest them. All clear. Tonight's menu is going to be vegetarian. I want to keep the high-energy dehydrated food for as long as possible. If we have to break camp and move on, we'll need all the nutrition we can get.

"Where's Ellie?" Cam asks. I noticed she wasn't in the area and presumed she'd just gone inside. Apparently not.

"No idea, I'm sure she won't be too far." I refuse to go out looking for her again.

"Hey, I had an idea," Mic chimes in. "I know that the show is obviously not going to happen because well…" He waves his hands around, highlighting our current circumstances. "But I was thinking that we could all document our time out here. We have individual GoPros. I was thinking we could keep our own journals. Then if we get rescued, we have something to show the world, and if we all die, we have a last will and testament if the equipment is ever found." Jesus, that's morbid!

"Christ, Mic, negative much?" Cam laughs.

"No, I don't mean to be, but I think we have to be realistic. We have no idea if we'll be found, and let's be honest, there are many things here that could hurt us. I'm just saying it would be a good idea to document our wishes. Plus, it might be therapeutic to get our thoughts and feelings out."

The man has a point. Before each mission I went on, I would draft a letter stating my wishes if anything happened to me. Of course, I had an actual will, and the military knew what to do if I died, but I still liked having that letter on me. "I'm in," I say. "I'll happily do it. Will you remind me what I need to do?"

"Sure, hang on." Mic skips into the plane and fetches the camera equipment. The camera itself is small. Mic attaches it to a tripod that can bend 'round things, meaning I can set it up practically anywhere.

The device isn't difficult to use, so after a quick recap from the guys, I head into the plane to make my first log.

I hit record. "My name is Robin Stuart. I'm the survival expert on *Wild Celebrities*. Two days have passed since the plane we boarded crashed. I want to take this time to explain what happened." I go into precise detail about José. The landing and everything that has happened since. Mic was right, it's quite therapeutic. "I intend to record daily. I will note this as day one." I take a beat. "If I'm honest, I'm fucking exhausted already. We have little food and very little water. I have no clue where in the Amazon we are. When José collapsed, his body caused the plane to veer off course. I have a map, but unless I can get my bearings, it's pretty useless. The radio on the plane is broken, and I hold little hope that we'll be located via the plane's tracker. So far, we've set up a makeshift camp by the wreckage. Luckily, the cabin is in good shape, and we can lock ourselves away at night. We have foraged for some food, but it's not sustainable long term. Once the water runs out, we're going to have to move on.

"So far as a group, we're doing okay. Mic and Cam are old friends. Their banter certainly lightens the mood. I can't say I've had an easy ride with Ellie. We'll see how that progresses. I'll check back in tomorrow. Hopefully, I'll have had a better day than today." I wave at the camera for some reason and then hit the stop button.

"How was it?" Cam asks when I return to our parachute hangout spot.

"Pretty good. I think we should all do it."

"Yeah, I will. Do you think Ellie will want to?" Cam asks. Of course she won't.

"Is she back yet?"

"Nope," Mic replies. There's a very long line of expletives running through my mind right now. She's leaving me with no choice but to go searching for her. Again!

"All right, I'll go look for her. Back soon." They give me a nod of understanding. I think my feelings for Ellie are written all over my face. It takes me several minutes to pick up her trail. For once, I'm glad she's wearing those stupid sandals, it makes finding her easier. Ten minutes pass, and then I hear it. Sobbing coming from behind a tree. So I guess she's crying again. Helpful.

Rounding the tree, I take her in. She's slumped down, there's blood on her thigh. Crap, she's injured herself. I kneel next to her and survey the wound. It isn't deep. Ellie is still sobbing. She hasn't even noticed I'm there. "Ellie," I shout. Her eyes snap open, but they look unfocused. "Ellie, can you walk?" Her gaze is trained on mine, but she looks thoroughly confused. Something isn't right with her. "Ellie, have you eaten something, something from here?" I ask, gesturing to her surroundings.

"Where am I?" she asks. Shit, I don't think this is an act. Ellie looks out of it.

"Ellie, you're in the Amazon, remember? We had a crash." Her eyes slip closed again. This isn't good.

Chapter Eleven

Ellie

Oh, there's a really nice breeze on my face. Damn, that feels good. Hang on, why are my eyes closed? What happened? Oh, no. I had an episode. Crap, how am I going to explain this?

"Hey, I think she's coming around." That's Cam's voice.

"Stop waving that stupid leaf at her," Mic replies. I hear some movement.

"Ellie, can you hear me?" Robin's voice is close to my ear, she's practically purring at me. Or maybe my brain is just fried and I'm imagining her sultry tone. Yep, totally losing my mind. Excellent.

"I-I'm okay," I reply. My voice is almost a whisper, which is unintended. My throat feels like sandpaper.

"Mic, grab that water bottle," Robin says. A strong hand cups the back of my head and lifts it slightly. "Here, take a drink." I swallow greedily. It feels like I have no moisture left in my body.

"Thanks," I splutter. My eyes adjust to the sunlight. The heat is all-encompassing and uncomfortable.

"Let's sit you up," Robin says, her hands supporting my back. "How are you feeling now?" That's the million-dollar question, isn't it? I feel humiliated.

After Robin caught me eating those protein bars and went full drill sergeant on me, I could feel another anxiety attack coming on. That's why I'd left. This time, I didn't just blindly walk off into the rainforest, I left a trail so that when the attack had passed, I could find my way back. That was the plan, anyway. But I tripped and cut myself because of my stupid sandals. When I hit the ground, my emotions took over. Add that to my low blood sugar, and well, it was a recipe for disaster.

My memories are patchy after that. I know I was crying, which is shocking because I'm not sure I had enough water left in my body to produce tears. I remember Robin's voice, but then nothing. I must have passed out. Great! All I can hear is my mother's voice hissing in my ear that I have to keep quiet. No one can know about my "issues"—her words, not mine. God forbid anyone gets to know the real Ellie Bishop. So how do I get around this? I lie. Well, I can just blame it on shock and lack of water.

"I'm fine now. Sorry if I worried you. Just needed five minutes to myself, but I fell over something." That's when the pain in my leg rears its head. Fuck, I really scraped myself.

"Robin cleaned up your leg. It's only a scratch," Cam offers. Now I'm doubly embarrassed because I should apologize to Robin about the whole protein bar incident, but no matter what, I can't tell her the truth, so I'm still going to come across as an asshole who ate everyone's food. Plus, she rescued me again without question, so there's that. Robin Stuart is a hero, and I am an entitled diva bitch. I internally roll my eyes.

"Thanks," I say quietly to Robin, who's surveying my leg.

"No worries," she replies with a tight smile. I'm feeling all kinds of awkward now. Cam and Mic are still standing over me, looking at the strained interaction between me and Robin. I can't take it anymore. All I want is for them to leave me alone so I can wallow for a little while. Actually, all I want is to pick up the phone and call Toni.

Toni is the only human on the planet who knows the shit I have to contend with. I know, I know, how bad can it be, right? I'm rich, living a life of luxury in the Hollywood Hills. Well, let me tell you, appearances are very deceiving, especially in my case.

Alas, I can't just call up Toni. I can't even shut myself away in my bedroom like I normally would when my emotions are too overwhelming. "I'm just going to…" I point to the door of the plane. Happily, I successfully pull myself to standing without help. On very unsteady feet, I stumble to the plane, climbing in on all fours. *That was not very dignified now, Ellie!* Holy crap, the plane is stifling. It's like a greenhouse, but I need some solitude, and this is the safest place right now.

Peering over my shoulder, I crawl to my pack. There are certain items in it that would really help me out. I'm scared, though. What if I get caught? That would open me up to all sorts of questions that I don't want to answer. The thing is, my nerves are fried, and I know that my blood sugar is still too low. Screw it, I need the help. Carefully and quietly, I unzip my pack and search for my socks. I'm just about to unroll them when I hear the door open behind me. Scrambling, I shove the offending sock bundle back into my pack and zip it up as fast as I can.

"Hey…" Robin says. I whirl around, and I know

I look guilty as hell. She's staring at me with quizzical eyes. Shit!

"Hey, hi," I stutter. *Nice work, Ellie, jeez.*

"I just wanted to make sure you drink some more water. You're really dehydrated."

"Right, cool, yeah, thanks." Good Lord.

"Okay. Right…also we decided to use the GoPros after all."

"What do you mean?"

"Cam and Mic brought GoPros for us all. It was supposed to be for the show, obviously. Well, we decided it would be a good idea to document our time here—"

"Why the hell would we want to do that? I don't know about you, but I have no intention of reminiscing about this shit when we get back." Um, I didn't mean to snap at her again. It's like shit just comes tumbling out around her.

"Well, you don't have to," she says.

"What do I have to say?"

"Anything you want. The three of us have already done a video today. It's actually quite therapeutic, but that's just my opinion."

"I'll think about it."

"Think of it this way. The video records will give you more ammunition for when you get back and sue the studio plus the rest of Hollywood." I don't know if she's being a bitch because I threatened to sue the pants off her or if she's making a joke. My silence has stretched on too long, and now I realize she was trying to be funny and probably thinks I'm a humorless douche. "Anyway, I'll leave you to it," she adds, turning on her boot heel and exiting the plane. I let my head drop to the seat behind me in defeat.

It's official. Robin and I are destined to be enemies. Awesome.

❧ ❧ ❦ ❦

The bird song is like a lullaby. I can't remember the last time I could really listen to nature. It's not like I've got tons of time to hang out in the wilderness at home. Ha, funny, as if I would do that anyway. I'm a city girl through and through, but at this moment, I'm really enjoying the peace that nature is providing me. It's the first time since this nightmare began that I feel calm. I'm not Zen, but I'm not about to lose my shit, either. I'll call that a win.

The water Robin gave me is gone, and the plane is still stupidly hot, but I'm not quite ready to leave my sanctuary yet. Over to my left is a GoPro that is set aside from the others. I presume it's the one that was assigned to me. The other three have got scraps of paper under them with their names scribbled on. Someone is organized. Probably Cam. He's the camera expert.

Huffing out a breath, I take the camera and attach it to the tripod that's with the other cameras. I'm not thrilled to be documenting my time here. I can't understand why we would want any of this shit preserved. Whatever, if Mic, Cam, and Robin are doing it, I should, too. What if we get rescued and the camera footage is used? Surely, people will wonder why I didn't contribute.

The camera is easy to use. It's not the first time I've played around with one. Toni bought one as a present for this girl she was seeing a few years ago. Said girl was an adrenaline junkie. Well, they lasted two weeks after that. Turns out the adrenaline of cheating was just as addictive as throwing herself out of a plane. Toni kept the GoPro, and we had a blast filming utter shit while we drank and cussed out her ex.

I set up the camera and press record. Instantly, I transform into Ellie Bishop, actress supreme. "Hi, everyone, welcome to the 'we crashed in the rainforest' program. Coming live from the Amazon." My megawatt smile is going to break the equipment if I don't tone it down. I don't know why I'm performing. Yeah, I do. I'm performing because I don't know how to let the real me shine through. Not when there's a chance someone could see this. *Optics, Ellie, remember the optics.* Ah, there's Mother's voice again.

"So let's get you all caught up on the shenanigans that are happening in our little camp. Robin Stuart, that's our survival expert, has built us a great camp. We have an awning and everything." Big-ass smile again. Shit, people are going to think it was a holiday at this rate. Maybe that's a good thing. What I really want to say would definitely bring the mood down. "Mic and Cam, that's the two crew members that traveled with us, are also awesome. What nice guys. I have to give a moment of silence to poor José, our dedicated pilot that unfortunately fell in service." I bow my head and stay silent for a couple of seconds. Jesus Christ, I'm appalled at myself right now!

"Rest in peace, José," I say before moving on. "The area we landed in is a little scary. The plane brought down quite a bit of the forest, so we have a clearing all around us. The sun is super hot. Glad I brought my factor fifty." I laugh at the lens. What a moron. My brain is screaming at me to be genuine for once. Just once in my life, I want to forget about the opinions of others and how everything I do is scrutinized. I want to cry in front of the camera and confess how goddamn terrified I am. Not just because we're stranded with little hope of being rescued but that I could die here, and the only thing people will remember is the false me. I will be immortalized as Hollywood's perfect princess when the truth is so different.

Tears fill my eyes. I'm helpless to stop them. I stop the camera recording. My fingers work automatically. They press the relevant buttons until I find the mp4 file on the camera and delete it. If that shit got watched, I would just be proving that I'm some vapid airhead. The usual internal voices are desperately trying to shout at me, telling me to hide myself behind the mask of my preconceived character. I can't, not now.

Repositioning the camera, I hit the record button again. After a couple of calming breaths, I look directly at the camera. Here goes! "I think it's day two, or is it day three? Honestly, I'm not sure anymore. So much has happened in such a short amount of time. Before I get into it, I need to say a couple of things first. This part of the video is in case we don't make it back home. Hopefully, one day this video will be found and will give you all a good idea of what went down.

"Toni Fresh, you are my absolute favorite person. You have been my friend and confidante for so long. I'm sorry I'm not around anymore. Please know that I'm holding you in my thoughts, always. Mother, Gabe, I wish I could say the same was true for the both of you. My biggest regret is that I never struck up the courage to tell you how your behavior affected me so badly. I suppose it doesn't matter now. For my fans, I love you all." I draw a breath. My mind already feels lighter for sharing that tiny bit of myself. "Food is short. I'm not sure how much water we have. I can't imagine it'll last long, though. The heat is so intense we're sweating more than we can consume. I'm scared. I know I'm not acting how Robin wants me to. We haven't exactly hit it off. I'm pretty sure she hates me and will offer me up as food if it gets that desperate." I give a mirthless laugh. I bet she would be happy to get rid of me if she could. "We're all sleeping in the plane's cabin. It's safe at least. For now. I'm struggling with my anxiety. I can't seem to get control of it at the minute. Let's hope I can soon. I don't know what will happen if I continue to spin out." That simple bit of talking has exhausted me. "I'll check in again tomorrow." I press stop.

Wow, that felt equally wonderful and terrible at the same time. The cabin is starting to feel claustrophobic. It's time I went outside.

The sun is a lot lower in the sky when I jump down to the ground. Robin, Mic, and Cam are all lying down under the canopy. I hesitate for a moment. They're used to me sulking in a corner by myself, but I don't want to be alone anymore.

"Hi," I say nervously. Robin lifts the cap she had draped over her face.

"Hey." She smiles, and I think it's genuine.

"So I did a recording. I don't know if it's what you guys wanted, I just rambled."

"Well, I had a full meltdown." Mic laughs.

"Me too," Cam adds. I nod and smile, thankful for their effort.

"Say whatever you want, it's your recording,"

Robin chimes in. Her tone is friendlier than before. Maybe we can build on that. If I can remember to stop snapping and getting shitty with her.

"So any news?" I ask with a chuckle.

"Well, Mic got hit in the face by this massive flying bug. It was hella funny." Cam laughs.

"Fuck you!" Mic laughs back. "You squealed like a bitch," Mic retorted.

"Hell yeah, I did. Did you see the size of it?"

"You both are ridiculous. It was a butterfly," Robin says, her tone mocking. I can't help but laugh out loud. Robin grins, but she's looking at me weirdly. Our eye contact goes on a little too long. I snap my gaze to Cam and Mic, who are now in a full-on banter war. My tummy does a little flip as I replay Robin's steely eyes on me.

Robin suddenly jumps up. "Just need to grab something," she says. I try subtly to watch her walk away. Not sure it worked. Her ass is so good it's really hard not to drool. Buns of steel are a real thing.

A few minutes pass, and Robin hasn't come out of the plane. Maybe it would be good for us to clear the air properly. I don't particularly want to have that conversation in front of the guys. I slip away and head for the cabin. Mic and Cam are busy talking about a project they hoped to work on after *Wild Celebrities*. Boy, do I hope they get to do it.

The door of the plane is ajar. I climb in and nearly collapse. Robin is on the floor with my pack. She's steadily making her way through my belongings. I can't believe what I'm seeing. "What the fuck are you doing?" I hiss. Surprisingly, Robin doesn't flinch. In fact, she continues to root through my things. I swallow hard as she takes out my bundled socks. Jesus

Christ, she's feeling them up, like she's looking for something. "Robin, get your fucking hands off my stuff," I seethe.

"No." she replies. I'm ready to go full fucking diva on her ass, but then the worst thing that could happen happens. With a flick of her wrist, she shakes my sock bundle, and the unmistakable rattle of pills echoes through the now silent cabin. Her gaze snaps to me. Those eyes bore into me as she unwraps my socks. Inevitably, my pills drop to the floor. Robin doesn't stop there. She continues to search until she unearths all my secrets.

Vomit makes its way up my throat. I count furiously in my head, trying to keep my breathing steady. "You're an addict," she says matter-of-factly. "That's why you're shaking like a fucking leaf all the time. The excess sweating. I bet you've vomited, too."

My voice is gone, I can't answer. Hell, I can barely keep myself conscious. "I-I'm…"

"I take it you're in withdrawal. Couldn't just nip in here and get a hit, right? Not with us three just outside." She's shaking her head. "Jesus fucking Christ."

"I'm not an addict," I say, but my voice is barely a whisper. Something at the bottom of my pack grabs her attention. I know what it is. She reaches in and picks up the box of my blood sugar tests. Her eyebrows scrunch as she takes in what she's seeing.

"I'm not an addict," I repeat. Nope, not an addict, just someone who needs medication to function.

Chapter Twelve

Robin

Going through Ellie's bag will seem like a dick move, but it really is necessary. The way Ellie has been behaving is a giant red flag. I've been around enough ex-service people to know when someone is struggling with addiction. It's a sad reality for a lot of men and women when they leave the military to develop drug problems. War zones have a way of scrambling the brain.

After finding Ellie confused in the woods, that red flag became a friggin' flare. It didn't take long to put two and two together. Her trembling hands, sweating far more than the rest of us. Her pale skin and confusion. Clearly, Ellie is in withdrawal. The pill bottles littered around my feet would back that up. How she can stand there and tell me she isn't an addict is laughable. Although the blood sugar tests are a little confusing.

"Shut the door, Ellie, you and I need to have a conversation."

"I can't believe you went through my things. How dare you?" Ellie cries. She's trying to come across as aggrieved, angry, but all I can see is a scared woman. A prickling sensation is working its way up my spine. It's like my own Spidey-Sense, and it's telling me I'm off the mark in my previous assumptions. There's something going on with Ellie, that's for sure, but now I think I've made a mistake accusing her of being a drug addict. Shit!

"You're right, I shouldn't have done that, but at the time, I didn't feel like I had much choice. Ellie, you are not right, and it goes beyond dehydration. Plus…well, look." I point down to the pill bottles. "I wasn't wrong about the drugs, was I?"

"Did you read the labels?" she asks, her voice void of emotion. I scratch the back of my neck because I feel uncomfortable. She knows I didn't read the labels. She saw me toss them out of her socks, straight to the ground. "No, you didn't. Maybe you should." She nods at the bottles. I bend down and pick up the closest pill bottle. There's a prescription for Clonazepam. If memory serves, that's an anti-anxiety medication. I swallow hard.

"Pick up the other one," Ellie says. I don't want to. What I want is to rewind twenty minutes and stop myself from invading Ellie's belongings. "Go on, you might as well follow through now." I bend down and pick up the second bottle. It's Metformin, a medication I'm not familiar with. My creased eyebrows give me away. "It's medication for diabetes."

"You should have told me," I say weakly. After all, I'm the one trying to keep her safe. Knowing someone has medical issues is the first thing that should have been disclosed.

"Nobody knows."

"What do you mean?" How can she say that? She's a world-famous actress, there's no way she's kept this a secret.

"My mother and brother know. Obviously, my doctor, but he has to sign so many legal documents he wouldn't dare utter a word about my conditions. Toni, that's my best friend, knows I have some anxiety issues but not the diabetes."

"Why in God's name have you kept it hidden? How could you not think it was vital information to share with the studio? Fuck, just me would have done. We're in a godawful situation as it is, and now I find out you have serious health issues. That's why you've been so off lately, isn't it?" At least she has the decency to look embarrassed. Yes, I should not have gone through her things, but shit, I'm glad I did now.

"Yes, it is. I haven't been taking my meds. I don't have an endless supply, and I... Well, I thought I should save them, you know, in case we're out here for a long time."

"I just...honestly, I'm gobsmacked you didn't tell me."

"Look, my life is complicated, okay? I don't know you well enough to give you my life story, just like you haven't told me a single thing about you, and yes, I know my attitude hasn't helped us get to know each other—"

"I don't need your life story, but I could have helped you. I wouldn't have gone off at you for eating those protein bars. I take it you were suffering with your blood sugar." Ellie nods at me. "And what about your anti-anxiety meds? I know from experience you can't just stop taking them. No wonder you're suffering."

Ellie slumps to the floor, her back against the seat. "I'm sorry I didn't say anything. I should have, you're right. I just...I don't find it easy opening up to anyone. I'm including my friends in that, so the idea of telling you something so personal doesn't, or didn't, compute. It was too risky."

"Risky? Who the hell would I tell?"

"Cam, Mic, the press. I'm hoping we get home one day. What's going to stop you from selling my health issues to the press?"

"No offence, but your celebrity life is of no consequence to me. I have no interest in talking to the press."

"That may be true, but I've got enough experience to know that I can't trust your word."

"Wow, that's some pessimistic shit right there. Aren't you supposed to be the All-American girl next door? Positivity seeping out of every orifice?"

"I'm a superb actress. What you and pretty much everyone sees is a mask. One I have spent my entire career sculpting."

"Why?"

"That's personal. Look, I think we're getting off topic."

She's right, our little *tête-à-tête* is starting to resemble a therapy session. "Fine. Can we agree that from now on you keep me apprised of your health? I want to get us all home in one piece. I can't do that with half the information."

"Fine."

"I won't tell Cam and Mic," I say because I want her to trust me. I'm starting to see behind the curtain of the Ellie Bishop Show, and what I'm seeing is a surprise. I can't discount my initial assessment of her. It's too early for that, but I can see there's a lot more to her.

Ellie blows out a big sigh. "I should probably tell them. What if you're not around and something happens?"

"Okay, it's your call." I hesitate because I want to delve a little deeper. "What…can I just ask one thing?"

"Sure, why not?" she mumbles, rubbing her forehead.

"How have you gone all this time with no support? I mean, what happens if you have an issue on set or something? If no one knows, how do you explain it?"

"It's easy. Most people I work with aren't that interested in getting to know me past surface level. Saying I have a headache or feigning a hangover usually gets me by. I've not had a health scare in a while. I have my diabetes under control, and the anti-anxiety meds do their job."

I can't imagine living that kind of life. I haven't got a million friends, but I do have a small group of people I would trust with my life. Colin knows everything about me. We bonded over something most people will never experience. Our unit became my family. Ellie has probably never had those kinds of bonds.

There's nothing for me to add. I look around my feet and realise I pretty much threw her clothes and shit everywhere whilst I hunted for drugs. Without a word, I drop to my knees and start folding her clothes, placing them back in her pack.

"You don't have to do that." She scrambles over to me, taking her clothes out of my hand.

"I made the mess, I should clean it up," I continue to pick up her clothes, but then I feel something wrapped in a T-shirt. Stupidly, I shake it out, and oh, look, it's a vibrator. A bright pink vibe. Oh, crap! We both freeze as the vibe kicks into life after thumping on the floor. Neither of us moves as the enthusiastic silicone toy buzzes around. When it hits my leg, I shoot to my feet. "I'll just let you…" *Get the fuck out of there, you idiot!*

It's my turn to scramble, but I'm heading for the exit as fast as my legs will take me. Pushing the door open, I hop to the ground and slam it closed. My face feels like it's on fire. It's not the fact that I found her vibrator. Jesus, most women have them, right? It's that as soon as I saw it, my mind was flooded with very, *very* inappropriate images of Ellie. If things weren't strained between us before, they are close to breaking now, surely. The one thing I garnered from my interaction with Ellie—pre-vibrator—was that she doesn't like people knowing anything personal about her. And here I am getting a front-row view of her most personal items.

❧❧❧❧

Thirty-three minutes have passed since our unfortunate incident, and Ellie is still in the plane. Mic and Cam didn't ask what happened. I think they would see by my face that I did *not* want to relive it with them.

The plane door opens and out steps Ellie. Her hair is perfect again, and she's changed her clothes. I'm impressed. She's decided against being a fashion model and put on suitable attire. Her arse looks amazing in her shorts. Those legs are…wow, breathtaking. I can't even describe her top half. Lord, have mercy! Why am I so horny? The night with Della should have tided me over for a few months. Nope, not with Ellie Bishop standing in front of me looking edible.

That's enough of that! Get it together. Jesus, one

half-honest conversation with the woman, and you're forgetting how much of an arsehole she's been since you met.

"Mic, Cam, can I have a word with you?" Ellie says, striding over with a confidence I haven't seen since the airport. The guys nod, and Ellie takes a seat on the ground in front of them. Without delay, she tells them about her medical issues. I take that as my cue to record my day's diary. I've had enough of the interior of the plane, so I grab my GoPro and head a few metres into the forest. Balancing the tripod on a fallen tree, I clear a space and put some palm leaves on the ground. It's quite a comfy little seat, if I'm honest. Pressing record, I settle in.

The report I give doesn't mention anything to do with Ellie's health conditions. That's for her to document if she wants. My diary highlights that we're running dangerously low on water. I haven't told the others yet, although they aren't stupid. For the most part, Cam has been in charge of the rations, so he will have noticed. My reticence in telling them is because I can't decide what to do for the best. It's clear we need to break camp in search of water, but I don't think all four of us going is the best play. Ideally, I should just go alone. I'm fast and experienced. Having anyone else with me will only slow me down.

I say all this into the little lens, hoping it will pave the way to a decision. Now, though, I have to take into consideration Ellie. My leaving could put her at further risk. I'm no doctor, but I have extensive medical training. I doubt Cam or Mic would know what to do in a genuine emergency. It's possible that I could teach them, but we don't have that kind of time. The water will be long gone.

I sign off, still undecided as to my next step. By the time I make it back to the others, they're laughing with one another. It's nice to see. This is the first time I think the real Ellie Bishop is in control and not the vapid actress. "Hey, we need to chat," I say. Three sets of eyes turn to me. I can see they're worried. "The water situation," I add.

"I wondered how long it would take." Cam grins.

"Are we almost out?" Ellie asks. I nod. Ellie runs her hands over her hair.

"It's crunch time. We have a decision to make."

"What are the options?" Mic asks.

"Staying here with no water isn't possible. It's suicide. However, I'm reluctant for us all to leave. There's still a possibility of a rescue team finding the wreck. I don't want them to find it but not us."

"So you think someone should stay here?" Cam asks.

"Yeah. If we leave the rest of the water and the majority of the food, that should allow two of you to stay with the plane. At least until me and whoever else comes along returns with water."

"So who's staying?" Ellie asks, her eyes shimmering with concern.

"I take it you've told the guys," I say directly to Ellie. She nods. "Considering Ellie's situation, I think it best she comes with me. How do you two feel about staying here?"

"Well, my shoulder still feels sore. I'm not sure how much I could help you out there if something happens," Cam says honestly, and I agree.

"I'm happy to stay here, too. Hold down the fort," Mic chimes in. Okay, this is good so far. Now I just pray that Ellie doesn't have an issue with it.

"I agree with the plan," she says quietly. I doubt she's happy about any of it, but there really is no choice.

"Right, we'll head out at first light. Ellie, there are two small rucksacks in the bottom of my pack. Can you grab them? We need to travel light, so only take essentials." Without arguing—halle-fucking-lujah—Ellie scampers into the plane to get the travel packs. "Let's get the rations divvied up. You two are going to have to be diligent, gents. If you blow through all this before we get back, you're fucked. Understood?"

"We understand," they answer together.

"I'll leave you my guidebook. It has everything you'll need to forage. If you're not one hundred percent sure that what you've collected is safe, don't eat or drink it, okay?" I arch my eyebrows to get the point across.

"We can stick to the stuff we've already collected. We know that's safe."

"Good. Now don't leave it too late to bunk down. You triple check the door is shut securely. Don't leave any food lying about and do not venture outside at night. Use the empty water bottles to piss in if you have to go in the night."

"Aye aye, Captain."

"That's Sergeant to you, mate." I wink. "We'll go as fast as we can, but I can't promise you it will be in a day or two. I have no idea where we are or if there's a water source nearby. What I do promise is that I will get back here pronto."

"We know, Robin. We have every faith."

"I'm going to take a look at the radio while you're gone," Mic says. "It might be kaput, but you never know, right?"

"Absolutely, get cracking. I'll keep my fingers crossed."

Ellie jumps out of the plane with two packs. "I packed myself, but I didn't know what you would want to take, so I'll leave you to do that." She smiles, handing me the empty travel bag. I smile back. *That was considerate of her.*

"Great, thanks. The lads know what they're doing. I'll just go stuff some things in here." I'm a dab hand at getting my pack done in a few minutes. I put one change of clothes in alongside several pairs of socks. My hunting knife gets strapped to my thigh. The compass and map get shoved in the front pocket of my bag.

Back outside, the three amigos are working quietly to divide up the food rations. I'm impressed with how well they're suddenly working together. It's amazing what the attitude of one person can do to a group. With Ellie participating and helping, everyone is visibly more relaxed. The stiffness that's been hanging over us is gone, and it's nice.

"How's this, Sergeant?" Cam asks with a grin. That's going to be his thing now, isn't it?

"You were a sergeant?" Ellie asks, her voice tilted in surprise. I bet she thought I was a lowly private.

"Certainly was." I smile. "This looks good, although you two can keep more of the food. We'll take a couple of packs of the dehydrated food. The rest we can forage. I'll fill our canteens with water and leave you the rest."

"Sure, that's enough for you?" Mic asks, his eyes betraying his meaning as they wander to Ellie. He's worried about her blood sugar.

"Yep, don't worry." There are things in the

forest I can give Ellie to sort out her blood sugar if needed. "Ellie, did you pack your meds?" She nods but turns away. I don't understand why she looks so embarrassed or ashamed. Not wanting to draw any more attention to her, I look at Mic and Cam. "It's possible that we'll get rainfall whilst we're here. Cam, Mic, make the most of it. Use whatever you can to catch the water. It could be what saves your lives if something happens to us, okay?"

"Sure thing. We'll get something rigged up."

"Hey, I found these," Mic says, handing me a short-range radio. "I don't know exactly how far they'll reach, but we could use them for a little while, keep in touch with each other." Yes, finally something good. I feel much better knowing I can communicate with the guys, at least for a time.

"Excellent. Right, well, it looks like we're all sorted." I peer up at the sky. The sun is still high, but I want Ellie and I to set off early. "I know it's still early, but I think we should turn in. Ellie, we need to be up and gone by dawn."

"Okay," she says. I really like this Ellie, she's so much easier.

"Here, before you go, eat this," Cam says to Ellie, passing her one of their food bags.

"Oh, no, I..." Ellie protests.

"Take the food, Ellie," I say, hoping not to come across as bullish. She needs to replenish her body, especially now that we're about to go wandering through the forest.

Chapter Thirteen

Ellie

I slept exceptionally well, considering we all went to bed in the daylight. The noise of the rainforest never stops, but instead of it being disturbing, I find it calming. If we get home, I'm going to have to listen to bird sounds to fall asleep, I think.

From what I can see, the sun is just starting to rise. Robin is asleep behind me again, just like the first night. Once again, she's snuggled up to me, which makes me involuntarily smile. I didn't let on the first time that I'd felt her lips on my neck or her hips pushing into my ass. We weren't exactly on the best terms, but I think that's changing.

Having to admit to Robin that I have an anxiety disorder and diabetes was one of the most nerve-wracking things I've ever done. Finding her rooting through my bag had almost made me faint. It had also made me so angry I contemplated murder. My murderous mood was quickly replaced with embarrassment as I watched her discover my pill stash. I don't want to get into why telling people about my conditions is the last thing I want to do. That opens up a can of worms that I don't think I'm mentally capable of handling right now.

What I need to do is concentrate on the task ahead. It's likely I'm not up to the challenge of searching for water. Robin only wants me to come along because she's worried about my health, not because she thinks I can add anything of value.

Robin shifts behind me, and my nipples react instantaneously. The woman might drive me to distraction, but I can't deny her body is fantastic. Is that shallow? Whatever, she's gorgeous. I keep as still as possible. I don't want us going back to being at odds. We're forming a tentative bond. Whether that turns into friendship, I don't know. I just don't want to argue anymore. Now if I can keep my inner bitch tucked away for a little while, that would be great.

"Ellie," Robin whispers. She thinks I'm asleep. I turn my head slightly and have to swallow hard. Robin is hovering just above me, her hair a little mussed from sleep. Her eyes are clear, and her skin looks flawless. Damn, this woman has great genes.

"Morning," I mumble.

"We need to get moving. Come on, let's wake the guys and get ready." I just nod and wait for her to move. I could do with a few seconds to calm my raging libido. Once she has shifted away, I sit up. I've already picked out the clothes I'm going to wear. Ridiculous, I know, but I want to make a better impression than the one I did in the airport. Paris did a fab job of packing stylish clothes. The problem is, now that I'm here, I realize how impractical they are. Great if I were lounging by a tropical pool like I thought I would be. But for hiking in the rainforest, not so much.

Thankfully, Toni was level-headed and packed two pairs of cargo shorts and some vest tops. It's the closest I'll get to looking the part of Jungle Jane, but it has to be better than the shorts that lived in my ass for the first two days. Shoes are a problem. Paris packed sandals and flip-flops and some sneakers. Robin is wearing some serious hiking footwear, which I now wish I had, too. The sneakers will have to do.

Another hot and muggy day bitch-slaps me as I climb down from the plane. How the hell anything or anyone survives in this place is a mystery. Cam and Mic are lounging under the canopy. Robin is going through her pack for what is probably the tenth time. My nerves are building. It's one thing being in the rainforest with a secure area to sleep and the possibility of someone finding the wreck. It's a whole other scary-ass thing to go wandering in the forest with God knows what lurking out there wanting to eat us. My mind drifts back to that session I had with the nature guy. I remember thinking that I was going to die in this place. Ha, for once, I hate I might be right.

"Okay, I think we're good to go," Robin calls. She hefts her pack onto her back. I feel like I'm about to embark on an adventure with the female Indiana Jones. Wow, that visual is hot!

"Ready," I reply. I'm not ready at all, well, not emotionally, but what can I do?

"Fellas, you good?" Robin asks Mic and Cam.

"Good, you guys be safe. You have your radio. Set it to channel five."

"Got it. Let's go, Ellie."

Here goes nothing. I pick up my pack, which isn't too heavy, and fall in line behind Robin. It takes all of ten seconds to realize I'm going to be physically fucked in under ten minutes. Robin is charging through the brush like she's on a mission.

"Um, Robin, could…could you slow down a little?" I pant after five minutes.

"Shit, sorry." She grins. "I kind of get into an

automatic marching pace." She laughs. "My friends hate walking with me." That little insight sparks my curiosity. Robin has had a whole life. I know she was in the British forces. I'm sure she has lots of stories. I wonder if I'll ever get to hear them.

We fall into a comfortable silence. Robin has slowed down considerably. I take the opportunity to absorb our surroundings. So far, the rainforest has just represented anxiety and fear. I've heard the birds and bugs, I've seen the trees, but I haven't taken the time to really let it all sink in.

Over my career, I've traveled the world but never to a place like this. My travels usually include five-star luxury hotels with on-call facilities any time I want them. I'm also usually surrounded by people. The best times I've had are when it's just me and Toni. We have fun together, but she also gives me space. Just like Robin is now. She's not trying to talk my ear off or find out all the secrets of Hollywood. She probably couldn't think of anything worse to do. That thought makes me smile. Robin Stuart isn't like anyone I know. Maybe that's why I'm so intrigued.

A rustling above our heads catches my attention. The canopy of the trees is dense, and I can't find what's making the noise. The next thing I know, I've slammed into Robin, who apparently stopped without me noticing. It must be a record. We've only been walking twenty minutes, and I'm already flat on my ass.

"Shit, sorry." Robin grabs my arm and yanks me up.

"No, that was on me. I didn't see you stop. I got distracted."

"That's why I stopped. Look." Robin points up

into the trees. For the life of me, I can't see what she's looking at. Robin moves to my side. Her face comes alarmingly close to mine. She tells me to follow her finger, which is pointing above us. All I can think of is what those long slender fingers could do to me. Holy cow. Finally snapping out of my sexy fantasy, I narrow my eyes, and then I see it. Or I should say them.

"Oh, wow." I gasp. Sitting high in the branches above us are monkeys.

"They're called howler monkeys. At dusk and dawn, they let out loud howls. They're the loudest land animal in the world. You can hear their howl up to three miles away."

"They're big. Are we safe?"

"Don't worry. They'll keep their distance." We stand there for a few more minutes taking in the wondrous sight. I never thought I'd experience something like this. Something so real. Silently, Robin walks off. I take an extra beat to sear this image into my head. Then I remember I brought my GoPro. These sights are definitely worth recording for posterity. Much better than me moaning on camera for half an hour.

Quickly, I whip out the camera and press record. I know it's probably going to piss Robin off, but it's worth it. To my surprise, I look over and find Robin smiling at me.

"Sorry, I'm ready now." I smile.

"Hell, you might as well enjoy it."

"Have you been here before?" This seems like an excellent opportunity to get to know her a little better.

"Yeah, for training when I was in the forces."

"Did you enjoy being in the…Marines, right??"

Robin huffs out a breath and chuckles. "That's a tough question to answer. Yes, I enjoyed the camaraderie. I made friends for life, but I also experienced things I wouldn't wish on my worst enemy."

Okay, wow, that was a lot. I don't know if I should push it. I can't help it, I want to learn more. "When did you sign up?"

"I was sixteen. My whole family has been in the forces. It was a no-brainer for me. I'd wanted to be a Royal Marine Commando since I was a kid."

"Isn't it full of buff men that have too much testosterone?" I ask, hoping she knows I'm joking.

Laughing, Robin nods. "Oh, it's definitely full of those. They're good men, though. And women. I was one of three women when I joined up. We all got through basic training together. I feel like they're family now. Most of us got shipped out to different units. My unit was full of tough guys. Colin Berk was one of those guys."

"Oh, isn't he one of the hosts of *Wild Celebrities*?" One of the guys Toni was creaming over.

"Yeah, but he had an accident. Damaged his junk." Robin laughs. I look at her, wondering if I heard correctly. "Yeah, you heard me. Broke his knob, the bloody idiot. Anyway, I stepped into his place and, *voilà*, here we are."

"Wow, Colin owes you," I say, laughing along.

"Fuck yes, he does."

"So when did you get out of the military?"

"Oh, it's been a few years. I generally work in private security now."

"And you like it?"

"Only when I don't have to put up with entitled arseholes."

"Like me, you mean," I say, smirking. She definitely means people like me.

"Yes, like you." She winks. My new goal in life is to get Robin to wink at me like that again.

"I didn't come off great when we first met, huh?"

"Maybe we both kinda acted like arses."

"I know why I did. What about you?"

"Simple. I didn't want to do the show but was strong-armed into it. I didn't want to be responsible for you and the other two. And I'll admit that when you turned up, I judged you pretty quickly."

"And let me guess, my behavior played right into that judgment you made."

"Yup, one hundred percent." Robin laughs.

We continue to walk. The silence is comfortable. "I got pulled into this, too," I say. I'm not sure why I'm telling her this, but it feels right. "My brother, Gabe, who is also my agent, signed me up without telling me. I was not pleased."

"Wow, that's out of line. Why didn't you just back out?"

"Why didn't you?" I shoot back.

"Colin would have had to pay to get out of the contract. He's going to be a dad soon, so I couldn't see him get into financial trouble."

"That's kind of you. For me, the optics would have looked awful if I'd backed out."

"The optics?"

"Yeah. My life is run on optics." I laugh mirthlessly. It's sad how true it is. "Gabe would have already started marketing the show. If I pulled out, I would look like a difficult woman. That's not an image I want."

"Surely your PR person could have put a spin on it or something."

"Maybe, but I couldn't take the risk." Robin is

looking at me as we walk side by side. I can tell she wants to say something but is holding back. I can also guess what she wants to say.

"Well, it doesn't matter now. We're in it. Do you think you can pick up the pace a little? I don't want to push, but I would like to put some more distance in before we have to set up camp."

That wasn't what I was expecting. "I can go faster."

Robin walks off, and I regret not being physically fit. I imagine Robin is a fitness freak after so many years of having to keep her body in optimal shape. I drop behind her again, my gaze firmly on her ass. If I'm going to work out, I need an incentive.

Sweat is pouring off me. The day is passing by and still we walk. I should say something because I can feel myself getting a little dizzy. Suddenly, Robin stops again and whirls around. "You haven't eaten," she declares.

"Nope, I could do with taking a rest."

"Shit, Ellie, why didn't you say anything?" Her tone is a little harsh.

"I'm saying something now," I protest. Dropping her pack to the ground, she digs through it until she finds a protein bar. She shoves it at me, grumbling under her breath. I roll my eyes.

"Eat and drink. We'll stop here for the night."

"I can still go on."

"No, you've walked enough."

"I'm not a fucking invalid," I bark. Nothing pisses me off more than people deciding what I can and can't do.

"No, you're not, but you are someone who needs to rest. We've put in some solid miles. It's better to rest up now and have you ready to go fighting fit tomorrow."

I flare my nostrils because my anger is still near the surface wanting to boil over. My brain knows that she's right. I do need to stop and rest. Counting in my head, I calm down and nod my agreement.

"Good. Let's set up over there." She points to an area to my left. There's a low-hanging tree branch. It's a natural rooftop. "I'm going to show you how to construct a basic shelter and get a fire going. Everyone should know basic survival skills."

"Yes, because I'll need them in Hollywood." I snicker, rolling my eyes.

"Hey, you never know! What happens if the area suffers a massive earthquake, hmm?"

"I have people for that," I say. I'm being obtuse because I find it amusing to wind Robin up.

"What if those people can't get to you?"

"I would wait for emergency services."

"You could be waiting hours, even days."

"Oh, God, are you one of those survival nuts?" I laugh.

"Nope, I'm a practical person. I could outlive ninety percent of the population in a crisis." Now that I believe. "Plus, wouldn't it be good to test your mettle? Show the world what you're capable of. I'm guessing not many of 'your people' would think you can look after yourself." That statement jars me. She's right. I rely on so many people for the most basic of things. I really would be fucked if anything happened. Let's be honest, without Robin here, I would have already perished. I know it.

"Okay, Robin Bear Grylls Stuart. Show me what you've got." Robin laughs at the name.

Over the course of the next hour, Robin shows me how to bind sticks together to make a simple frame. We collect fallen palm leaves and add them to the top of it. So far, it's looking like a tiki hut, but that's cool. I can fall asleep imagining I'm in Tahiti, sipping on a cocktail by the ocean.

Once the shelter is finished, we set about making a fire. We collect firewood, and Robin shows me how to set it up. After several failed attempts and a little temper tantrum from me, I finally get the fucker to light.

"You did great. It's not easy getting it to light in these conditions. You should be proud of yourself." Robin doesn't look like she's blowing smoke up my ass. Hey, maybe I just did something good. I'll take it. It's the first time in a long time that I've done something worthwhile. "Let's get some water boiling and have a cup of tea."

"God, could you be any more English?" I laugh. "It's boiling hot, and you want to drink tea?"

"Tea solves everything." She grins. Leaving Robin to get the water boiling, I continue to clear the surrounding area.

"Stop," Robin almost shouts. Her tone is commanding and a little terrifying. Instantly, I freeze. What the fuck is going on? "Ellie, I need you to stay absolutely still, okay?"

"W-why?" I stutter.

"A meter to your left is a bushmaster."

"What the fuck is a bushmaster?" I hiss.

"It's a highly venomous snake." *Oh, fuck. God, no, I can get killed by a snake.* I can feel my skin crawl. Everything in me wants to sprint away. "Ellie, focus, listen to me. You're fine. Stay still and let me deal with it. Trust me."

I look into her eyes, which are imploring that I listen to her. "Please hurry," I whimper. Slowly, Robin picks up a long sturdy stick. She circles me. Her footsteps are precise and quiet. I naturally scan the area, looking for the snake. Probably a bad idea because I know I will freak the fuck out if I spot it. This shit doesn't happen in L.A.!

Robin takes a few more careful steps before she suddenly launches the stick toward the ground. I can't look. I'll throw up or faint. "Okay, Ellie, slowly make your way toward the fire." I do as she says. When I feel the heat of the flame on my legs, I stop. Robin has the snake's head trapped under her stick. Reaching behind her, she pulls out a knife. With skill and precision, she severs the snake's head.

I vomit instantly.

Chapter Fourteen

Robin

Well, that was an exciting few minutes. Ellie is still looking green around the gills. What an introduction to the Amazon wildlife. A South American bushmaster isn't anything to sniff at. If Ellie had been bitten, she would have been in all kinds of trouble, and there would have been nothing I could have done. I'm just really thankful she listened to me and followed orders. Crisis averted.

What a shame we can't eat the snake. Well, technically we could, but it's a risk and not one worth taking in light of Ellie's medical issues. I discard the reptile's body in the bush a few metres away. Some creature will come along and make use of it.

Ellie has sat herself down under our makeshift hut. "Welcome to the Amazon," I say, laughing, hoping to dispel some of her anxiety.

"We haven't even been out here a full day, and I already almost got eaten."

"Not eaten. Bitten. But yeah, I get it's a shock."

"Thank you, you know, for saving me."

"All in a day's work." I laugh again. Do you think she'll figure out I'm nervous? Not because of the snake thing but because now I have to bunk down with her. The space isn't very big, and we all know I'm a bloody sleep snuggler. That will be three nights in a row I'll find myself pressed into Ellie. Not sure how much my lady bits can take if I'm being honest. Bloody hell, I can't even masturbate to relieve some of the tension.

"Are we going to be okay tonight? What if another snake comes along?" I can feel the anxiety radiating off her. The fact is, she is right in her worries. I can't protect us entirely from all the things that live in the forest.

"You sleep closest to the back of the shelter. I'll sleep behind you. I'll be your personal bodyguard. Literally." I smile, squeezing her shoulder.

"And what if you get bitten? Can't we like sleep up a tree or something?" I suppress my laugh because I know she won't appreciate it right now.

"Snakes are found in trees, too. Look, I know you're nervous, but trust me, okay. I will keep you safe. I'll build up the fire to keep any animals away."

Begrudgingly, she shuffles over to the back of the shelter and lies down. I didn't mean she had to go to sleep right now. We haven't eaten yet. I turn back to the fire, stoking it up, adding a couple of logs to get it going. I can feel Ellie's gaze on me, scanning my body. Not going to lie, I like it.

The water I put on earlier is boiling away. Setting our tin cups down, I pop in a couple of tea bags. Yes, I absolutely brought Tetley English Breakfast tea bags with me. I don't leave home without them. Ellie is right because it is a tad warm to be drinking tea, but I want her to have something relaxing. I even have a little sachet of sugar I add to hers.

"Do you need to test your blood sugar?"

"Oh, Jesus, now that you know, are you going to turn into my nursemaid?" Her eyes sparkle, and her dimples show as she smirks.

"Maybe. It seems you need looking after," I reply, only half joking. It surprises me how much I like the sound of taking care of Ellie.

"Well, no need, Mom," she mocks. "I'm a big girl, and I learned my lesson." All that said, she still takes out a little testing packet and sets about pricking her finger, dropping a little bit of blood on the strip. "All good," she chimes. I hand her the tea and start organising our dinner. Oh, dehydrated mush, how I've missed you.

Watching Ellie's expression as I hand her a packet of food that resembles cat vomit is highly entertaining. I can tell she's trying hard not to come across as ungrateful, but her eyebrows are scrunched so tight they form one well-shaped unibrow. Her nostrils flare, and her jaw tightens. I tuck into my mush as if it's a dish from a Michelin star restaurant. Ellie looks from her mush to me, eating happily, and back again.

"Do we have the same thing?" she asks eventually.

"Yup," I mumble through a mouthful of food.

"And you...you like it?"

"Course, it's yummy." My face is so serious right now. Ellie scratches her head in confusion, and she is adorably cute. Shrugging, she gingerly takes a small sporkful of mush and pops it in her mouth. Oh, she has her eyes slammed shut, which makes me snicker. Chewing like her life depends on it, I finally see her swallow. She takes a beat before opening her eyes again.

"That's..."

"Gross? Hideous? Not fit for human consumption?" I laugh.

Laughing with me, she nods furiously. "Yep, all the above," she croaks, diving for her tea.

"I bet you're glad I gave you a cup of Tetley, now aren't you?"

"Yes, I'm forever in your debt." She laughs. "Fuck, is this what you had to eat in the Marines?"

"In the field, yes. Otherwise, we had decent chow in the mess hall."

"I don't know what any of that meant, but I'm going to go ahead and say how sorry I am that you had to eat this crap."

"Food is food. Don't think you're getting out of eating it, Ms. Bishop. You need the energy."

Screwing up her face, she pouts. I'm getting a glimpse of teenage Ellie right now. After a few moments of sulking, she eats her food. I hear her grumble now and then, which makes the whole situation hilarious. I should have scavenged some grubs or something. I wonder if she would have eaten them. Ha, that's tomorrow's lunch sorted. She's going to kill me!

⁂

So my nighttime cuddling has progressed. I was suitably alarmed to find my hand groping Ellie's boob this morning. I snatched my hand away so fast it made her jump out of her skin. To cover up the fact that I had been playing with her nipple in my sleep, I lied and said there was a bug that I batted away, hence the sudden movement. I didn't stick around to see if she bought my bullshit. Instead, I made myself very busy getting us breakfast.

Now we have been walking for five and a half hours with a couple of ten-minute rests in between.

We will have to go through the whole process of picking a place to camp for the night and building a suitable shelter. I think we could get a couple more hours under our belt before we do that, though.

The majority of our hike has been in companionable silence. Honestly, there's so much to take in around here. I'm grateful we gave each other the chance to do so. The last time I was here was for training. Let me tell you, there isn't much time for sightseeing in the Marines. As the time marches past, I'm becoming more and more interested in learning about Ellie. There are definitely two sides to this woman. I'm guessing that few people get to see the side I have glimpsed recently. Well, here goes nothing!

"So," I begin, turning slightly so she knows I'm talking to her. "What's it really like being you?"

"Being me?" she parrots, looking confused at my question.

"Yeah, being you. I mean I'm sure it's a lot of parties and glamorous events. But I'm guessing it's not all rainbows and butterflies."

"Why are you asking?" I can see the paranoia shooting off her like a laser. Wow, she really doesn't trust anyone.

"I'm genuinely interested. Look, we both admitted that when we first met, we were both acting... well, not being ourselves." Her demeanor is telling me to back off. "Sorry, never mind, you don't have to answer." I turn away from her again and concentrate on the path ahead. A few beats go by, and then I hear her suck in a breath. Is she going to speak?

"I never wanted to be an actress," she says quietly. I stay silent, hoping she's going to continue. "My first love was a mutt named Arnold. He was our cook's dog. I'm sure you know I grew up rich, even before the acting."

"Yeah, I've read your IMDB." I grin over my shoulder.

"Ha, right? So you know my mother's side of the family is old money. Anyway, I really wanted to be a vet."

"Really, a vet?"

"Yup. Not what you expected, right?"

Her tone is light, which I'm glad for. "Very surprising. So do you have a bunch of pets in your Hollywood mansion?"

"No."

"Okay. So why didn't you go to vet school?"

"My mother felt it wasn't suitable."

"But acting was?"

"Yes, she was the one who got me my first audition. Money opens doors, don't you know?"

"Do you not like what you do?"

She blows out a breath in frustration. "It's not that, it's just sometimes…sometimes I wish I could make my own choices."

"Why can't you? You're in your mid-thirties. A grown woman."

"It doesn't work like that, not with my mother. Appearances are everything. And I mean everything. All my choices and actions are subject to public opinion…that also reflect on my mother."

Ellie Bishop is starting to make sense to me now. The higher-than-mighty attitude has been ingrained in her. Oddly, she still has a very humble side, too. I wonder where that comes from.

"If my father were still here, my life would have been so much better," she comments. I look at her fully now. She's staring off to the side wistfully. "He didn't come from money. He was such a laidback guy. When I told him I wanted to be a vet, he was so enthusiastic. Hell, he even bought me a bunch of books on animal biology. I was like seven." She laughs, then her eyes water. "He had a heart attack when I was fifteen. One minute he was there, and the next…"

"That must have been tough," I say. I can't imagine losing one of my parents at such a harsh age.

"It was the hardest time of my life. Shortly after, I started having anxiety issues."

I'm a little lost for words. Ellie seems so vulnerable, a far cry from the woman I met at the airfield. Everything in me wants to turn around and take her in my arms, but that would cross a line. Instead, I slow my stride so she's walking next to me.

"I don't know why I'm telling you all this," she says after several minutes of silence. "I never speak about my private life."

"You must speak to someone."

"Toni, but that's it."

"That sounds lonely." We go quiet again. "I told you all my family has been in the forces. Well, my older brother Andy was in the Royal Marines, too. He was six years older than me—"

"Was?" Ellie interrupts.

"Yeah. He was killed in action two weeks before I shipped off to basic training." It's been a long time since I've spoken about Andy.

"Oh, Robin." Ellie gasps, her hand gripping mine as we walk. I don't pull away, and we end up walking hand in hand. "My mum tried to stop me from going. It was a really tense time. To serve in the forces was a point of pride in our family, but after Andy, well, my mum wanted nothing to do with it."

"So what happened when you left?"

"She didn't speak to me for a year. I know she was grieving. We all were. My grief pushed me to be the best Marine I could be."

"What about now? Are you okay with your mom, I mean?"

"Yeah. It was tough. My dad got her into counselling, which helped. We have a great relationship now."

"Are they back in Britain?"

"No, they live in Florida. My mum is American. We lived in the UK for all my childhood. After Andy died, things changed. Mum missed her family, and Dad was more than happy to move to the States. When I got out of the forces, I decided to follow them over there."

"I wish I had a great relationship with my mom." Ellie's hand snaps to her mouth. "I didn't mean to say that out loud."

"Hey." I stop walking and squeeze her hand that is still firmly in mine. "You can say what you want to me. I promise I have no desire to sell your story. I would never do that."

"Thank you," she replies, a small smile on her lips. I have the irrational urge to kiss her. Those lips have been taunting me for days. I feel my body sway slightly forward, and that's when I see her eyes go wide. Shit, I've ballsed this up.

Quickly, I take a step back and drop her hand. Whatever moment we were sharing is well and truly kaput! "Um...we should..."

"Do you hear that?" Ellie beams. I'm thoroughly confused by her reaction. I tune my ears to our surroundings, and that's when I hear it. The sound that makes my heart soar above the treetops. A sound so magical I could fall down crying. It's the sound of our survival. My eyes snap in the direction of the thundering noise. How the hell I missed it is worrying. I was so caught up in Ellie, I didn't register anything.

"Let's go," I practically shout. Ellie is hot on my heels as we run. It's only a few minutes before we break through the trees and lay eyes on the most beautiful thing I have ever seen.

"Oh, thank God, thank God." Ellie laughs manically. I stand staring at the most glorious waterfall ever created. We have fresh water! Ellie wastes no time wading into the crystal-clear pool. I laugh along as she splashes and dives into the water. "Come on, Robin, get in," she shouts from the middle of the cove. The water is up to her chest. Oh, her tank top is now see-through. Marvellous. Can't I have five minutes without some part of Ellie's body turning me on?

I throw down my pack next to Ellie's and wade in. The water is so fresh I dive under immediately. I'm a water baby, so this is heaven to me. I twist and turn underwater until I see Ellie's lovely legs a few feet from me. My mischievous side takes over, and I grab her legs from beneath the surface. I hear her scream, but then she laughs, tugging at my top, pulling me up. I burst through the surface, splashing her with a wave of water. We're both laughing hard. It's clear the weight of our search was a heavy one. We can relax a little knowing that we can take water back to Cam and Mic.

After we've splashed and played for a while, I reluctantly leave the pool. Daylight is fading fast, and we need to build our shelter. Ellie is having so much fun that I leave her to it. I can get the fire and shelter done quickly, no need to spoil it for her. This is the most relaxed and happy I've ever seen her. Actually, the smile on her face is like nothing I've ever seen.

I've seen Ellie on plenty of magazine covers, in films and on TV, yet none of those award-winning smiles she gave are a patch on the one she has plastered on her face right now.

"Hey, grub's up," I shout an hour later. Tonight's menu is another packet of mush but with some berries I foraged. I know how to treat a lady!

"Oh, my God, I don't think I have ever been so happy to see water." She laughs, plonking herself down next to me. I laugh when she enthusiastically wolfs down her mush packet. Ellie's good mood is infectious.

We eat and chat about nothing and everything. It feels like a massive barrier has come down since Ellie opened up to me. It's a little heartbreaking to hear the restrictions and rules put on her by her mother. I wonder if her mum can see the damage it's doing to her daughter. No one should feel like they have to hide themselves away. From what she's telling me, Ellie has been living a very lonely life. I'd like to meet Toni. She sounds like a good person. Not sure about the other people in her life. Gabe sounds like a Grade A twat, in my opinion. The more I listen to her, the angrier I get. It's clear that the world has no idea who Ellie Bishop is, and it's my strong belief they are seriously missing out.

Once the food is gone and we've talked ourselves to the point neither of us can string a coherent sentence together, we get comfy. Oddly enough, Ellie backs herself into me so we're spooning. I know that's how we've woken up every morning, but I thought I'd done a decent job moving away from her before she realised our position. Perhaps Ellie has been aware all along and is okay with it.

Not one to pass up the chance to feel her body, I shuffle closer. The firelight is shining off her hair. It's mesmerising.

"Thanks for today, Robin," she whispers. I stay quiet because I'm not sure what she's thanking me for. "You're easy to talk to."

"Anytime," I reply softly. Ellie lets out a contented sigh, and I feel my stomach flutter. My heart thrums just that little bit louder. I close my eyes and breathe her in. We fall asleep to the sound of the rainforest, and quite frankly, I've never been happier to be lost in the wilderness.

Chapter Fifteen

Ellie

Last night sucked! Like really fucking sucked. Everything was perfect to begin with. Robin held me tight. She's a massive snuggle monster. Then the fucking heavens opened. I have never seen rain like it. Add the fact that every raindrop hit a leaf on the way down, which made our evening deafening, as well as soggy.

Robin had done a great job on our little hut, but there was no way it could withstand the beating rain. I woke up soaking and not in a good way! It took a good hour or so before we could sleep again. Robin volunteered to fortify the hut's roof, which worked well. We snuggled closer and managed to get a little more sleep.

I woke up ten minutes ago and nearly had a mild panic attack. Robin wasn't behind me; in fact, she was nowhere to be seen. Not unlike an Olympic pole vaulter, I launched myself out of the makeshift bed and searched frantically for her.

That leads me to the present. I found her, all right, and I'm not embarrassed to say I'm watching her from behind a tree. Yes, I'm full-on stalking her. Why? Because Robin Stuart is buck naked swimming in the pool by the waterfall. Damn! That woman is giving me hot flashes.

Her clothes are piled by the bank. That gorgeous mane of black hair is flowing freely around her as she floats. I know it's wrong for me to be looking. Actually, it's super fucking creepy, but I can't help myself.

Things have been changing between us lately. My gut feeling tells me I can trust her. I certainly feel like we're closer now that we've shared such intimate details about our lives. I know that doesn't automatically translate into a relationship or anything. It certainly doesn't give me the right to spy on her when she's going *au naturel*, but once again, I'll reiterate that I just can't help it. She is…just wow!

"You do know that you're not invisible because of the tree, right?" Oh, crap, she knows I'm here like a creepy creeper. I'm pretty sure my entire body goes beet red. Excellent.

"I…sorry, I didn't want to disturb you." *Smooth, Ellie.*

"You're not disturbing. Well, okay, it *is* a little weird knowing you're there watching." She chuckles. "Why don't you join me? There's nothing better than swimming naked. Don't worry, I won't ogle you." She laughs again.

My breathing is a little erratic now because my body really wants to be naked with her, but let's be honest, we aren't compatible at all. Not one bit. Just because we've had a few personal conversations doesn't mean I should read anything into it. Plus, Robin was in the military, so I'm pretty sure that being naked in front of another woman isn't a big deal to her.

"I'm good, thanks. I'm finally dry after last night. I think I want to stay that way for a while." I smile.

"Okay, well, I'll just be another few minutes. Fancy putting some water on? I need my morning cuppa before we set off."

"Sure," I reply before—begrudgingly—leaving Robin to go back to the camp. I've got this whole fire-making thing in the bag now. I feel like a regular survival expert nowadays. Ridiculous, I know. I'm nowhere near Robin's level, but I think I would do okay on my own. I could at least build a shelter and fire. That's like rule number one and two of survival.

My musings are interrupted by a damp Robin sitting next to me. Her hair is still loose and wet. My nether regions are making themselves known. I can feel the pulse in my clit radiating into my tummy. I am so fucking turned on by Robin. Laughable, really, considering it's only been days since we met and the majority of the time I wanted to slap her. Now the only slapping I would like is a bit of spanking. *Wow, Ellie, calm the hell down.*

We sit quietly, enjoying our beverage. I'll never admit it to her, but I'm starting to appreciate a good cup of tea. It occurs to me that we should check in with Mic and Cam. I laugh out loud when Robin reaches for the radio Mic gave us.

"What are you laughing at?" she asks, amused by my sudden outburst.

"I was literally just about to suggest we try contacting the boys. And then you go and pick up the radio before I even say anything. Are you a mind reader, as well as a Jungle Jane?"

Robin laughs, shaking her head. "So far, I've been Indiana Jones, Lara Croft, G.I. Jane, and now Jungle Jane. That's a lot of nicknames."

"How did you know I called you the other names?" Have I accidentally called her them to her face? That's completely embarrassing.

"Let's just say that you rant when you're pissed." She grins. That's fair. I do tend to rant out loud to myself. "Don't stress. I've been called worse, trust me."

"Like what?"

"My training sergeant called me a worthless garbage rat once. Oh, my favorite, though, was being called a walking fart nugget. To this day, I still have no clue what it means."

"That's fantastic." I can't help but laugh. My shoulders are shaking, and my belly hurts. Robin is smiling at me with her big beautiful blue eyes sparkling. Everything between us feels different. Surely, I'm not imagining it. My laughter has died down, and now we're just staring at each other. I wish I was brave enough to make a move. If we were back home, I would have, but then again, it's unlikely Robin would be smiling at me like this if we were in L.A. I wouldn't have shown her the real me, and she would continue to think I was just a privileged asshole.

Robin is the first to break eye contact. She jumps to her feet and starts collecting our cups to wash out. I lean back on my hands and watch her a little longer. Robin turns to me again, and that's when I register a flicker of something in her eye. It's not lust because in a flash she's whipped her knife out of her leg holder and has launched the fucking thing at me. Naturally, I scream bloody murder.

What the hell is she doing? My hands have flown to my face, as if that's a good defense against a flying hunting knife. Blood is pumping loudly in my ears. I snatch my hands from my face and glare at Robin, who is standing calmly in front of me. "What the fuck was that?" I scream, staggering to my feet. I look around and see the knife buried in the ground just to the left of where my right hand was sitting moments ago. "Are you completely insane?" I scream again, this time louder. Robin remains quiet. Slowly, she walks over to her knife and yanks it out of the ground. That's when I see what is impaled on it.

"Didn't think you wanted to get stung by this fella," she says. My mind is a tornado of anger and confusion. My eyes aren't computing what they're seeing. Hanging limply off the end of her blade is a black scorpion. I visibly shiver because it is *so* gross. "It was right next to your hand. I didn't want to wait until it had hurt you to do something, so I'm sorry we didn't have a chat about it beforehand," she finishes sarcastically.

"You could have said something. Anything would have been better than nothing. You just threw a knife at me."

"No, I threw a knife at this," she says, waving the knife around. The scorpion's tail flops from side to side.

"I hate this place," I whisper. I do, genuinely. I hate it. I don't care how fucking beautiful it is or how cute the monkeys are. I want out of here now! Everything wants to kill me. Suddenly, I feel the need to go and wash this morning off myself. Without another word, I stalk off toward the pool.

The playfulness I shared with Robin earlier is completely gone. I don't swim naked, I strip down to my underwear instead. I wade into the pool and dunk myself. I scream at the top of my lungs underwater. The adrenaline I felt continues to course around my body. Needing to take a breath, I resurface, take a large breath, and repeat my underwater scream therapy.

By the fourth time, I can feel myself calming down. Swimming around the pool helps burn off the last remnants of anger. I know I shouldn't be angry with Robin. She saved me again, but seriously.

Once I've dried off, I dress and head back to camp. Robin is sitting with another cup of tea, radio in hand. She's fiddling with the dial on top. The distinct crackle of static noise shatters the peace. "Rob… Robin, can you…hear?" That's Mic's voice.

"Mic, you there, copy?" Robin replies. She hasn't acknowledged my return, which hurts a little.

"Yeah, I'm here, Robin. Over."

Robin laughs. "Good to hear your voice. Is everything okay back there? Over."

"Yes, all fine. We had a good drenching last night. Managed to collect a lot of water. Still working on the radio. No luck so far. What about you? Over."

"We hit the jackpot. Came across a waterfall yesterday evening. We're just about to start heading back to you now. Over." Robin has her two foldable water butts by her feet. To her utter astonishment, I walk over and take the radio out of her hands.

"Hi, Mic, it's Ellie." I wait but nothing, then I roll my eyes. "Over," I add.

"Hey, Ellie, good to hear you're okay. Over."

"You too. Look, there's a change of plans," I say. Robin is scrunching her beautiful face up in confusion. She's going to hit the roof when she hears what I have to say. "We're not coming back to the camp just yet. Over."

"The fuck we aren't," Robin barks. She goes to snatch the radio back, but I duck out of her way, running around the closest tree. "Ellie, stop it, come here," she yells as I evade her by running around the tree. We must look ridiculous. "Robin, just hear me out," I plead.

"Ellie, we need to get back to the wreck."

"No, we don't. Can you stop chasing me?" I shout.

"Fine." Robin throws her hands up in defeat, which makes me smile. I keep my distance but approach a little so she can hear me talk to Mic and Cam.

"Mic, you there? Over."

"Yup. What's the new plan then? Over."

"We continue to follow the river. I think this is our best chance of getting help. Where there's water, there are people, right?" I'm asking Robin as much as I'm stating it to Mic.

"Ellie, we need to discuss this," Robin says, her muscular arms crossed against her chest. She's doing her brooding warrior stance, and I'm here for it.

"Mic, give us a few minutes, okay? We'll radio in ten. Over and out." I place the radio in my back pocket. "I'm not going back to the crash site, Robin."

"Right, so what's your plan, hmm? Just continue wandering around the rainforest until we die of starvation?"

"Fuck off, don't talk to me like I'm an idiot. You and I both know that we can survive out here. No one is coming for us. We are *alone*. The only way we get out of here is if we find someone to help us. Now we've found a water source. We can follow it upstream. That gets you a better vantage point from which to survey the landscape, right? Hopefully, you can see something that shows our location on your map."

Robin studies me with piercing eyes. She's not saying no, so that's something, right? "And what about Mic and Cam?"

"They have water. They've listened to you, and they have your survival guide. We have zero chance of getting home if we go back. At least this way, we're giving ourselves a fighting chance. Once you can pinpoint us, I know you can figure out the location of the wreck. We can get help to the boys once we find it."

"There's no guarantee we'll come across anyone."

"True, but at least there *is* a chance if we're looking. Come on, it makes sense. You know it does."

Turning her head away from me, I watch and wait. I know she's running it all through her head, deciding what's for the best. "Okay. We'll continue on. But only if Mic and Cam agree. It's their choice, too." I nod happily, pulling the radio from my pocket and handing it over. Robin wastes no time contacting Mic and Cam, relaying our plan. To my relief, they agree to it.

Am I stupid for suggesting we remain out here? Probably, considering I've already had two close calls with the local wildlife, but I know in my gut it's the right thing to do.

Robin is quiet with me now. I can't tell what's pissing her off. Is it because I screamed at her for throwing the knife? Storming off? Or changing our plan without consulting her first? I don't want to make the situation worse, so I stay silent as we pack up our things.

With full water canteens, we head upstream. It's less than five minutes before we come across the first hurdle. Because we want to follow the river to higher ground, it means we need to do a bit of climbing.

The last time I climbed anything was a stripper's pole during Toni's last birthday bash. I can successfully dangle upside down while looking super sexy. Scaling a slippery rock face, not so much.

"Ready?" Robin asks me as she grabs the rock, preparing to ascend. I nod dumbly. I'm not going to voice my concerns because I'm pretty sure Robin is super tired of me and all my problems. Or the problems I cause her.

I take a step back, allowing Robin to start her climb. Every muscle in her tanned body flexes. Oh, momma! Clearly, this isn't the time for me to be getting hot under the collar, so I focus all my energy on watching where Robin puts her feet and hands as she confidently makes her way up the small cliff.

The height doesn't stress me. Even if I slip and fall, I don't think I would get seriously injured. Still, I don't want that to happen, so I concentrate harder on each of Robin's movements. In no time at all, she's hauled her fine ass over the top. I look up to see her peering over the edge. "You got this, Ellie, just take your time. Don't rush your movements, okay?"

Here goes nothing! The first few feet were easy enough, but it's getting harder. I have the upper body strength of soggy lettuce. Must hit the gym when we get home.

Robin continues to give me encouraging shouts from up above. I know I'm taking way too long, but she did tell me to take my time. I finally make it to the top third of the cliff. "Give me your hand," Robin says, extending her arm toward me. Now it's not natural to let go of the thing that's keeping you from tumbling to the ground, so I'm finding it challenging to acquiesce to her demand. "Let go, Ellie, trust me."

Sucking in a big breath, I peel my hand off the stone and thrust it into Robin's. "Use your feet to climb the last bit," she says as I feel her pull me up.

With a heave of pure power, Robin grunts and yanks me the rest of the way up. She's so strong she pulls me right into her body and we fall back with me firmly on top of her. If I wasn't so fucking tired from the climb, this would be really sexy. Instead, I let my head flop to her shoulder. My breathing is that of a chain smoker. Hell, I even start coughing just to make the whole thing worse for both of us.

"You okay?" Robin asks after a few moments of hyperventilation. I nod wordlessly. Not wanting to cause any more awkwardness between us, I roll off her. *The sky is so blue.* That's the limit of my brain function at the minute.

After a few minutes, I'm able to sit up. "That was fun," I say, causing Robin to laugh.

"You did good, princess." I don't know how I feel about her calling me that. Does it mean she's back to thinking not very good things about me? I really hope not. I offer her a tight smile until she bumps my shoulder and gives me one of her sexy grins and that oh-so-delicious wink. "Let's go." And just like that, we leave any unease we had at the bottom of that waterfall.

We walk for a few hours, stopping now and then to cool down or snack. I've noticed that Robin is eating half of what I am. There's no point in me saying anything. I know why she's doing it, and it's very sweet. So far, my blood sugar is stable. I'm not overly worried, so I wish Robin wouldn't worry so much.

"Hey, I was thinking," Robin begins as we take

another water break.

"Thinking what?"

"Thinking it might be a good idea for me to show you a few things with my knife."

I swallow hard. "What kind of things?"

"Well, how to use it for one thing." She laughs. "I could teach you how to throw it accurately. Basic defense stuff. Could come in useful one day." She shrugs. Is she blushing?

"O-okay, yeah, I'd like that. But I think you should limit your expectations, Rob." I laugh. She grins at me.

"And I think you should have more faith in yourself, El."

Chapter Sixteen

Robin

Do I regret letting Ellie talk me into continuing our search for help? A little. We've been following the river for two days, and there's nothing! Don't get me wrong, there's plenty for us to see. The rainforest is pretty magical, but a pleasant view doesn't help us get the hell home, now does it?

We're down to the last packs of food. I've been trying to eat as little as possible so that Ellie has enough. That's my primary concern now. What the hell am I going to do if we run out of food before we get help? If Ellie gets sick, we're screwed. Safe to say, I'm internally kicking myself for going along with her plan.

"Why are you scowling?" Shit, I didn't realise I was. How do I explain how I'm feeling without Ellie getting upset or pissed at me?

"Just thinking."

"Vague."

"I suppose I'm getting a bit antsy at the fact we haven't found anyone yet."

"I get it. I really think we'll find someone, though." Her optimism is refreshing but misplaced, I think. I give her a courtesy smile and continue to analyse every decision I've made since we crashed.

"Robin," Ellie hisses, which makes me stop and

turn. Her eyes are wide, and she's staring to our right, into the trees. I follow her gaze. Standing half behind a palm tree is a young boy. He must be around six. "Please tell me you can see that kid, too. I'm not losing it, am I?"

"I see him," I whisper. Unlike Ellie, I'm not overly surprised to see the boy. His attire tells me he's part of the Yanomami tribe. That's great for two reasons. One, I now know the region we're in. The Yanomami tribe is between Brazil and Venezuela. Granted, they have a large section of land, but it's a start. The second and probably most important thing for me and Ellie right now is that they're a friendly tribe. One less thing to worry about.

"Um, so what's the plan? Do we run or what?" Ellie asks me.

"No need to run. In fact, this could be a really good thing. Some of the Yanomami tribe have contact with the outside world. They could be our ticket out of here."

"Yanomami?"

"Yes, that's who they are."

"How the hell do you know that?"

"We spent some time with the tribe when we came here to train. The Yanomami are expert hunters and fishermen and have vast amounts of botanical knowledge."

"Great, so you can talk to them then?"

"Nope, we had a translator. I don't speak Xiriná, do you?" I ask. Obviously, I know she doesn't.

"Oh, yeah, I'm fluent." She huffs, rolling her eyes.

There's a rustling noise. A woman steps out from behind the tree, laying her hands on the boy's shoulders. From the corner of my eye, I see Ellie blush and avert her gaze. I can't help the chuckle that rumbles in my chest. The woman has a simple loincloth covering her lower half. Apart from that, she's naked. I can't believe Ellie is blushing at the sight of a pair of boobs.

Things are about to get a hell of a lot more uncomfortable for our resident movie star. If a pair of bare breasts embarrasses her, just wait until she finds out how the Yanomami greet each other.

I approach the woman and child slowly. I keep a smile on my face. I wait patiently. After a few moments, the woman approaches me. Now this is where it gets super uncomfortable. The Yanomami tribe has an... *interesting* way of greeting. To put it bluntly, they fart. Can you imagine the response of my unit when we first learned about the custom? Let's just say my male colleagues were delighted. Not that they needed a reason to pass gas.

Anyway, that's how it's done in the tribe, and that's what's about to transpire here. I'll spare you the details. Let's just say that Ellie turned the colour of a tomato, and I had to stop myself from hyperventilating with laughter.

The woman beckons us to follow, which we do. It's only a few minutes until we reach a clearing where there are around twenty other females with children. I know that the women in the tribe tend to the crops and kids. We're ushered into the centre of the group, and that's when I decide to take out my map. It's difficult to communicate because we don't speak the same language, but I find visual cues are a good way to overcome that barrier.

I lay the map out. I gesture to our surroundings

and then point to the map with—what I hope is—a questioning face. The woman who found us first bends over the map. She looks around at her friends and family before standing back up and gesturing for us to follow her again.

Ellie has been deathly quiet. I bet she's terrified. It's understandable, I suppose. At least I have some knowledge of the tribe and their customs. Ellie is flying by the seat of her pants, trusting me to guide her through these interactions.

A few minutes later, we break through the trees and into the tribe's home base. The Yanomami live in a giant oval hut. All of them together. Damn, what's it called…um, oh! I remember a shabono. The shabono is where they live, feast, and celebrate.

We continue to follow the woman into the shabono. She leads us to a man who, I presume, is her husband or something. The Yanomami people live in independent communities. This is a small one, by the looks of it. They don't have a chief; all matters are decided amongst them equally. World governments could seriously learn a thing or two from these people.

The woman takes my map and hands it to him. Like the women, the men are dressed in loincloths. Many of them have black and red body paint on their faces and torsos. The other really cool thing is their piercings. Long sticks protrude from their noses, cheeks, and chin. Some of the sticks that are used are decorated with colourful feathers. They all look really awesome. Wonder what my mum would think if I added a couple of sticks to my face.

I feel a presence behind me, but before I can turn, I feel Ellie's body close to my back. I don't even need to look to know it's her. I have snuggled that body every night so far. I could tell her curves blindfolded. Her breath dances across the skin on my neck. I have to close my eyes and calm myself before speaking.

"What's going on?" she whispers.

"I think the woman has given my map to her husband. Hopefully, he'll understand that we're lost."

"And if he doesn't? Are we prisoners?"

"No, I don't think so. Just try to remain calm. Friendly faces, okay?"

"I always have a friendly face." She grumbles, making me grin. Yeah, she has a friendly face, usually for everyone but me.

The sound of people talking catches my attention. Good job, really, this isn't the time to be zoning out, lusting over beautiful actresses. I lightly shake my thoughts away and concentrate on the people in front of me. The woman walks over to me, pulling me to the table where her husband is talking rapidly.

On the map are three markings he has crudely drawn. The man leans over, pointing at the first marking he's made. It's an oval, I think that's supposed to represent their shabono. Farther north, the man points to a cross. He's talking so fast it's hard to believe anyone could make out what he's saying. He abruptly points to the third marking, which is east of the oval. More rapid conversing.

"Do you have any idea what he's saying?" Ellie whispers out the corner of her mouth.

"I think he's trying to tell us where we are. I presume the oval mark is the hut." Ellie nods. "It's the other two markings I'm not sure of. Maybe one is somewhere we can get help."

"And the other?"

"No idea. It could be another source of help or

somewhere we should avoid."

"Great." She huffs again.

"Hey, if you think you can do better, princess, take it away." My sarcasm isn't needed, but sometimes she doesn't half get on my nerves.

"I didn't say I could do better, and I'm not criticising you. I'm just frustrated."

"Yeah, me too, but instead of huffing and puffing, maybe try to help." It's then I realise our discussion has gone from whispers to almost shouting level. Looking around, I see that everyone in the shabono has stopped what they're doing and are watching us. Crap!

I hold up my hands in a surrender-type action, hoping they understand. I say sorry and lean back over the map. Ignoring everything and everyone, I study it. My gut is telling me that one of those marks is our salvation, and the other is a warning. I know from the news and my time spent in the Amazon that there are plenty of things and people to avoid. Illegal gold mining is rife here, and those people don't take well to outsiders. The last thing we want is to run into anyone like that.

Once again, my wandering mind is interrupted by the woman. I need to give her a name. I hate referring to her as "the woman." Maybe Carla. Traditionally, Yanomami don't have individual names. They call each other sister, brother, cousin, et cetera. Well, I don't have the foggiest idea how to say those words, so I'll just stick to giving them names.

Right, so Carla starts to drag me again. This time, we head over to the opposite side of the shabono. Each family has their own section. We're being taken to an empty part, so I'll assume that's where we're meant to stay. Christ, Ellie's going to throw a fit. She's not happy about being here one bit. Although, if she does kick off, I'll have to remind her gently that going off plan was her bloody idea in the first place.

Dropping my pack onto the floor, I pointedly stare at Ellie to do the same thing. At the end of the day, these people have taken us in. The least we can do is be polite. Ellie rolls her eyes at me again! But she drops her pack. Carla hands me a red loincloth. Um…

"Why is she giving us these?" Ellie asks, not at all quietly. I can see her cogs turning from here. Yup, I think she's got it right. Carla is trying to lift my tank top off me. Christ almighty, she expects us to dress in their clothing—or lack thereof, in this case.

Fuck it! I gently take my top out of Carla's hands and lift it over my head. Carla takes my top and then stands there, waiting. She wants the rest of my clothes. I'm not shy, so I strip off my shorts, handing them to her. I don the loincloth and slip down my knickers. I kind of hoped that Carla would forget about my sports bra, but alas, she's pointing at it. Here goes nothing. It wasn't the way I wanted Ellie to see my boobs up close, but what are ya gonna do?

Let's take a second to really bask in my reality. I'm thirty-five, stuck in the Amazon rainforest in an indigenous tribal hut with my tits on display. Excellent.

Carla promptly turns to Ellie, who is shaking her head so hard I'm afraid she's going to sprain her neck. "Robin," Ellie says to the floor because she hasn't looked at me since I got undressed. "I'm not wearing that. Not a chance."

"I think you're going to offend them if you don't. Look, it's not a sexual thing. It's hot here, they wear very little to combat the heat. Get out of your head and just strip. Bloody hell, you've seen boobs before. I'm sure you've done a lot more than look at them, too." I grin.

"Not the point," she shoots back, but I can see a glimmer of amusement on her face.

"Ellie, just think of it as part of the experience." I laugh. "We won't be here long. We can afford to take their generosity with some humility, right?"

The huffing returns, but to my surprise, she starts fumbling with her clothes. I turn my body away from her to respect her privacy. Not that she'll have very much once her bra comes off, but I least want her to know I understand she's feeling uncomfortable, and I'm not taking advantage of it.

Carla bundles our clothes together and then walks off, leaving me and Ellie alone. I can't help but look after a few minutes of silence. The whole situation is ridiculous. I catch her eye, and we both fall into hysterics. "So this is awkward," I say.

"Oh, you think?" she laughs.

"Okay, let's just get it over with, all right. We're two lesbians with our boobs out. I know I can't speak for you, but I'll admit it's in my nature to look at breasts, and, well…yours are right there."

Ellie shakes her head, laughing. "I can't believe this is my life right now. Okay, sure, fuck it. I'll admit it, too. I'm obviously gonna check out your rack."

"See, that wasn't too hard now, was it?"

"Right, you have thirty seconds to look with my permission."

"Fine, I give you permission, too. On three. One…two…three."

Our gazes take a southward dip. First thing I

can tell is Ellie has very, *very* nice breasts. They would definitely fit in my hands. With her being a blonde, I'm not surprised that her nipples are pink. Mine are more brownish. I guess that's the Italian I have in my ancestry. Have thirty seconds gone by yet? God knows, but until Ellie tells me to stop, I'm going to get my fill.

"You've got your nipple pierced," Ellie says without looking away from my ladies.

"Yeah, got it done after I left the Marines."

"Did it hurt?"

"Like a bitch. That's why I only got the one done." This is possibly the most surreal conversation I've ever had.

"I wanted to get it done, but I chickened out. I did get a tattoo, though."

"Really? Where?" I ask, scanning all that delicious skin that's on show.

"It's on my hip. It isn't big."

"What is it?"

"That's for me to know, Ms. Stuart." Hang about. Is she flirting with me? It's well past the thirty-second mark now, but we're still checking each other out. My gaze has strayed from her boobs to the rest of her body. "Do you have any tattoos?" she asks.

"Just this one." I point to the regimental coat of arms on the underside of my left biceps. It's an outline, so it's not overly noticeable.

"You're very fit." Ellie is appraising me, and I like it.

"I work out a lot."

"I can tell."

"Do you...work out? You're..."

"I'm what, Robin?" Oh, boy, that's a sultry voice

if I've ever heard one.

"Gorgeous," I say because she is, and every woman should be told they're beautiful because they are. I'm so happy to be a lesbian.

"Thank you." Our eyes lock, and I know that things have irrevocably changed between us. Yes, Ellie is annoying, rude, and privileged, but I see the other side to her. The soft, caring funny woman who has hidden herself away for far too long.

Carla is back. This time, she takes Ellie by the arm, which I'm grateful for. We end up in the open area of the shabono. A group of men have turned up. By the looks of it, they're a hunting party. A wild pig has been strapped to what looks like a stretcher made of bamboo. I think we're being invited for dinner.

Ellie had the brilliant idea of using her GoPro to record our time with the Yanomami. None of the tribespeople seemed to mind. Ellie even spent some time over dinner showing Carla and a few others some of her previous videos. It wasn't the best showing, not on a two-inch screen, but they appeared to be fascinated all the same.

The wild pig was delicious. We had a veritable feast of meat and vegetables. The community sat eating and chatting for hours. It was all a little overwhelming, to be honest. Never in a million years did I think I would get the chance to experience something so pure as what I have tonight.

Even Ellie seems relaxed. We can't exactly have open conversations with anyone except each other, but it's more than enough to just observe. Their culture is fascinating. For a brief period, I think we've both forgotten why we're here in the first place. Worries about water, food, and finding help blow away with the smoke from the fire.

"Tonight has been...wow." Ellie sighs as she shifts into me once we arrive back at our little section of the shabono. As usual, we sleep holding each other. Well, me spooning Ellie. Her hair smells of smoke, and her skin is warm from the fire.

"Yeah, it was something to remember, all right."

"They just live so..."

"Happily?"

"Yeah. They don't care what people think. They just look after each other."

"They have problems, though."

"I know that...I'm just...I don't know."

"You're experiencing a different side to life. I know we're in a shitty situation but...being here, experiencing all this, is giving you a glimpse at a life away from expectations and judgments. This isn't the Ellie Bishop Show, and I don't mean that nastily. I mean *you* get to take a break and just be. No mask."

Ellie has gone silent, and I'm panicking that I've said too much. Then I feel her shoulders shake. *Oh, well done, Robin, you've made the woman cry. Again!*

Chapter Seventeen

Ellie

I cried again! It's getting a bit out of hand, really. Every time Robin says something remotely nice to me, the waterworks start. Jesus, have I been deprived of affection for so long that the hint of warmth shown by another woman sends me off the deep end?

As usual, Robin was entirely sweet about the whole incident. Instead of trying to talk, she just held me tighter while I cried. I found it a little confusing because as lovely as her support was, she was still holding me while we were both topless. I tried very hard not to react to her nipples poking me in the back.

I'd love to blame my emotional meltdown on my meds, citing anxiety as the cause, but that would be false. Every word Robin said to me last night was true. Being here, stranded in the Amazon rainforest, has given me a tiny glimpse of a world outside of Hollywood and all the pressure that it brings. That's not even including the overwhelming standards I have to keep for my mother.

Here, though, I've been able to open up a little. Robin is teaching me things I would never get the chance to learn in my regular life. Not without my mother interfering. How am I in my mid-thirties and so thoroughly ruled by her and my brother? It's times like this that I miss my dad so fiercely.

Anyway, I woke up this morning feeling better for crying and worse for, once again, blubbering all over Robin. I'm not some weak-willed girl. I know I'm strong, independent, and powerful. Unfortunately, I'm none of those things around the people who influence my life. Things *need* to change. If by some miracle we get a second chance and can go home, I can't go back to how it was.

"Hey, breakfast," Robin calls, interrupting my life-affirming decisions. A thought flitters across my mind. Will Robin be in my life if we get home? I truly hope so. The woman drives me nuts, but she also calms me. I feel like I can do anything when she's around.

"What's on the menu?"

"Fruit."

My mouth waters. We've been stranded for a week, yet it feels like we haven't had authentic food for years. Wasting no time, I savor the two bananas Robin brought over. It's only after I've scarfed the second one that I realize that was probably for her. With my mouth full, I grin at her. "Sorry," I mumble. Robin laughs at me, shaking her head.

The awkwardness that we felt yesterday about being half naked has dissipated. There's nothing sexual about it, and it's really nice not to have a sweaty top on. The breeze under the loincloth is pleasant, too.

"So I was thinking that we could spend a couple more days here and then head out."

"You don't want to get going now?"

"No, I think it's a good idea to rest up. We can plan our route now we have an idea where we are. I also want to pinpoint the wreckage. If we can find someone to help, we need to get them to Mic and Cam

ASAP."

"That makes sense."

"I'm betting that we'll be expected to follow the women as they tend to the crops today. Take the camera. It would be interesting to document our days here."

"I got so much cool footage yesterday."

"Carla seemed to enjoy watching what you've recorded so far."

"Carla?" Did I miss a memo or something?

Robin smiles shyly. She's too cute. How can someone go from a strong warrior goddess to a shy and adorable woman in the blink of an eye? "I've given her a name. I don't know how to address them in their native language, and it feels weird calling her 'the woman,' you know what I mean?"

"Totally. Do you think she would mind?"

"I doubt she understands."

We continue eating until Carla comes over like Robin predicted and gestures for us to follow. However, Robin got one thing wrong. We aren't following the women into the rainforest to tend to crops. Instead, we're placed in the center of the shabono. I look at Robin with questioning eyes. She shrugs at me, clearly having no better understanding than I do of what's going on.

A few minutes pass, which is unnerving. Do you know *how* long a few minutes feel when you're in this kind of situation? Let me tell you, it's a goddamn lifetime! My palms are sweating, and my mind is coming up with all sorts of scenarios. What if, all this time, the Yanomami have been buttering us up to…I don't know, eat us or something. That's stupid, right? Yes, stupid. Um…maybe they just want us to leave.

That would be the best case. Oh, God, I can feel my nerves fraying.

"Calm down," Robin whispers, her hand gently squeezing mine. I close my eyes and count in my head. When I open them again, I'm even more confused. There are three boys—well, young men—maybe in their early twenties, standing in front of us. Each of them is dressed in the customary red loincloth. Their bodies sport different painted patterns, and two of them have multiple piercings, where the third just has a stick through his nose.

"Um…any clue what's happening right now?" I ask nervously.

"Nope." *Well, that's super helpful, Robin.*

Carla's husband is speaking. He's pointing at the young men and then at us. I'm starting to get an uneasy feeling. I turn to Robin, who's looking just as concerned as I am. Bruno has stopped talking. Oh, that's Carla's husband, by the way. I've just named him. So, Bruno has gone quiet and is looking at us. I have no clue what we're supposed to do.

Robin has that look she gets when she's trying to solve a puzzle or problem. I stay frozen in place, afraid that any movement will give Carla and Bruno an excuse to do something. I don't know what that something would be, but I'm sure I wouldn't like it.

Then Robin is moving closer to me. "Trust me," she whispers. I watch Robin point to me and then at herself. Robin then slides her hand into mine, entwining our fingers. I'm completely lost. What the fuck is going on? Whatever it is, Bruno seems to understand. He nods and waves the young men away. "Time for us to leave," Robin says quietly. She's still holding my hand.

I wait until we're back in our section of the hut before asking Robin what the hell just happened. I feel like I missed something important. We find our clothes that Carla whisked away neatly stacked by our packs.

"Get dressed," Robin orders. Her soft tone has been replaced with what I can only imagine is her military voice. It's hot.

"What's happening?" I waste no time putting on my clothes. It feels weird to have panties on again.

"That was some kind of setup, I think."

"Setup?"

"Yeah."

"Robin, you're gonna need to say more than that."

"When we've left. Come on."

I can see there's no point in pushing it. I haul my pack on my back and follow Robin over to Carla and Bruno. There are several other people hanging around. We spend a few minutes saying goodbye. Hopefully, the tribe got our meaning.

"Will you tell me what the hell I missed back there?" I'm agitated that Robin is acting the way she is. I don't understand why she's so different all of a sudden.

Robin continues to march on. Gone is her laid-back attitude. Here walks Sergeant Stuart. "They were looking for us to match with those men."

We continue to march through the forest at an alarming speed. "Match? What do you mean?"

"Marriage probably." Those two words have me stumbling over my own feet.

"Marriage," I screech. "What? Why? We're strangers. Why the hell would they want that?" No way.

Robin must have misread the situation. I'm no expert, but I can't see an indigenous tribe wanting to introduce outsiders to their community.

"I think, and I'm just guessing, that they haven't got enough eligible women. The Yanomami usually marry cousins. That community was small. If I had to hazard a guess, I would say they've had some problems with illegal gold diggers. I think they've lost some members of the community."

"Sorry, back up. Gold diggers?"

"Yeah. This area has a lot of them, unfortunately. Some are families just trying to make some extra cash. The rest are brutal groups who don't think twice about attacking tribes to get them off the land."

"So you think the tribe we were just with has been attacked by gold diggers?"

"That's exactly what I think. It makes sense that they would want to marry off their young men to available women. They need to make their communities whole again, and that means babies."

"Fuck me!"

"That's what they wanted to do." Robin laughs.

"You're hilarious. So how did we avoid getting hitched?"

"I indicated we were together."

"Together?"

"Yup. The Yanomami don't actively encourage homosexuality, but they also don't stress about sisters being *sisters*, if you know what I mean."

"So why did we practically run out of there if they aren't bothered?"

"The fact that they were trying to match us was worrying. Better that we left."

"Okay, so now what? Do you have a direction

for us to go?"

"Well, that's our choice to make. There are two options on the map."

"Can I see?"

Robin stops walking and hands me the map. "We're here, I think." Looking at the map, I try to decide which cross we should head for. It's a toss-up. The marking farther north is by the river. Maybe that would be the best one.

"Our original plan was to follow the river. Let's stick to that."

"Okay." Robin nods.

"Okay, just like that?"

"Well, it's as good a choice as any." With that, Robin stuffs the map back in her pack and continues marching. I trundle along, half jogging to keep up with her. There's something going on, and I don't know how to ask her what. I really thought we'd broken through this bullshit but apparently not.

"Robin, can you slow down?" I growl eventually. It's never a good thing when I'm given time to overthink things, and that's exactly what I've been doing. Robin is acting different, and it has to do with me, I'm sure of it.

"We can't go at a snail's pace."

"I'm not saying we should, but I'm getting tired, and we haven't had a break in a while."

"We'll stop in a couple of hours." I should probably tell her I'm feeling woozy. Since the fruit this morning, I haven't eaten, and we've been on the move all day. I also haven't checked my sugar levels in over twenty-four hours. The problem is, Robin has now ruffled my feathers with her behavior, and I'm being stubborn and sulking, so I don't want to tell her I'm feeling faint. Nope, I soldier on, just like she wants until I collapse. Oops.

What in God's name is that noise? If I've died, this is not heaven. Sweet Jesus, what a horrendous racket. My eyes flicker as I try to open them. My mind is fuzzy, and I feel light-headed. A small groan escapes my lips when I try to move. Ugh, that doesn't feel good. My ass hurts and my arm. I probably landed funny when I passed out. Shit, I fainted. Robin is going to be pissed.

"Don't sit up." Robin's voice is coming from a few feet away. I expected to have her glaring at me, but I'm shocked to see pure panic written across her face. This is a woman who served in war-ravaged hellholes, yet me fainting is causing her to panic. Weird.

"I'm fine," I mumble, ignoring her and sitting up.

"You're not fine, you passed out."

"Stop worrying. I'm good now."

"Only because I shoved some berries in your mouth. Why didn't you tell me you needed to stop?"

"I—"

"I thought we promised to talk to each other. You told me you would let me know if you weren't feeling well." Okay, so she's full-on ranting at me now.

Anger boils in my veins. "I *did* tell you I needed to slow down, but you wouldn't listen. For whatever reason, you've been acting like an asshole since we left the Yanomami."

"You could have told me you were feeling faint," she yells back.

"I told you I was getting tired, but you wanted to march on, so that's what we did."

"If I'd have known—"

"If you hadn't been acting like that, you would have known. What the hell happened? Yesterday we were getting along great. God, you held me all night while I cried, and then today it's like we're strangers again."

Robin starts pacing back and forth in front of me. She's furiously rubbing her forehead. Maybe she has a headache. Whatever is going on with her, she's not telling me. I'm done playing the guessing game. If Robin wants to be all dark and moody, that's fine, but I'm not going to be her whipping boy. I stagger to my feet, grab my pack, and start walking again. It's only a few seconds until Robin catches up with me, grabbing me by my elbow and swinging me around to face her.

"Where the hell do you think you're going?"

"I'm going to that little mark on the map, so I can get the fuck out of here and go home."

"Ellie, you need to rest."

"No, I need my normal life back. I need to see Toni and drink three Starbucks a day. What I don't need is this bullshit." I yank my arm from her grip and march on.

"Will you just stop?" she yells. Like hell I will. "Ellie, for Christ's sake, just stop." Nope, not gonna happen. Oh, apparently, it is because Robin has just grabbed me by the waist. "Just stop," she pants. Her breath tickles my neck as her body pushes in behind me.

Now if this were a movie, I'd spin around in her arms and kiss her. Let's be honest, that's where this is leading. Our back-and-forth arguing is pent-up sexual tension. Don't get me wrong, it wasn't in the beginning. I genuinely didn't like her one bit, but that's changed.

Alas, this isn't a movie, it's not some rom-com where everything can be sorted with a kiss. I peel her arm from my body and take a step forward. I can't look at her because my resolve will crumble, and I will kiss her. Instead, I take a breath first, *then* I turn around. "I'll rest for half an hour and then we carry on."

The disappointment in Robin's eyes is crystal clear. Hopefully, my amazing acting skills are masking my own regret at not planting one on her fine lips.

Dropping my pack and myself to the ground, I avoid eye contact with her and set about drinking some water and nibbling on some berries. Robin walks a few feet away and does the same. The atmosphere is strangled with tension.

True to my word, I pack up my gear and set off walking after half an hour. Funny, I'm taking the lead considering I have no clue where we need to go. The thing is, I just need an ounce of control. Something to cling to that will stop me from unraveling. "Hey," I say suddenly because a thought has just occurred to me. "What the hell was that noise? It sounded like a bunch of banshees when I came round."

For the first time in hours, I glimpse a smile on Robin's face. "Howler monkeys. You fainted under a tree full of them. It was a little early for them to be calling, but they did. That's what you heard."

"Jesus, they were deafening."

"Told you." Robin walks past me, taking the lead, which is fair. I could be leading us anywhere.

The pace is a lot slower now. Robin is being cautious. My mind wanders as we walk. I'm thinking of home. My life in general, really. I do want to get back. I want to see Toni, and I absolutely want a caramel frap. Oh, and pizza. What I don't want is to slip back into how I was living. I just don't know how to change it.

Toni would tell me that the first step would be to fire Gabe, and she would be right. That would mean that I was prepared to face my mother. I've always done what she wanted just to keep the peace. Of course, I don't want my personal shit splashed over the tabloids, so I understand where she's coming from.

What I *don't* agree with is that every one of my actions needs to be analyzed. I shouldn't be worrying that the brand of toothpaste I buy might offend my mother. That actually happened, FYI. I bought some AquaFresh once, and my mother reamed me out for an hour. Sometimes I think she just loves the control. Who the fuck cares what toothpaste I use? And how does that in any way make the family look bad? That's how dire it's gotten. Is it any wonder I hide away in my house most of the time when I'm not working?

Even though acting was never my dream, I do love it. So *if* we get home, that won't change. My gaze wanders to Robin. I hope we can have some kind of friendship when this is all over. I need people like her in my life.

We break through the dense trees, and my heart soars. We've found a camp. We have found a camp with people! People who have cars and tents and whatever equipment that is. Holy shit, we're saved!

Chapter Eighteen

Robin

You know when something bad is happening, and the entire world seems to slow? It's like you can see everything happening in slow motion, but you can't do anything to stop the bad thing from happening. That's where I'm at now.

Today has just been one disaster after another. It started out pretty great. I woke up to Ellie tucked into my chest. She'd cried for a while, but then she'd finally fallen asleep. In the night, she'd turned over and cuddled into me, her face buried in my neck. There's no denying that I'm developing some serious feelings for her.

After breakfast, everything went downhill fast. As soon as I realised that Carla and her husband, plus the rest of the adults in the tribe, were trying to match us up to those blokes, my stomach sank. We were in a really tricky situation. I'd taken a gamble by indicating that I was partnered with Ellie. I wasn't too worried that they'd be upset with the sapphic thing. It was more that I was scuppering their plans.

The longer we spent with the particular group of Yanomami, the clearer it was to see that they'd suffered some losses. There were parts of the shabono that looked as if they'd been recently occupied but had no personal belongings in them. I remember learning that when a member of the tribe dies, they're burned along with every possession they own.

Last night at the feast they threw for us, I noticed them conducting some sort of ritual. I couldn't be one hundred percent sure at the time, but now I'm convinced they were enacting a death ceremony. There were no dead bodies or anything. If memory serves, the bodies are burned, and then the bones are ground down with the ashes of the body and mixed with bananas to form a soup. Ellie and I weren't offered to partake, thank fuck.

Ellie was right when she said it was unlikely they would try to welcome outsiders into their midst, but I suppose if they were desperate to populate their community enough, it could happen. Hell, maybe I got it completely fucking wrong, and they were offering the men up to escort us somewhere. Shit, now I think of it, that seems more likely. Jesus, what a mess.

Anyway, I thought it best we get out of there. We had the map and a couple of places to go looking for help. I was so thrown by the events of the morning that I was too in my head to realise that Ellie hadn't eaten or drunk for hours. How stupid could I be?

When she hit the deck, I thought I'd lost her. She was so pale and sweaty. I crammed as many sweet berries in her mouth as possible. Thank God it brought her around. My relief was immeasurable, and then we got into a fight.

I know my mood was off when we left the Yanomami. It wasn't just the possible matchmaking thing. It was how I felt when I'd taken Ellie's hand in mine and declared her as my partner. It was like a wrecking ball slammed into my chest. I have feelings for her, but so what? Where could it possibly go?

Ellie Bishop is adored worldwide. Our lives are so different. As soon as we get home, everything will go back to normal, and where does that leave me and my feelings? Up shit creek, that's where!

My natural tendency is to retreat into myself when I'm faced with a problem I can't fix. Yes, I was a dick to her, and I should have just been honest, but at that moment, I couldn't. Ellie was rightfully irritated with me. We've been doing this dance since the day we met. Most of it's sexual tension now, though, not outright disdain.

So that leads me to the present. Us busting through the trees to find this camp. It takes me all of five seconds to know we do not want to stick around, but unfortunately, Ellie doesn't pick up the same message. And that's how everything comes to slow down. Time almost grinds to a halt as Ellie throws her hands in the air and starts calling out excitedly.

There's nothing I can do to stop her. She's running head on into the camp thinking we're saved. We are most definitely not. My heart shudders when two men armed to their back teeth step out from behind one of the vehicles. They have their guns raised, and I see Ellie screech to a halt. She turns to me with eyes so wide and so full of fear I want to weep. If she'd just taken an extra second to look around, she would have seen that we've stepped into an illegal gold mining base.

The men are screaming at us. I shout to Ellie to get down on her knees. I need her to listen to me. I drop to the floor with my hands above my head and my face down. Ellie is screaming as they drag her away. Everything in my body is wanting to run after them, but I can't. That's a surefire way to get us both killed.

Moments later, I feel rough hands grabbing me. My hair is pulled as I'm carted towards a shack. My Marine Commando training is kicking in. If it were just me alone, I would have fought them and made a dash for the trees, but that's impossible with Ellie here.

My body slams to the floor of the shack with an almighty thud. The air is knocked right out of my lungs, and I'm struggling to inhale. "Robin," Ellie cries. She drops to the floor next to me. The men have already shut and locked the door. The room we're in is only lit by the natural light shining in through two small windows. They have bars across them, so no chance of escaping that way.

"Are...are—"

"I'm okay," Ellie says quickly. "Are you hurt?" she rushes to ask. I feel her hands snaking around my body, checking for wounds.

"No, I'm good. Just hit the floor with a bit of a wallop." I sit myself up. We should be thankful they haven't bound our hands.

"What do we do? Who are these people? Oh, God, Robin, I'm so stupid. I just ran us right into trouble." She sobs. Yeah, she did, but I'm not about to make her feel worse. No point in playing the blame game. We need to think about how to get out of here.

"Listen. You have to stay calm, okay? Comply with them, don't fight."

"Robin, they could do anything to us." Her eyes are red and puffy, and her skin is pale but not with low blood sugar. No, this is pure fear.

"Those were likely just guards. They won't do anything until they speak to the leader."

"And what happens then?" God, I don't think she wants to know. My mind is already thinking up some pretty horrifying shit.

"I don't know. But hey, I will protect you, okay?" If the only thing I can do is make sure Ellie doesn't get hurt, then that's what I'll do. I was trained thoroughly to resist interrogation. I just have to make sure they keep their interest on me and not her. "I want you to stay behind me, okay? Don't look at them and don't speak."

The room has a chair and an empty desk in it. Not a cell, therefore it's possible we'll be moved. Trying to escape in transport is always a good idea. That's usually when opportunities arise, especially if they only send a couple of armed men with us. I can deal with them.

The rattling of the lock jolts me into action. I shove Ellie behind me and brace myself against the wall flush to the door. As soon as that motherfucker pokes his gun barrel through the opening, he's mine. I steady my breath. This is what I was made for.

Everything around me goes quiet as I enter the zone. All the lads in my squad tried to get me to teach them my technique throughout my whole service. I can shut everything out completely and pinpoint my focus on my objective. Colin used to call me a war machine. None of the instructors ever wanted to fight me when I got into that mode. That's what made me such an effective weapon.

The barrel of an assault rifle inches slowly through the door. I wait until just the right moment and then I attack. Pulling the barrel through the door unbalances the guy on the other end of it. He stumbles in, and then I incapacitate him. It's so fast he has no chance of stopping it. These bozos think they've captured a couple of defenceless women. Not this time, fellas.

I take the rifle and do a quick check. It's primed and ready to go. There's a shout from outside. I presume his buddy is calling out to him for a sitrep (situational report). I bide my time. I take the opportunity to check on Ellie. She's tucked behind me like I told her to be. "Stay calm," I whisper. To my shock and delight, Ellie isn't a dribbling mess of panic. In fact, she looks strong and confident. She gives me a swift nod, allowing me to turn my focus back to the other armed assailant.

It's a waiting game now. Unlike the movies, I'm not going to go out there with guns blazing. That would just get me filled with bullet holes. No, this is a game of patience. I guarantee the man outside will break before I do. I smile to myself when I see a second gun barrel poke through the door. Showtime.

Now I have *two* unconscious arseholes on the floor. Go me!

I have no idea how many other gun-toting dick-wads are out there, so I need to be careful. I take the shoelaces off their boots and tie them up. Carefully, I peer through the crack in the door. So far, I can't see anyone else. I edge myself a little closer to the door. Still nothing.

"Okay, Ellie, listen to me carefully. When I tell you to go, I want you to run to the trees. You don't stop and you don't look back. Just concentrate on putting one foot in front of the other. I will be right behind you. Got it?"

"Got it." Her voice is firm. She's doing so well. I poke my head out ever so slightly to confirm the coast is clear. "Go now," I whisper. Ellie takes off like a rocket towards the trees. There are no shouts, no gunfire. I follow behind her as quickly as I can. As soon as we hit the treeline, I throw my body behind the thickest one and raise the gun ready to fire on anyone who may be following.

Holy hell, we did it. We escaped. I turn to look for Ellie. She's still running. Crap, I need to catch up and get her to stop. My daily running comes into use as I sprint after her. It's a few hundred metres before I catch her. "Ellie, stop," I call.

Putting on the brakes, she stops and whirls around toward me. She's breathing hard, her face is flushed from the exertion of running so fast. I'm positive this is the most running she's ever done, and I am so bloody proud of her. I go to tell her that, but I'm left speechless when she crushes her lips to mine. Her hands grab my face firmly as she moves her mouth against me.

My brain takes a couple of seconds to register what's happening, but when it does, I'm all in. I thought we were going to kiss earlier when she stormed off from me and I caught her by the waist. It didn't happen then, but I don't care, not when she is giving me the kiss of my life.

Hands wrap around my neck as she pulls me in closer. I plant my hand right on her arse because it's the one thing I've wanted to do since I met her. I feel her mouth part and her tongue tease my lips. This isn't a soft kiss, this is a battle. It's a *we survived* kiss. Everything about this kiss makes me want to shove her up against the closest tree and sink my fingers into her folds. I want to take her over and over again. I want Ellie Bishop screaming my name in ecstasy.

Shouting behind us rips us apart. It's not close,

but it's definitely coming from the campsite. "Run, Ellie." I grab her hand and pull her along. We have to put distance between us and them.

Pulling the map up from my memory, I know which way we can't go, and that's back to the Yanomami. Leading an armed group back to their home would be a grave error. No, we have to lead them away. We have to get to the mark that was east of the Yanomami home base.

Straining my ears, I try to pick up every noise. We're being pursued, that's for sure. At least this time we have a weapon, although I'm not sure it's of much use if there's an entire army of bad guys behind us. I pull Ellie as hard as I can. She must keep up with me.

More shouting pierces the forest, but this time, it's coming from our right. Goddamn it. Reinforcements must have been called in. There's no telling where they are. "Robin," Ellie screams. I look behind us and see four men running at full speed. The echo of a gunshot rings through the air. Ellie screams again. I pull her so she's catapulted in front of me. Another shot, and I feel the sting of a bullet hit my side.

Burning, that's all I can feel. It's like a red-hot poker has been pressed to my skin. The bullet knocks the wind out of me, and I stumble. I hear Ellie scream my name, but I can't see her because I'm falling forward. "Run, Ellie," I shout, but I know she's not going to leave me.

"Get up, Robin." Ellie is pulling at my hand. I try to get up, but it's no use. I can't believe I've let her down like this. I promised to protect her, and I'm failing. The men's voices get louder. Ellie drops to her knees with her hands behind her head. My arms are forcefully pulled behind my back, and this time, I am bound.

With a goon on either side of me, I feel the forest floor scrape across my knees as they move me. This can certainly go down as being one of the shittiest days on record.

Ellie is being dragged by two other dudes in front of me. She doesn't seem hurt, just frightened. I have to do something, but what? I can't fight four of them, not with an injury.

The men talk rapidly in Portuguese. I can make out some of their conversation. Thankfully, it doesn't sound like they plan to off us straight away. I think they're taking us back to their main camp. Not the one we stumbled across.

They bundle us into the back of a waiting SUV. This group is organised. I'm gonna take that as a positive. If they're taking orders, it means they at least have a pecking order and are less likely to act on their own volition.

Every bounce of the car sends pain through my side. Nausea crashes over me. I will not pass out! Now we're on the move. I need to refocus. Ellie is sitting next to me. I can feel her trembling, but God love her. She's not giving them the satisfaction of seeing how scared she is. I actually want to laugh when I look at her face. She's wearing the same *go fuck yourself* face she gave me at the airfield.

We arrive at our destination a few minutes later. It's similar to the camp we found, but this place is much bigger. Multiple shacks litter the area. The place has been stripped of trees. Several cars are parked next to the biggest hut. Everyone is armed. Fantastic! Our hopes of escaping this are dismal at best.

"Out," one of the men shout. The door is ripped

open, and we're practically thrown out of the truck. "Move," the same man shouts. So they speak some English, good to know.

"In," he barks when we arrive at a building that is definitely not an office. As soon as we step into the room, the door bangs shut.

"You're shot." Ellie wastes no time lowering me to the ground. "Let me see." Carefully, she peels my tank top up. "It's a graze. A deep one." Music to my ears. A graze we can work with.

When Ellie stands and unbuttons her shorts, I'm a bit confused. "Erm…El, as much as I'd love to, I don't think this is the time." She looks down at me, scrunching her eyes. Then she does her oh-so-practised eye roll at me.

"Don't be stupid." Not a very nice way to talk to an injured person, but whatever. Ellie's shorts hit the floor. I can't help but look up. Supergirl panties. Who'd have thought? "I put these on earlier," she says, rolling down what I now see are tights. "You need your side wrapped up. Pantyhose are good for that, right? The animal man told me they were good for keeping ticks and spiders off my legs." She's rambling, but she's right.

"Yeah, tights are good."

"Let's get you wrapped up." I'm sad to see her shorts go back on. "Careful, don't get a run in these. They're my good pair."

Chapter Nineteen

Ellie

The guilt I feel right now is unbelievable. It's my fault we're here in this godawful shack, bound and injured. Not me, I'm not hurt. Robin is. I can't believe she got shot. I can't quite comprehend a lot that has happened. Robin put herself in harm's way to protect me.

I *would* like to revisit the fact that Robin is a real-life Rambo. The way she took down those two men the first time we were caught was…sexy as hell! She was a real-life hero straight out of a movie, I swear it!

After we had escaped, I had no choice but to kiss her. She was and is phenomenal. It's likely that the kiss was fueled by adrenaline, but who am I kidding? I've wanted my lips on hers for a while. Even though we were in obvious danger, my body just wanted her to take me up against a tree and fuck me into oblivion. I've seen what those capable hands can do, so I know damn well she would be masterful in bed.

Our fantasy was very much shot to shit, quite literally though, when the assholes from the campground chased us. I have never been so terrified in my life, and that's after I've experienced a plane crash!

Robin is sleeping on the floor now, my pantyhose wrapped around her torso as a makeshift bandage. There's no way in hell I'm going to be able to sleep. We're trapped. Our packs have been taken, which means my meds have been confiscated, too. God knows what these barbarians plan to do with us.

The light outside has dimmed to the point that I can only see Robin's outline. Are we just going to be left here? Maybe that's preferable. The night is silent. It feels like even the birds and monkeys are avoiding this place.

Robin shuffles on the floor. A small groan leaves her lips. I wish I could do something to ease her pain. Even though I won't sleep, I settle behind her, hoping that it provides some comfort. This is the first time I get to play the big spoon.

I must have eventually fallen asleep because now I'm being woken by Robin calling my name. I crack open an eye and gasp. Robin is kneeling in front of me with her hands behind her head and a gun barrel pointed at her temple. My gaze shoots up to the maniac who is brandishing the weapon. To my surprise—although I'm not sure why it's a surprise, I suppose I just expected to see a man—there is a tall, muscular woman holding the gun. Her hair is a shaggy brown mop. Her eyes are almost black. She's wearing khaki green shorts and a black vest top.

"Do whatever they ask, okay?" Robin's voice is steel. She's not letting on that she's in pain.

"Robin," I whisper. My voice is struggling to work.

"It's okay, everything is going to be all right."

"Oh, I don't think it is." The woman sneers. Her English is very good but heavily accented.

"What do you want?" I surprise myself at the level of venom I put into those few words. Remember when I said I was terrified? Well, that's been replaced with a burning anger. Something in me has snapped. I am so goddamn sick of other people fucking with my life.

"Oh, we have a feisty one." The woman laughs. Then she squints at me, and in that moment, I know she's recognized me. Her face lights up like she's just unwrapped the best Christmas present ever.

"I don't believe we've been introduced," she continues. "My name is Antônia." Is she seriously thinking I'm going to engage in conversation with her? I cross my arms over my chest and stare at her. We're in this weird standoff. Suddenly, a smile creeps across her face, and I don't like it one bit. "Cat got your tongue? Let's see if we can loosen it." The gun she was holding to Robin's head drops to her side hanging from its strap. Reaching down to her thigh, she unclips a small knife. My heart is racing. What the hell is she going to do to me?

With speed, she slashes at Robin's face. My stomach drops, and all I want to do is get to her. A firm hand grabs my hair from behind. I didn't even notice there was someone behind me. Robin has her eyes closed. I can see her jaw flexing, but she hasn't made a sound. "Please," I beg. I can't believe I've just caused Robin to suffer, again.

"Care to introduce yourself now?"

I swallow hard. "Ellie," I splutter.

"Ellie. Hmm, now isn't that a pretty name?" Antônia is still way too close to Robin with her knife dripping with her blood. I want to curl up into a ball, just like when we crash landed. I want to close my eyes and will all this away. I want to wake up in my king-size bed and have all this just be one awful nightmare.

"Are you ready to introduce yourself yet?" Antônia aims the question at Robin, who now has her eyes open staring at me. There's no emotion on her face.

"Robin."

"Another pretty name." Antônia is caressing Robin's face with the end of her knife. "Now, Robin. You and I have some business to settle. I have two men that seem to have come to harm by your hands." Robin stays silent. "What do you say?" Silence. Antônia sighs and slashes at her face again. I can't help but cry out.

"Robin, please," I say. I'm not sure what I'm asking for.

"Now, now, Ellie, don't get yourself worked up. This is between me and Robin. Unless…"

"Unless what?" I ask. I'll do anything to make Robin's suffering stop.

"How about you and I get a little better acquainted?" What does that mean? Robin is glaring at me. I know she's telling me not to agree to anything. Clearly, I've taken too long to answer because she takes another swipe at Robin. My God, her face is pouring with blood.

"Fine," I shout, "but please stop." Robin's shoulders drop, and she closes her eyes. I don't care, I *cannot* sit here watching her get sliced up.

"Excellent." Antônia speaks to the guy behind me who drops my hair. She walks behind Robin and brutally shoves her forward with her boot-clad foot. Robin hits the floor with a crack. "Up you get, Ellie." She beckons me to rise.

Slowly, I get to my feet.

Antônia resheathes her knife and walks out of the shack. The asshole behind me gives me a shove. The sunlight makes me wince when I step out. It takes a few seconds to focus on my surroundings. There are several other men and a few women scattered about the place. All of them have weapons. I'm not an expert, but I'd say this is a pretty serious operation they have going on.

I follow Antônia over to the largest building that we saw when we arrived. The inside is a stark contrast to the derelict shack we've been kept in. There are several large windows. No bars on them. That's something I need to tell Robin. It's set up like a studio apartment. It doesn't take a genius to figure out these are Antônia's private quarters.

My pulse spikes as I'm led farther into the space. My gaze darts to the double bed at the other end of the room. When she asked to get better acquainted, it didn't occur to me that she might mean sexually. Shit, why didn't I think of that? All because she's a woman doesn't mean she's above being a pervy fuck.

"Sit," she says, pointing to the dining table in the middle of the room. I let out a shaky breath. The table is adorned with every fruit you could think of. There's also bread and meat. This is a proper villain's lair. I'm just waiting for her to walk out with a tiger on a chain or something. That would just finish the whole image off. Irrational laughter bubbles up and out. "Something funny?" she asks.

"I mean, really?" I say, waving my hand around. *What the hell are you doing?* "Did you Google how to make a villain's lair and go all in?" I can't explain why I'm poking the bear. This bitch could shoot me anytime she wants, and I'm here mocking her house.

"You don't like my place?"

"Oh, no, it's great if you're in a James Bond or Indiana Jones movie."

"I like luxury," she says. A silence descends on us. I fidget in my chair, not sure what to do or how I'm going to get through this with everything still attached to my body. "Wine?"

"No, thank you." I could swallow the entire bottle if I'm being honest.

"Your loss. It's a good year." Antônia pours herself a generous glass. She stalks over to the chair opposite me. Sitting down, she begins filling her plate with food. I want to roll my eyes at how absurd this all is. "You're Ellie Bishop." The statement takes me by surprise. "Don't deny it. I'm a fan. Plus, the world news is going *loco* over your disappearance."

"We just want to go home."

"I'm sure you do."

"Then just let us go. We won't say a word. What you do here means nothing to us."

"And I'm just supposed to take you on your word, hmm?"

"Yes," I say emphatically. "I have no reason to lie."

"I could ransom you. I'm sure I'd get a pretty penny."

I can see she's playing with me. Does she want me to beg? Should I beg? No, I don't think so. Antônia seems like she'd get off on it. "You could, or you could let us go, and I'll pay you whatever you want. I have the money. You know that if you're a fan."

"I loved you in *Mountain Heart*, one of your best films."

Ugh, I want to cringe. That is *not* my best film, it's a ninety-minute bag of crap. It's so cheesy and hetero I want to gag. Obviously, I don't say that out loud. "I'm glad you enjoyed it."

"What's your next movie going to be?"

"I have nothing in the works."

"Well, that's disappointing." I bite back a sarcastic comment. "So..." she continues after a charged silence. "What should I do with you and your friend?"

"Just let us go."

"Tempting, but I have a debt to settle with her," she spits.

"She was just protecting me. That's her job."

"Her job?"

"Yes. She was hired to be my survival guide."

"No, she's more than that to you."

"No, she's not. I might classify her as a new friend, but that's it." I don't want Antônia thinking that Robin means a lot to me.

"So you won't mind if I have a little fun with her?"

"What do you mean?"

"Well, apart from the bloodied face, she's good-looking. I could have quite a bit of fun with that body of hers." Bile rises in my throat. "Hmm, maybe you'd like to take her place instead?" Oh, dear God.

"Please, just let us go home." I beg now. She's won. I can't play this twisted game. If she needs to see me break, fine. I'll give her that.

"Not so feisty after all." She chuckles. I hate her. I physically hate this woman. "I'll tell you what. You have dinner with me tonight. Let me wine and dine you. We'll chat about your films, and then I'll decide if I'm going to let you go or not."

That sounds too good to be true. "Okay." What choice do I have? Either I have dinner with her and hope that I can persuade her to let us go, or I decline and she probably murders us both.

"Excellent. I'll have a dress brought over. Wouldn't want you to have to sit there in dirty clothes, and this will be a formal affair." The bitch is deranged! "Get comfortable, Ellie. I have some business to attend to now. I'll see you later." And then, just like that, she's gone.

So what? I'm just supposed to wait here? I thought I would be escorted back to the shack until it was time for this horrendous dinner. I scan the room. I might as well take advantage of the time to try to figure out a way to escape or something. Truthfully, without Robin, I doubt I could get very far. Maybe there's something I can stash on my body to give to Robin.

A dreadful thought enters my mind. What if the business Antônia was referring to *was* Robin? What if, while I'm in here, surrounded by comfort, Robin is being hurt, tortured? I make my way to the door. Of course, there's an armed guard outside, but that's not what I'm interested in. I need to get eyes on Antônia.

There, I see her, and thank God, she's not walking toward the hut that Robin is in. Pictures of Robin's slashed face haunt me. She needs help, and I'm fucking useless. *Come on, Ellie, think.*

Okay, so I can't help physically. I'm not dumb enough to believe I can help that way, but there must be something else I can do. I try my hardest to recall the conversations I've had with Robin the past few days.

After she threw that knife at me—all right, not at *me* but at Mr. Scorpion—she began to teach me some things. We had a session on knife throwing, which went well. I was able to hit the target in the end. She also showed me some basic self-defense moves, also a handy skill to add to my repertoire.

But the one thing that I think I can actually use in this situation is the skill of observation. Sounds lame, right? I said the same thing to Robin at the time, which earned me one of her sexy-ass scowls. Anyway, Robin explained that one of the most useful things I could learn was proper observation and reporting.

In cases like this—according to my British Rambo—captives are usually so scared they don't take in what's going on around them. Robin said that learning about who has hold of you and where you are is vital information. She said it can help lead to escape or help apprehend the baddies once free. So that's what I'll do.

Memorizing things comes naturally to me—except dangerous plants and animals and people's names apparently. I can read a script once and know my lines almost perfectly. I can adapt that to the here and now. So first thing. I need to count the number of people. From my vantage point—which isn't great—I can see four men to my right. They're guarding a building. Two men and one woman just to the left of me. They look like they're taking a break, so no telling where they're supposed to be stationed. I know there are more assholes than that, so I'll presume they've been sent away to do jobs. Maybe they're guarding the smaller outpost.

Next, the location. Not my strong suit. Robin is the expert map reader. *Think, Ellie*! Right, I know the outpost is north of the Yanomami. When we escaped, Robin took us... I visualize the outpost, turn around so—in my head—I'm facing back toward where we came from. I look like a dork as I use my hands to point left and right, trying to remember which way we went. Left, we went left, so that means we went east. Yes, that's it. We went in the direction of the other spot marked on Robin's map.

How far did we get? Maybe a mile? Possibly a little less than that. When we got caught again, they dragged us in the same direction we were running. So still east, but then in the SUV, we swerved, so we were going north again. If I'm right, we're a little farther northeast of the outpost. I'll need to tell Robin that.

My attention turns back to the room. I quickly head over to Antônia's bedside tables. There's a desk, but she's not stupid enough to leave anything of value in it with me here. Her bedside table, though, might hold something. Rummaging through her drawers, I find a pen knife. Not massive, but it will cut her, if it comes to that. I tuck it in the side of my bra. After a few more moments searching, I realize there's nothing else of interest.

The knife is concealed for now, but what happens when I have to change into a dress? I swallow hard because I'm about to do something that I never thought I would have to even consider, let alone do. I *will* do it, though, and then I will *never* speak of it again. Removing the knife from my bra, I close my eyes, suck in a breath and deposit it somewhere… private. Oh, shit, it's cold.

With everything stored in my memory, I take a seat—gently—at the table. My stomach rumbles, and as loath as I am to accept anything from Antônia, I know I have to eat. Once I've consumed my body weight in bread—because I normally abstain from eating it, carbs are bad, right?—I play a few rounds of I Spy with myself. It's not a riveting game.

The sun has almost set by the time I'm handed a dress to change into. It's a black off-the-shoulder. The hemline reaches just above my knees. Where the hell did Antônia get this from? I doubt there's a Dolce & Gabbana store in the Amazon.

Speak of the devil, Antônia has just walked in wearing a very smart tux. This is like an alternative universe. She has a wide smile as she approaches me. Her hands skim my curves as she appraises the dress. I can't stop the shudder that runs through my body.

"Let's eat," she says, ignoring the obvious disdain I have for her hands being so close to me. I have no idea how this evening will go, but the one thing I do know is that as soon as I'm back with Robin, we have to get the hell out of here.

Chapter Twenty

Robin

Blood is running into my eyes. I need to get out of my bonds. I can't do very much tied up and injured. There's no choice now, though. Not when Ellie is with that psycho. I can't believe she went with her. Christ, I glared hard enough. Surely, that should have told her not to go anywhere.

My side is aching like a bitch. I know it's only a surface wound, but hell, it's nasty. Now I have to contend with cuts on my face, too. Ugh, I'm gonna have scars, although they won't be the first.

As soon as Antônia left, so did her men. I half expected them to stick around and kick the crap out of me for a while, especially after what I did to their buddies. Well, at least I'm alone now, and I can start to plan. There's a rusty nail hanging out of the wall. That will do nicely. I can rub the string binding my hands on it. Hopefully, it won't take too long.

Now my hands are free, I can clear the blood off my face. I gingerly dab my wounds with my tank top. I don't think the cuts are deep. There's one on my left cheek. One above my right eyebrow and a small one across my nose.

It hasn't escaped my notice that Ellie is still not back. I have to fight the dread that is trying to settle in my stomach. I head to the door. Through the slats,

I can see one guard smoking a cigarette. There are several others milling around but no sign of Ellie or Antônia. I will do unspeakable things to that woman if she lays a finger on Ellie.

Pushing those thoughts aside, I continue to collect information. It's clear that trying to escape in daylight would be suicide. I'm guessing there will be fewer people around tonight. Most of them will probably have a few drinks, which will increase our chances of escape.

It's a waiting game now. I can only hope that Ellie gets returned to me soon. If she isn't back when night falls, I'll go after her. It won't be too hard to get the guard's attention. I just need to decide our plan after I've secured Ellie.

The cars are tempting. We could certainly hot-wire one, but I don't know the terrain. We need to head to that other mark on the map, so going by foot would be the most sensible option. Then again, am I being stupid holding out hope that the other mark is help and not another gang of gold diggers?

At the end of the day, we need to put distance between us and the bad guys. What's the fastest way to do that? If this was an op, we would use the river. Granted, we would be kitted up to the eyeballs with flippers and portable air tanks. We don't have those things, but the premise is still the same. We can use the river's current to take us downstream quickly. I'm not keen on the idea that we swim because you know, piranhas and all. Yes, they really will take a bite. What's the likelihood these dicks have a boat or something? Only one way to find out.

There, decision made. As soon as I have Ellie, we'll make our way to the river.

Adrenaline is starting to pump through my body. The sun is rapidly setting, and there is still no sign of Ellie. It's still too early for me to make a move. Most of the guards are still hanging around. I pace the floor because I need to do something.

Hours pass as I pace, becoming more and more hyped up on worry and adrenaline. I feel like a caged animal. Taking another look out between the door slats, I note the moon is out now, but it isn't full. The sky is also partially clouded, which will benefit us. I haven't spotted any towers, so I doubt they have spotlights.

My face feels tight. The cuts have scabbed over quickly, but they're burning, and I know the skin around them is red and swollen. What I wouldn't give for a bag of peas to slap on my face.

The sound of raucous laughter grabs my attention. The drinks are flowing finally. I peek at the guard stationed outside my door. He keeps looking over to the shack where the noise is coming from. I smile because I know he's distracted. Probably monumentally pissed off that he's missing happy hour with his arsehole mates.

Across the way, I see a door open. The light from inside spills out, and my breath catches. I'd know that figure anywhere. My heart skips a beat knowing that Ellie is alive, and by the way she's walking, she isn't hurt, or not too badly. Antônia is escorting her over. Is that a fucking tux?

Standing back from the door, I drop to the floor and feign sleep. I'm not going to make a move yet. I want Antônia to think I'm not a threat anymore. Footsteps get closer, and then Antônia speaks to the guard. The door opens, and in walks Ellie. In a cocktail dress. In. A. Cocktail. Dress!

My eyes are half open. I want them to think I'm either half asleep or semi-conscious. "That was a lovely dinner, Ellie. I appreciate the company. See you in the morning." Well, my mind is going all kinds of crazy. What the hell has been going on in that shack? What company is she referring to?

When the door closes, I wait a second before opening my eyes. Ellie is facing the door. I quietly get up and peep through the slats. We still have the same disgruntled guard, but he has taken several steps away to smoke. He also has a hip flask he's draining quickly. Excellent.

"Robin," Ellie says quietly. I turn around and marvel at her beauty. Even in a fucking crappy hut in the middle of the rainforest, Ellie Bishop is a knockout. "Robin, my god, your face." She's stepped into my personal space, and her hand is hovering above my cuts.

Now I'm not sure what comes over me, but I'm suddenly furious with her. Here I am, worrying my arse off for her, after she fucking volunteered to go off with a loon, and she's been playing dress-up. "What the fuck, Ellie?" I hiss. I can't shout because I don't want to alert douchebag numero uno.

"Wha…Robin?"

"What were you thinking, you stupid woman? Why did you go with her this morning? That was the most irresponsible, most reckle—"

"Are you shitting me? How dare you get angry at me for doing the one thing that stopped you from getting chopped into tiny pieces? Fuck you."

"Fuck me? Fuck you. I have never met such an infuriating person in my entire life."

"And I've never met such a stubborn, controlling asshole." We're breathing heavily, and both our faces are flushed. Her chest is rising fast, and her breasts are straining against her dress. I don't know which one of us makes the first move, but suddenly, we're together. Our bodies crash into each other with force, but it doesn't deter either of us.

The pain on my face is forgotten; all I can feel are her lips and teeth biting my bottom lip. I let out an involuntary growl. God, she's vexing. I need her out of that dress. I roughly grab the hem and rip it up. "Don't damage the dress," she hisses.

I ignore her and in one motion take it up and over her head. I hear a rip but don't give a shit. She's not wearing a bra. Thank Sappho. My mouth takes her left breast greedily. I suck her into my mouth, nipping at her nipple as it pops back out. She moans and grips my head harder. With my free hand, I rip at her knickers.

Her back hits a wall. I have no idea which one. I'm in a sex fog. There is only Ellie and her body. My mouth moves to the other breast as I continue my quest to get her knickers off. Finally, they hit the floor along with my knees. I'm going to make her come in my mouth, and then I'm going to fuck her.

She smells divine. I feel like a cat that's just been handed a pound of catnip. My fingers travel to her folds, opening her up. She is fully bared to me, and I'm in heaven. There is a small patch of dark blond hair leading down in a strip to her lips. I trace that line with my tongue. She has both hands firmly on my head now.

"Suck me." Oh, yes. Oh, yes, yes, yes. I enjoy taking orders. "Robin, suck my clit." Yes, ma'am.

Burying my face in her silk, my eyes roll back in my head as I experience what I can only describe as a divine act. She is so wet and warm. I can already feel her coat my chin. I want more. I cup her bare ass, pulling her even closer.

"Faster." My tongue swipes her fully, and she gasps. I double my efforts, sucking in her lips. I don't want her to come too quickly, so I'm avoiding her clit. I can tell she's getting frustrated, which makes me smile. I don't mind taking orders, but that doesn't mean she's in charge. "Robin." She growls, which makes me chuckle. Suddenly, she rips my face away from her. "I'm not fucking around. Make me come." Then she slams my face back into place.

I am so turned on I have to relieve some tension. I pop open the button of my shorts. When I take her clit between my teeth, I start rubbing myself. I'm so close already. Ellie's moans of ecstasy rev me up even more. Her hips are rocking wildly. The hand that isn't on my clit grips her ass again.

"Oh, yes…right there…keep going, Rob." The use of my nickname sends me over. I give her one last hard suck, and she unravels violently. I'm going to have scratches on my scalp, that's for sure. When she's finally come down, she pushes me back. "Did you touch yourself?"

I nod. Ellie looks from my face to my hand, which is still lodged in my shorts. Dropping to her knees, she pushes me on my back, grabs my shorts, and rips them down my legs. Holy hell. "Keep stroking yourself," she says, bringing two fingers to my pussy. I whimper as she coats her fingers in my come. With no warning, she enters me and starts thrusting.

"Jesus," I cry a little louder than I should have,

but there was no stopping it. Ellie is killing me. I feel her weight on me. Then I feel her wetness on my thigh. Lord almighty, she's rocking herself against me as she thrusts. I bend my leg a little to give her some more friction.

Watching Ellie ride my leg is one thing. Watching her toss back her beautiful head in rapture is like being in seventh heaven. She is so beautiful. The orgasm that tears through me is sudden and so powerful I lean forward and have to bite something. That thing turns out to be Ellie's shoulder. In the explosion, I grab her, and hold her close. She comes on my leg, her screams are lost in my neck.

Our breathing is steadying, but she's still wrapped up in my arms straddling my thigh. It's a few minutes until she moves. Slowly, Ellie pulls up, her eyes shining brightly as she looks down at me.

"I was so scared." She sobs. I lift my head and kiss her tenderly. I know my anger was down to the fact that, like her, I was terrified. I don't know what I would do if anything happens to her.

"We're okay," I whisper against her lips.

"We have to get out of here. Now." I nod gently. Our foreheads are pressed together, and we're just being in the moment. Life is about to get really shitty, we both know it. If things go wrong, we might not get another chance to be together like this. I think we both realise it, which is why we aren't rushing to move. Both of us need this moment.

"I'll get you home, Ellie, I swear it." Leaning in, Ellie kisses me again. "Ready?"

"No."

I smile against her mouth. No one can really be ready for what we have to do. "We can do this.

Together we can do it. Okay?"

"Okay."

We separate and get dressed. My side pinches as I stand. Ellie catches my wince. "I'm fine." I need her to be strong right now.

"Oh, shit, I forgot," she says. I watch with a curious gaze as she reaches under her dress and enters herself. Before I get the chance to ask what is happening or give her a hand, she produces an object. "Meant to give this to you." My mouth opens and closes a couple of times. I wasn't expecting that.

"Anything else in there?" I joke. I get the eye roll, which makes me happy to see.

"Um, I can wipe it on my dress," she says, which makes me laugh.

"El, you're all over my face. Relax." I flick open the little knife. Its size isn't relevant to me. In the right spot, the knife can inflict some serious pain. Good job. I know just where to shove it. "How the hell did that stay up there after what we just did?"

"Kegels. Now what's the plan?"

I hold up my finger, asking her to wait as I take a look at our guard. Just as I thought, he's passed out. In fact, it sounds like most of the camp is in an alcohol-induced coma. "Help me with this," I say, pointing to a floorboard in the corner of the room. Antônia needs to do a better job of keeping her shacks in a good state of repair.

Together—and with the help of Ellie's vagina knife—we manage to pull up the old rotting board. The wood makes a few creaking sounds, which leads me to check our drunk douchebag. Still out like a light. We continue to pull up the boards. I drop down first, helping Ellie into the hole. Her dress isn't exactly helping. Using the knife, I slice up her dress, ripping twenty centimetres off the bottom. "Did you really need to do that?" she whispers.

"Yes, you need to be able to move. Where are your clothes?"

"Antônia kept them." Gross. I take a beat to get over the fact that Antônia is probably sniffing Ellie's clothes or something equally pervy.

"When I go, you follow. Stick to me like glue."

"Okay."

"We need to be silent, Ellie." She nods. It's now or never, I suppose. I crawl out from underneath the shack first. My head is on a swivel as I look for any potential dangers. So far, so good. I make it out and turn to help Ellie.

We both stay low. The guard is snoring like a freight train. I'm tempted to relieve him of his weapon, but it's risky. No, we just need to go.

There are a couple of buildings with lights still on. We can avoid them, so I'm not too worried. I notice that Antônia's light is on. As quietly as possible, we slowly creep across the camp. That's when I see our packs. They're sitting propped up against the wall of Antônia's place. Ellie must know what I'm thinking because she's shaking her head at me.

"Your meds," I mouth at her.

"No," she replies.

"Stay here," I say when we crouch behind a car. Ellie has gone too long without her medication. There's no telling how long we'll be out there. I can't let her get sick, not when the answer is a few metres away. Ellie is tugging my arm furiously, but I ignore her. I have my objective.

There's no sign of anyone as I make my way over

to the packs. I reach them and root through Ellie's bag. I'll just take her meds so Antônia doesn't suspect we've escaped. With the meds safely stowed in my pocket, I take the opportunity to swipe a fresh bandage for my side. Ellie's tights were a good temporary aid, but they're a little coarse and are rubbing. I reach under my top and unfasten the knot. The tights drop to the ground.

With everything quiet, I set about wrapping my side. Ellie is going to rip me a new arsehole. I've been way longer than I should have been. Just as I go to leave, I hear it. The distinct sound of a boot walking over foliage. "Well, well, well," the voice whispers. "Look what we have here."

I'm at a complete disadvantage. Antônia looms over me, knife in hand. "I was going to wait until the morning, but I think I'll do it now."

I frantically look around for Ellie. Thank God, she's out of sight. I just hope she runs and doesn't do anything foolish. After all, it's my stupidity that has got me caught. She doesn't need to suffer for it. I plead with the universe to keep her safe as Antônia's boot connects with my head.

Oof, that one hurt. Lying on my back with my ears pounding, I watch Antônia slowly drop down until she's straddling me. "I'm going to enjoy this. No need for anyone else to get involved." That explains why she hasn't sent out an alert. She wants to do this personally. "It's a shame we don't have more time. I like to play for a little bit first, but I'll just have to be happy with what I have." Her hands circle my throat. Her legs have trapped my arms to my sides. I'm completely useless. The blow to my head has disorientated me too much, I can't focus, I can't fight.

I'm pretty pissed off this is the way I'm going to die. Looking into the deranged face of Antônia is not the last thing I want to see as I depart this life. Well, fuck. Blackness starts to invade the edges of my sight. Antônia is taking her time, squeezing just a little harder every few seconds.

My eyes start to close as the lack of oxygen takes effect. Hang on…the weight on my body is gone. I…I can breathe. My eyes snap open, and I gasp for breath. Where the hell is Antônia? There's a spluttering noise close by. I lift my head with great difficulty, I may add. That fucker knows how to deliver a kick.

"Ellie," I rasp. I'm not sure I'm seeing what I'm seeing. Ellie is standing behind a kneeling Antônia. Her knee pressing into Antônia's back as she tightens… are those her tights? Yup, Ellie has wrapped her tights around Antônia's neck, and she is pulling with all her might.

Chapter Twenty-one

Ellie

My hands are cramping, and my arms feel like they're on fire. I can't let go, though, not until I know Antônia won't get back up again. I've said it many times before that I'm a city girl. I rarely exercise. I shop and do lunch with my vast wealth. That's what I'm good at. I don't camp or go to the woods for a pleasant hike. Hell, I never cook my own food. I have bodyguards because I'm defenseless. All that *was* true, but now? Shit has really changed.

We were so close to escaping, but Robin just had to play the hero again, didn't she? I would have been okay without my meds for a while. She didn't need to take the risk, but she did. And then! She stopped to change her fucking bandage. I mean, come on! Up until that moment, I was Ellie Bishop, helpless movie star relying on Robin to get me home, but then Antônia appeared.

All the fear and trepidation left my body when I saw Antônia kick Robin in the head. Something animalistic, almost primal took over when I saw *my* Robin get hurt. And that's how it felt. Like Robin belonged to me, she was mine to protect. My body moved before I was aware of it. I approached silently, watching as Antônia clamped her hands around Robin's neck.

I should have been panicking, frightened at the scene in front of me, but I wasn't. Picking up the bloodied pantyhose Robin had discarded moments ago and wrapping them around Antônia's neck seemed like the only option. The only way to incapacitate her.

So here I am, with my knee lodged between Antônia's shoulder blades as I pull with all my strength on the pantyhose. I can see her clawing at the fabric, desperately trying to loosen it. She won't, though, I'm pulling too hard. Time is passing so slowly; how long should it take for her to pass out? Goddamn it. My hands hurt so much.

Finally, I see her sag. The hands that were clawing are now hanging limply by her side. Her head has dropped forward. I know I need to let go, but I'm frozen. How do I know she's really unconscious? "Ellie," I hear Robin rasp. My eyes shoot to her. There's blood coming from her head again, and her eyes look unfocused. "She's down," Robin wheezes.

I don't know why I do it, but I unwrap the pantyhose. When they're free, I stuff them back in my pack before scrambling over to Robin. "We need to go now!" I whisper. It's a minor miracle that we haven't been discovered yet. Robin must have been right about the guards going heavy on the drink tonight.

Hauling both our packs over my shoulder, I take Robin's hand and help her up. She's really unsteady on her feet. "The river," she says through gritted teeth. I can only imagine she's in a world of pain.

"Which way?" I feel completely turned around.

"There," she replies, nodding slightly to our left. We need to stay low, which is proving difficult. As well as my arms and hands, my back is now protesting loudly. Robin is all muscle, and my scrawny ass is really not built to take her weight. Nevertheless, we keep going. Yes, we have to stop multiple times behind cars and equipment for Robin to get her breath, but we're almost to the treeline.

A noise behind us sends my adrenaline through the roof. There are two men laughing and shouting. They must be the last ones in the whole campground still standing. If they find us, I'm going to have to defend us. I suppose if they're inebriated enough, I might have a fighting chance.

We crouch and wait. The men seem to be getting closer. I close my eyes and pray that we aren't found. The car we're behind rocks as the back door on the opposite side opens and then shuts with a bang. So far, the car hasn't been switched on. We wait longer but still no movement. Well, that's not strictly true. The body of the car starts to rock gently.

"Let's go," Robin says in my ear.

"We can't," I reply, indicating the men who just got into the car.

"They're fucking. They won't notice us, let's go."

I peek my head up and look into the car. Yup, they're really going at it! Okay, that's our cue. The treeline is roughly twenty yards away. With one cursory glance around, I haul Robin as fast as I can to the nearest tree.

"We made it," I huff out. I'm going to need to see a chiropractor when we get back. "Where now?"

"Keep us in this direction. We should reach the river soon."

Robin's wheezing is really concerning me. What if Antônia damaged something in her throat or worse, her brain? I have no clue as to what a brain injury looks like or what symptoms I should be looking out for. God, I wish I had Robin's guidebook with me. "How do you feel?"

"Sore."

"What about your head?"

"It hurts." Well, no shit!

"Robin, focus. Do you feel lightheaded, or um… is your vision blurry?" They're good questions, right?

"I'm fine, Ellie. We need to go. They could find Antônia at any time, and we won't be able to outrun them." I can't argue with that.

With no need for further discussion, I brace to take Robin's weight again. This would be so much easier if I weren't in a fucking dress! There are some clothes in my pack. I can change when we get some space between us and them.

Robin is breathing hard, her hand is clutching her ribs. We stumble more times than I can count. Navigating the rainforest in the dark is a novel experience I won't be in a rush to try again. Actually after this, I'm not sure I will want to see a tree for a very long time.

Now and then, the moon shines through the canopy, lighting up the forest floor. I strain my ears, hoping that I'll hear the rush of water soon. We continue for what feels like hours. Honestly, I'm at the point of collapse. Robin has slowed down, too. She's losing the battle to stay awake, and I'm in no state to help her.

With Robin out of action, I need to take point. We probably should continue to search for the river, but I make the decision to bunk down for the night. Ha, listen to me using the term 'bunk down.' Robin has really rubbed off on me.

There's no time for a shelter, and building a

fire seems like a stupid idea, so I settle us under the branches of a large palm tree. Robin sits beside me, her head on my shoulder. "Sleep," I say into her temple as I kiss her.

Her slow, rhythmic breathing works to calm me. I can't hear any shouting or car engines, so I'm sure Antônia hasn't been found yet. How long will she be unconscious for? I close my eyes and replay the past hour. I can still feel the burn of the pantyhose on my palms. It's too dark to see now, but I bet that the morning light will reveal I have contusions on both hands.

When I startle awake, it takes me a second to orient myself. Robin's head is still perched on my shoulder. The birds are singing loudly, and the sun is shining. We have to move now. Crap! I can't believe we slept here for so long. If the douchebags haven't figured out we're gone, they will very soon.

"Robin." My voice is strong and commanding. I'm ready to get the fuck out of dodge.

"Mmm" is her only response. I shift so her head rolls off my shoulder. The sudden movement jolts her to life.

"Robin, we have to go now." Jumping to my feet, I waste no time getting the packs on my back and gripping Robin's hands. She's not fully awake, but there's no time.

"God, I hurt." She moans as she stands.

"I know, honey, but we have to go."

"I like that," she mumbles, and I'm convinced she's actually sleepwalking. Her voice sounds a little dreamy, you know, not quite with it.

"You like what?" I ask as I start the arduous job of moving.

"That you called me honey." Oh, that! It just slipped out. In all the hullabaloo of the evening, the fact we had sex a few hours ago has taken a bit of a backseat. We'll need to have a conversation, but not right now. Nope, now we need to haul ass.

"Let's go," I say, sidestepping her comment. Honestly, it felt natural to call her honey. Everything about Robin seems natural to me. Does that sound weird? Ugh, it's hard to explain, but…well, she just feels right to me. We've known each other, what? Over a week, and I can say with the utmost certainty that I have never felt so comfortable and safe with another woman. I have never felt compelled to share myself the way I have with her. She still drives me insane, but that's all part of it, of us.

It must be about an hour before I start to get this tingling feeling up my spine. I'm not into signs or fate or any of that stuff, but…I can feel that we're close to something. Hopefully, that thing is the river and not an army of bad guys.

Listening to my tingly feeling, I divert us a little. Robin is concentrating so hard on simply putting one foot in front of the other she's paying no attention to our change in direction. Another thirty minutes or so pass, and then I hear it. I have the same feeling as when we discovered the waterfall. Relief and pure joy.

"I can hear water," I say to Robin, who has been really quiet. I'm currently having an internal fight with myself. Half of me wants to break down and cry with worry because I know Robin isn't right. She's hurt a lot more than what I can see. The other half of me is refusing to give in to those feelings. That half is the warrior in me, the fighter. It's a surprise to know she exists, to be honest.

We walk toward the sound and finally break through to a river. It's not huge, but it's no stream, either. Propping Robin down against a nearby tree, I scan the area. There's nothing but water and trees. No sign of human activity.

Grabbing the map out of Robin's pack, I sit and study it. It's all guesswork, but I've been paying attention to our direction and how long we've been walking. There's only one river that's close to where I think we are. Is it the one Robin meant for us to find? No clue.

I follow the river with my finger on the page and note that if we can travel down it for a few miles, we could theoretically get ourselves within walking distance of that second mark. The one we think is where we'll find help.

How do we travel, though? Walking is out of the question. Robin has no strength. She needs help as soon as possible. Not a chance on this planet I'm swimming. I read about the things that live in the rivers here. Nope, not happening. So where does that leave us? Obviously, we need a boat or a raft. I rub my palm across my face in dismay. Where do I even start?

Okay, El, you got this. Take a breath.

"Robin," I say loudly. She's becoming less responsive as the day passes. I see her eyes flutter, but she doesn't say anything. I could really use her guidance right about now. "Robin, honey, please, wake up." Nothing.

All right then, time to wing it! What do I know about rafts? Well, Tom Hanks built one in *Castaway*. Tom's such a nice guy. So friendly. *Not the point, Ellie!* So what did he do? Shit, didn't he use some washed-up drums or something? Well, I'm fresh out of those, so what else? Wood, obviously. I can use Robin's hunting knife. Um…oh, I need to string it all together. So vines or something.

Good Lord, this is going to be a disaster. I have a moment of feeling sorry for myself until I look at Robin again and see how bad she looks. That fierce protective streak surges through my body again, propelling me into action.

With Robin's hunting knife in hand, I search the area. I could cry with happiness when I come across a patch of bamboo. That floats, right? I'll spare you the details of me hacking down the aforementioned bamboo. It's not pretty, and I have blisters on blisters by the time I'm done. Hauling it all back to the river was equally painful. I have to start working out. I feel a hundred years old, for Christ's sake.

With the bamboo laying in rows, I start to bind it all together. My gaze drifts naturally to Robin every few minutes. My heart clenches every time because I'm getting that sinking feeling that I'm going to lose something very precious if I don't get this right. Spurred on by my sheer refusal to fail, I work tirelessly until I have a raft. It's not going to win any prizes, and I hope to hell it floats.

The sun is setting by the time I have everything ready to go. There's no way we can ride the river in the dark. That would be dumb. I just hope that Robin can hang on until the morning.

⁂

Dawn hasn't even broken before I'm up and organizing. I managed to get Robin to wake up enough to sip some water last night, but it wasn't much. She hasn't eaten in forever, and she's sweating a lot. Time to get this raft on the water.

It's possible I've just experienced that superhuman strength phenomenon. You know the one where mothers can suddenly lift a car because their kid is trapped or something. The raft is beyond heavy, and at first, I simply couldn't get it to budge, but then I looked over to Robin, and I saw her pale as a ghost, and I knew we were running out of time. At that moment, I could have moved a car. Fuck, I could have moved an eighteen-wheeler.

Robin is lying on the raft on her back, and I can't get her to wake up at all anymore. The raft is bobbing in the water. It dips as I slide on. With an oar fashioned from another bit of bamboo, I push us as hard as I can into the river's current.

I studied the map before we set off. I tried to pinpoint something that would indicate where we need to stop. How the hell do I get us to stop? Okay, let's shelve that problem for now. On the map, I notice a smaller river that branches off. If I can spot that in time, we should be able to get close enough to the mark on the map for me to run and get help.

Robin isn't going to be walking anytime soon, so I make the decision to leave her by the river and search for help myself. I can't think of any other way. As soon as we have landed where we need to, I'll try Mic and Cam on the radio. Maybe they've had some luck with fixing the plane's transmitter or whatever techy crap Mic was going on about.

As we float, I keep one hand on Robin. She's my anchor, even though she isn't awake. I couldn't do this without her. There are monkeys in the trees overhanging the river. I can hear parrots talking to one another. There's a slight breeze that's whispering through the branches, and I'm trying so fucking hard to keep myself together.

Focusing on the landscape is helping. I keep my eyes peeled for that smaller river. As soon as I see it, I need to get us to shore. How do I do that? Ugh, I'm going to have to get in the water, aren't I? Oh, Jesus, there are piranhas in the Amazon and electric eels! So many things that want to eat me.

Shit, no time to dillydally because I can see the spot where we need to be. Slipping into the water, I audibly pray to any and every god that will listen. *Please don't let me get nibbled on by a fish, please!* I give it my all as I drag the raft over to the bank. There's a fallen tree trunk I can use to wedge the raft in place. My bones feel like jelly, but I can't stop. I have to get Robin onto dry land.

After another herculean effort, I lay sprawled on my back with Robin and our packs next to us. My breath is labored, and I'm beat. My eyes are trying to shut on me. "Get up!" I roar at myself. Placing Robin's pack under her head, I strip off that fucking dress and change into my spare clothes.

The hardest part is now to come. I have to leave Robin. Everything in me is protesting my decision, but I know I have to go. I must find help. I try Mic and Cam on the radio, but it doesn't even crackle. Are the batteries dead? Did it get wet?

After abandoning the radio, I manage to get a couple of drops of water in Robin's mouth. I cover her with some palm leaves. I kiss her forehead and then drop down to her lips. "Hold on, Robin," I whisper before setting off. *Hold on!*

I'm gripping the map in my hand so hard I'm afraid I might rip it. The trees are so dense I'm becoming disoriented. That can't happen! I have to find that camp. With the way Robin looked when I left her, the fear that she's already too far gone grips my heart like a vise.

My body is exhausted, but the thought of failing keeps my legs working hard, propelling me forward. Desperation is a powerful motivator. The sun is to my right, which is where I need it to stay if I have any hope of getting to my destination.

How long have I been running? I'm sure my legs and arms are covered in cuts and bruises as I crash through the undergrowth. Sweat is pouring from me, and I'm struggling to resist the urge to rest.

I'm snatched from my wandering thoughts when I hear a shout. My head instinctively turns in the noise's direction. *Please let that be help. Please.* Then the sheer elation I feel at hearing another human being gives me the boost I need. Pushing harder, I sprint through a set of trees, praying I find what I'm looking for.

Cars are lined up next to a building, just like they were at Antônia's camp. The sight gives me a moment's pause, but I ignore the fear. Even if these people are nefarious, I will do whatever they want to help Robin.

I must have made a racket as I tumbled through the trees because there are several people descending on me. Thankfully, none of them look armed, and their faces show only concern. "Whoa, lady," a young man says. His accent is English.

I could cry with relief. "Please, please help," I shriek. The adrenaline is pumping, and I'm shaking all over. The guy turns and shouts to someone in the distance. A woman approaches me and gently takes me by the shoulder.

"Calm down, tell us what's happening."

"My friend, you have to help my friend."

"Shit, Stacey, that's Ellie Bishop," another woman shouts. I don't give a rat's ass if they know who I am. I don't need them. Robin does.

"Are you Ellie Bishop?" Stacey asks.

"Yes, now please, help me," I scream.

"Brandon, Elliot, grab the medical kit and stretcher," Stacey commands.

Please let me find my way back to her!

I did my very best to track my movements, knowing I would have to find my way back to the river. In my fatigued state, I just hope I remember correctly.

"Come on, let's go," Stacey says, ushering me back toward the trees.

I only look back once during the entire journey back to Robin. As soon as I'm confident everyone is following, I barrel on, setting a scorching pace.

I scan the area, hoping to find anything that looks familiar. My heart soars when I hear the river in the distance and recognize a fallen tree I passed. We're close. My speed picks up, and eventually, I see the body-shaped mound on the ground. Robin hasn't moved, nor does it look like anything has disturbed her. Horrific images had flashed through my mind of finding Robin mauled by something.

"There, she's there, please help her." I sob.

A hive of activity erupts around me. Who are these people? They worked together like a team, each picking up a task, silently communicating with the others. Only minutes pass, and they have Robin secured to the stretcher.

"Ellie, come on, let's get you both back to camp."

Blindly, I follow the group back. I'm only vaguely aware that someone has their arm around me for support.

"I'm going to clean some of these cuts, okay," Stacey says, snapping me out of my comatose state. We're back at the camp, and I'm sitting under a canvas shelter, not too dissimilar to the parachute one we made back at the crash site. I nod numbly. "Can you tell me what happened?" Stacey asks.

"I...we..." Where do I start?

"It's okay, take your time."

"Who are you?" I croak.

"My name is Stacey Mathews. I'm a physician. I'm part of a group of doctors who travel to remote areas providing essential care."

Squeezing my eyes shut, I thank all the powers above. Robin has actual doctors taking care of her. My mind wanders to Mic and Cam. We need to get to them next. Yes, there's been plenty of rain recently, but that doesn't mean they can survive much longer. Surely, they must be out of food.

"There are two others out there. Mic and Cam, they stayed at the crash site while Robin and I went looking for help."

"Okay, could you tell us where the site is on a map?"

"Yes, where's the one I had earlier?" I frantically scan the area. My nerves are shot, and I'm falling apart.

"Hey, it's all right. Look, the map is here."

I take it with shaking hands. After a few moments, I'm calm enough to point to where the plane is. "They need rescuing," I say unnecessarily. Of course Stacey knows that, but I feel the need to voice it.

"We'll send a rescue party immediately—" Stacey begins before I cut her off.

"I'm going, too. I can help." Stacey smiles at me softly but puts her hand firmly on my shoulder, preventing me from rising.

"You will stay here. You need medical attention, Ellie."

"I'm fine," I protest.

"No, you're not. You have multiple cuts and are severely dehydrated. Let me look after you. I promise, your friends will be found."

There's no more fight in me. My body slumps under the weight of everything that has happened. "Can I see Robin?"

"Of course. As soon as I get an update, I'll take you to her."

Stacey must sense how tired I am because she doesn't probe further about the events that occurred that landed us here.

Once my cuts are tended to and I've had an hour hooked up to a portable IV line, I finally get permission to see Robin. Tears sting my eyes as I see her broken body. Her skin is pale and clammy. Her wounds look severe. I can't stop the emotion that spills out of me.

Stacey tries to get me to leave Robin a few hours later. My protests are waved away, and I'm led to a bed in another building. On the bedside table are two bottles of pills. It shouldn't come as a surprise that Stacey went through our packs, but the old feeling of needing to keep my medical situation hidden raises its ugly head. I want to snap at her, shout like I did at Cam and Mic when I thought they had invaded my privacy. But I don't. Instead, I listen to Robin's voice that tells me I need to let people in.

"When was the last time you checked your blood sugar?" Stacey asks. I couldn't tell her if I tried. Time has warped into a tangled mess. Stacey directs me to sit on the bed. She opens a test kit and pricks my skin. "Your numbers are good. Why don't you take your meds and sleep? Robin isn't going anywhere, and I promise to fetch you as soon as Mic and Cam are safe. We've already sent word of your rescue and are awaiting transport."

I want to fight her on sleeping. I want to return to Robin, but my body betrays me. As soon as my head hits the pillow, I'm out.

A gentle shake stirs me from a deep sleep. "Ellie, Ellie, come on." My eyes strain to open. Stacey is standing over me with a wide smile, instantly dousing any fears. *Robin is okay.*

"What time is it?"

"It's early morning. You've slept for quite a while."

"Robin?"

"She's still unconscious, but she isn't deteriorating, so that's the positive."

"And Mic? Cam?"

"Waiting for you outside." She grins.

My body is still protesting, but I ignore it as I tear myself out of bed. Ripping the door open, I sob loudly when I see Mic and Cam looking at me with big smiles on their faces. Our bodies crash together in a mass of limbs. All three of us are crying, elated at being reunited.

At that moment, I know we're going to be okay.

Chapter Twenty-two

Robin

*E*verything is painful. I even think I can feel my eyelashes screaming at me. Holy hell, I have never been this banged up before. It's really dark wherever I am. Oh, God, please don't tell me we got recaptured. I can't imagine Antônia holding us hostage again, not after what Ellie did. No, we'd be dead if she had us again.

Right, so where am I? Oh, hang about, my eyes are closed. Ow, ow, ow. How is opening an eyelid this painful? And why are there a million fucking lights on?

"Robin?" Antônia must have hit me harder than I thought if I'm hearing Colin's voice. "Stuart, thank fuck for that!" I pry my other eye open and give myself a second to focus on the world around me. It's not the rainforest, that's for sure.

"Colin?"

"I'm here, Stuart, I'm here."

"What…where?" My mind is foggy. I can't seem to string together a sentence.

"Hey, take it easy. You're in hospital."

"Hospital?" That means we made it, we got rescued. Ellie! Where's Ellie?

"Yeah, you've been here for a week."

"Ellie?" I croak. My throat is raw.

"She's fine. Everyone is fine. After Ellie found help, it didn't take long for the team to pick up the two Codys."

"Who?"

"The camera and microphone guys that were with you. Do you remember them?"

"Of course I do. You mean Mic and Cam."

"No, I mean the two Codys. Who the hell are Mic and Cam? Hang on, I'm going to fetch a doctor, you're clearly not right."

"Sit down, you arse. We called the two Codys Mic and Cam. We didn't want there to be confusion."

"Right, right. Makes sense." There's a beat of silence. My vision is clear now, and I take in the room. Nothing to write home about, it's a hospital room with a teal green chair on one side and Colin on the other near the window. The TV mounted to the wall is on but muted. "So how you feeling?" I hear the shake in his voice. Colin Berk is not a man to get emotional, but I can hear it plain as day that he's feeling overwhelmed.

"Well, everything hurts, but apart from that, I'm grand." I laugh and then regret it immediately. "Fuck me!" I wince. Did I break every bloody rib?

"You were in a real mess when they brought you in." My mind wanders back to Ellie. She did it, she got us rescued. I need to talk to her.

"Where's Ellie?"

"Already back in the States. She was okay, a little dehydrated, but nothing major. As soon as she was cleared, she was whisked out of here."

She's gone?

"Oh, right. Um…what about the boys?"

"Back home, too. They came in to see you, but

you were out of it still. They left me their contact details for you to call when you're feeling better. Nice fellas."

"Really nice. Did…um…did Ellie visit or anything?"

"She rode with you in the helicopter. As soon as you landed, Ellie was taken to a different room. The medics had their work cut out with you. No note or contact details were left, as far as I'm aware."

Well, that's fucking fab, isn't it? After everything, she's just gone! "Okay," I say, because what else is there?

"As soon as I got the call that you'd been found, I came here. Bloody hell, Stuart, you scared the piss out of me. Jill was beside herself."

"Shit, is Jill okay?"

"Yeah, she is now. She told you, didn't she? Before you left." He grins. He knows he's going to be a dad.

"Yeah, she did. You're going to be an epic dad, and if you fuck it up, I'll be there to be the best aunt and rub it in your face." Colin lets out a bark of laughter, which is music to my ears. After so long fearing I would never get to hear his voice again, I can't explain what a relief it is to have him here.

I feel his hand gripping mine. I look into his eyes and see unshed tears. "I'm all right, Berk."

"I'm gonna grab the doc. Be back soon." He doesn't wait for a reply. I know he needs a few moments to get himself together. This is not how our relationship works. Jill is the one I'm emotional with, not Colin. If we let each other get too emotional, God knows what torrent of shit we would unleash. We have experienced and survived way too much darkness to be each other's emotional support.

Stupidly, I try to move again. *Robin, you tit, stop moving!* I don't listen to myself and try again. It's amazing how stubborn I am, even with myself. The truth is, I detest feeling this powerless.

The door swings open and in walks Colin with a buxom brunette. She's hot. Yeah, my brain is fine! After a few minutes of her checking my chart and shining a light in my eyes, Dr. Castro—as her name tag states—looks down at me with a sweet smile.

"How are you feeling, Robin?" Her accent is delicious.

"Sore, a little confused about how I got here."

"To be expected. You came in extremely dehydrated. You've suffered several broken ribs, a bruised windpipe, facial lacerations, and trauma to the head. I believe you were attacked. Is that correct?"

"Yes," I say through the pain. Just hearing all the things that are broken in my body sends a wave of nausea over me.

"We kept you in a medically induced coma for a few days. Your brain needed time to heal. We reversed the coma yesterday, so I'm thrilled to see you awake and alert. I think it's safe to get you transferred to the U.S. now."

Yes, yes, yes, I just want to go home. I guess Dr. Castro can see how happy those words make me because she winks at me. "When can I go?"

"I'll get the transport arranged. I'll see you before you go for a final check-up."

"Thank you," I choke. This time it's through happy tears and not pain.

"Hey," Colin begins. His bushy eyebrows are furrowed. "Robin, I'm so sorry." He sobs. Oh, shit!

Now what? Where the bloody hell is Jill when I need her? Hell, Della would do.

"Marine," I bark, ignoring the burning sensation ripping through my chest cavity. It was worth it because Colin snaps out of it, discreetly wiping his tears. I'm not being an arsehole, both of us are emotional, but we have to express that in a certain way. To therapists or significant others, not to each other. "Berk, I'm going to be okay. We made it back. This is no different than…" I pause because he shouldn't need reminding that we've both come back from places that should have broken us but didn't. That's how I'm going to treat this, too.

"You're right," he says gruffly. "I'm going to call Jill. She's going to be over the moon. I'll try to get a sitrep on your transfer, too. Let's get you home, Stuart." That's better. That's normal, and that's what I need.

❧❧❧❧

There's very little difference between my hospital room in L.A. and Brazil. White and sterile. However, the constant flow of guests is nice. A little tiring, but it's good to be around the people I love. A stuttering thought crashes into my mind. Ellie's beautiful eyes appear, and I suddenly feel so alone.

I honestly thought I would hear from her. Mic and Cam have been by several times. I'm going to be lifelong friends with them, I know it. An experience like that bonds people in a way that's hard to explain.

The first time they visited, we all cried and then laughed at how ridiculous we all were being. I was just so happy to see them looking well. Mic told me he couldn't get the radio to work after all, but they did well foraging and collecting rainwater. Apparently, they had a close encounter with a jaguar on the last night there, but apart from that, they were good.

I tried to tell them about what happened to me and Ellie, but it was a struggle. Not because of the trauma, but because talking about her sometimes feels more painful than all my injuries. How could she have abandoned me like that? I thought we had something, or was it just pure delusion on my end? Maybe it was just the situation we were in. Ellie sure seems to think that.

Jill nearly flattened me when she first saw me. I gasped several times in pain as she squeezed my broken ribs. Then she spent the next half an hour sobbing. Colin eventually had to remove her from the room. That left me alone with Della, who kissed me within an inch of my life, which was just the perfect time for the one and only Ellie Bishop to stroll into the room.

"Oh, I'm sorry," she splutters, her face going red and her eyes looking everywhere but at me and Della, who still has her head bent towards my face.

"Shit, you're Ellie Bishop," Della blurts. Christ.

"And you are?" Ellie asks sweetly, but I know that tone. Oh, boy, she's pissed. Well, you know what, lady? Tough shit. I'm not in the mood for her to start acting like a petulant child.

"Oh, sorry, I'm Della, a friend of Robin's. I hear we have you to thank for getting her back to us." My gaze shoots to Ellie's and hers to mine. Our shared knowledge of all the crap we went through is silently hanging between us.

"Robin did most of the work," she says with a

genuine smile. Her eyes soften, and I know she's re-playing something in her head.

"Well, I'll thank you, anyway. This one"—Della points to me—"is way too important to lose." Oh, how I wish Ellie felt the same way.

"Del, can you give us a minute?" I ask quietly. Della doesn't always read the room well.

"Yeah, sure. I'll be outside with Jill and Col." Della takes one last look at me and then reluctantly leaves. Ellie stands about two metres away. She looks fabulous, but that doesn't come as a surprise. She's back in her element and Gucci. The silence between us is palpable, but I'm buggered if I'm going to speak first.

"How are you?" she asks, and I laugh, shaking my head because it's such a dumb question. "Robin—" she begins, but I slowly raise my left hand, which doesn't make me want to vomit when moved.

"No, Ellie, it's fine. I'm good. You didn't need to trouble yourself coming here. I'm being discharged in the morning. Healing well."

Her cheeks have heated. Is that because I stopped her talking or because she feels some sort of guilt for leaving me without a word? "I'm sorry I haven't been by."

"Why? You have no obligation to me. I *will* thank you for getting us home, though. I'm proud of you, and I hope you are, too. Mic and Cam told me about what you did."

"I only did what you would have done."

"Yep, but we both know it was a lot harder for you with me being injured, so thank you."

"Please stop talking to me like we hardly know each other." Her tone is a little sharp, which bugs the shit out of me.

"We don't know each other. We spent a few days together, and yes, we've connected through that experience, but now life goes on."

"Wow, you can be cold," she says, but her voice cracks. It's amazing how I'm being made to feel like the arsehole here. She's the one who vanished, not me.

"How can you pin this on me? After you just left and never looked back. No note, no number, nothing."

"As soon as my people heard I'd been found, they were all over me. I couldn't even use the bathroom without someone hovering. I asked to see you, but I wasn't allowed. Then, as soon as I was well enough to leave, I was ushered back to L.A."

"You're telling me you were forcibly kept from visiting me or leaving a note?"

"Well, no, not physically. Gabe and my mother said I needed to talk to a lawyer and a PR person first. Of course I disagreed, but I was tired and couldn't fight them on it."

"Okay." That's all I have to say. I'm not getting involved in her family shit. All I know is that nothing and no one would have stopped me from seeing her.

"That's it, just 'okay'?"

"Yup. Thanks for letting me know."

"Please stop being like this. I'm sorry. I should have been with you. Fucking hell, Robin, I watched you almost die in front of me. Do you really believe I would just abandon you after that?"

"But you did, Ellie!" My voice is getting louder. I don't know why I'm getting so wound up. It's the Ellie effect. Whenever she's around, she either incites lust or rage in me. "I woke up, and the one person I wanted to see was nowhere. Jesus, you weren't even in the same country."

"I told you what happened."

"Yeah, you did, and like I said, it's fine. We both knew that we'd end up going our separate ways when we got found, anyway."

"That's not fair."

"What's not? We never spoke about what would happen with us when we got home."

"Do you want something to happen?" That's a loaded question. If she'd have asked me that in the shack after we'd slept together, I would have said yes, but in the cold light of day, we are just too different.

"Maybe once, but I think we just need to draw a line under it. We'll always be connected, and I'm happy to send a Christmas card or whatever, but that's it. You have a life to lead, and I need to decide what I want to do next."

"Are you leaving L.A.?" No, I'm not, but she doesn't need to know that. After talking to Colin and Jill, I decided to make the city my home. I don't want to say that to Ellie, though, because I just want her to leave so I can start healing my heart.

Whenever anyone asks me about what happened in the Amazon, I have so far played the part where Ellie and I grew close down to a minimum because I realise how deeply I have fallen for her. Stupid, I know. We hardly know each other, but it doesn't matter. That infuriating woman has wormed her way in, and now I have to try to get her out. I can't do that if we're playing the role of best buds.

"Ellie, there you are," a man I don't know calls as he bustles into my room. He looks unctuous, so I automatically think he's her brother. Ellie had a few choice words to describe Gabe Bishop. I would have guessed by his looks because they do share some similar features, but it's his whole image that makes me think he's the arsehole who signed Ellie up to a show she didn't even want to do.

"Gabe, I told you to wait for me in the car!" Ellie spits. Wow, there is no love lost here.

"Yes, well, I have some business to attend to," he says, talking over her protests. "Ms. Stuart," he says, directing his attention to me.

"Yes?" God knows why he needs to converse with me. I'd quite like them both to fuck off now.

"Glad to see you well. I just have a few documents you need to sign." I look at Ellie, whose eyes have gone wide.

"Gabe, what are you doing?"

"I'm protecting your ass as usual, Ellie," he shoots back. "They're just standard NDAs covering all the things that happened when you were away."

"Are you kidding me?" Is he for real? "Why the hell do I need to sign NDAs?"

"You were made aware of certain things that need to stay out of the press," he continues. I dislike him a lot.

"I already told Ellie that I wouldn't say anything. I don't break my word, *Gabe*."

"I'm sure your intentions are good, Ms. Stuart, but Ellie can't afford for you to change your mind."

"Ellie, do you want me to sign them?" Fuck Gabe. If *she* wants them signed, I'll do it. I watch as she looks from me to Gabe, and my heart aches at the look on her face. She's so used to this prick bullying her into submission, I know she's going to say yes.

"Maybe...maybe just the one about my personal information," she says.

"No, Ellie, she needs to sign them all." Gabe scowls.

"I'll need my lawyer then," I say. Does this clown think I'm stupid?

"I don't think there's any need for lawyers, Ms. Stuart," he babbles.

"Well, I do." What game is he playing?

"Fine, fine, just the one pertaining to personal information regarding Ms. Bishop."

"Leave it here, and I'll get to it later. Now if you don't mind, I'm getting tired."

Gabe's face is going red. He hates I won't do what he wants. Ellie is pale, and I know she wants to stay and talk more, but I don't see the point. Ellie has Hollywood waiting for her, and I have a guest bedroom to occupy until I can figure out my shit.

"Gabe, leave me for a minute, please." He rolls his eyes and storms out. Not before slamming the paperwork he was holding on the tray by my bed. "I won't keep you. I know you need rest. I just want to leave you this." Taking a few steps forward, she lays a card on the tray next to her NDAs. I don't have to guess that it's her contact details. "Look after yourself, Robin."

"You too, Ellie." And then she's gone.

Chapter Twenty-three

Ellie

I wake up shaking as usual. The same nightmare has plagued me for over a month now, and I'm a nervous wreck. Mother keeps advising I take sleeping pills with a healthy dose of bourbon in the evening, but I'm not like her. I don't want to use chemicals to numb myself, not anymore.

My therapist has told me it may take some time for the nightmares to stop. I wish she could give me an exact time because I'm so tired. My schedule is as hectic as ever. The story of my disappearance shot my celebrity status into the stratosphere. Especially with the footage from the GoPro's being played on every news outlet in America. Gabe made sure to capitalize on it as much as possible. I sort of hate him for it.

From the moment I stepped off the helicopter with a broken Robin, my life has been nonstop. My gut still twists when I think of how I was too chickenshit to go against my mother and brother and visit Robin. After all the promises I made myself in that wretched rainforest, it took me point-one second to break them all.

My return to civilization was supposed to be a new start for me. I'd proven that I was capable of so much more, but the moment my old world came knocking, I sat back and let myself get controlled again.

In what way would my visiting Robin have impacted my image? Now I look back on the conversations I had with my mother and Gabe. I can't understand why I agreed to stay away. I'm so stupid.

Robin had every right to be furious with me. If only she knew how terrible I feel and how lost I am without her calming presence. The recurring nightmare isn't about Antônia or the shit she put us through. It's not about that fucking snake or scorpion. It's not even about the plane crash. No, the thing that my brain can't seem to process and move on from is the moment I had to leave Robin on the riverbank.

I play it over and over in my head. In my dreams, I try to run for help, but it's like my legs are stuck to the forest floor. All the time Robin is getting paler and paler until eventually she starts to bleed out of her eyes and nose. No matter how hard I try, I can't run for help, and I can't reach for Robin.

Beads of sweat sit on my forehead and upper lip. My breathing is labored just like every morning, so I have to spend several minutes trying to calm myself down. I have a meeting with a director today for a film that I really want to do, so I need to be on my game, not a blubbering wreck.

"Wakey, wakey, Ellie," Toni sings from the hallway that leads to my bedroom. I haven't managed to get rid of her since I got back. We've had plenty of chats, and I've told her I'm fine, but she's refusing to leave me, so for now, I have a housemate.

"Come in," I say shakily. I haven't hidden the nightmares or their effects on me from Toni. She's my constant, the only person who's getting me through my days without going insane.

"Oh, babe." She sighs when she sees the state

I'm in.

"I'm okay," I say, trying to smile. If I say it often enough, it might come true, right?

"Same one?" she asks. I just nod.

"You know…" she begins and then trails off.

"What?"

"Why don't you contact her? Maybe seeing her, actually seeing that she's healthy and safe, might help with the nightmares."

I shake my head and sit up until I'm resting against my many pillows. "If she wanted to hear from me, she would have called. I left my number." Even as I dropped my card on the table by her hospital bed, I knew she wouldn't use it.

"It's been a month now. Maybe she'd be open to it. What have you got to lose, honey? I hate seeing you like this."

I know what she means because I hate feeling like this. I may be living my old life, but I'm definitely not the same Ellie Bishop who went into the Amazon. The experience and the connection I forged with Robin and the boys has changed me forever.

"I can't see that anger in her eyes again, T, it's too hard."

"Then what ya gonna do? You gotta do something, babe, because this,"—she waves her hand up and down my body—"is not my bestie. I want her back."

What do I need to do? That's the question, isn't it? My struggling mind is interrupted by my phone. I'm quickly coming to hate that device, something I never thought I'd say. The screen flashes Sandra's name. Why is my lawyer calling me so early?

"Hey, Sandra, how are you?"

"Confused, El." Her tone is short, which is unlike her.

"Okay, what's the problem?"

"I've just been notified that you're transferring your account to another lawyer. What the fuck?"

"Whoa, whoa, whoa! What are you talking about?"

"I have an email with paperwork attached that's informing me of your intent to leave my practice. It's signed by you."

"Sandra, I swear to God, I have no idea what you're talking about."

"Is this Gabe?" she asks matter-of-factly. I close my eyes because, of course, it is. He's been trying to get me to leave Sandra forever because she does what I want and not what he demands. He's forged my signature. But why? Why now?

"It has to be." I sigh. "What do you need me to do to make this go away?"

"Well, go speak to your dick brother, for a start. He's just committed fraud. Considering he and your mother are so obsessed with optics, it's unbelievable he's pulled something like this knowing full well you would find out."

"He doesn't think I'll do anything." I sigh again. I feel like I spend my life now sighing.

"And is that true?" A beat goes by. "Ellie, it's time." Sandra's voice is all business. I look to Toni, who has heard the entire conversation, and she's nodding along. It *is* time. I really fucked up with Robin, and there's not much I can do about that, but if I ever want to be in a position where I'm happy with my life, I need to deal with Gabe and my mom.

"I'm on it. I promise," I say. "Can you try and find out if there's something circulating in your world?

There's a reason he's done this, and I'm getting that tingly feeling."

"The one that says he's being super shady?" Toni asks.

"Yup, that's the one."

"I'll reach out to some people and see if I can find anything. I'll keep the paperwork he sent over as evidence for now."

"Thanks, Sandra. Talk soon."

We end the call, and a fresh wave of fatigue rolls over me like a bulldozer.

"El?"

"Yeah?"

"It's time to make that change. Be the woman you want to be. I'll be right here every step of the way. It's time to take out the trash."

Knowing that Toni has my back gives me the courage I need. After I have met with the new director, I'm going to call a meeting with Gabe and my mother.

⁂

The conference room I'm waiting in has a wonderful view of L.A. I sit sipping on my bottle of water, gazing over the city waiting for Peter Burn to arrive. Gabe has no idea I'm at this meeting. Peter reached out to me personally a few weeks ago, offering me the lead in a new action movie. Something I've been trying to do for years, but Gabe has stopped me at every turn.

The woman who brought me into the room offered me my usual caramel frap. Strangely enough, since getting back, I've lost my love of them. I'm much happier drinking water. The large glass door swooshes as Peter enters the room. He's in his mid-sixties and has a string of award-winning movies under his belt.

"Ellie, darling," he coos. I've never met the man, and normally, the overly familiar way he greets me would irritate me, but it doesn't. I like the look of him. He feels safe to me. Since Robin, I've learned to trust my judgement when I'm around people. In a month, I've lost several "friends" who were in my life before the crash. They were all toxic, only around me for the fame. I did a bit of house cleaning. My pool of friends is only a handful now, but at least I feel good with them. I don't have to act.

"Hello, Peter." We air kiss before sitting at the table.

"I'm so excited that you agreed to do this film," he almost squeals. He's a flamboyant character, that's for sure.

"I'm thrilled you reached out."

"There was no one else who could fill the role, Ellie. Not after everything you went through."

The movie is set in the jungle. It's an action/adventure that pretty much re-enacts my time in the Amazon. I would have been majorly pissed off if anyone *but* me got the lead. "It does feel like it was written for me."

"So we need to get everything rolling. I want to start filming ASAP."

"Excellent. Can you send everything through to me? Not Gabe." If he's surprised, he doesn't show it. Peter has never met Gabe, but I bet a hundred bucks he's heard of him. Gabe's reputation has taken a hit lately. I don't want to know what he's done to piss people off. I find it incredulous that my mother hasn't gone nuts at him. For all the preaching she's done to me about protecting the family name and image, he gets nothing. Oh, no, Gabe is perfect in her eyes. Ugh.

We spend nearly an hour going over the movie. I'm getting so excited about starting this project. I want to push myself and play a role outside of my comfort zone. I wonder if the familiarity of the storyline will be difficult. I hope I can channel all my anxieties into the role. Turn the trauma into something positive.

It's time for something new, something I can sink my teeth into. Show the world why I'm paid exorbitant amounts of money and bestowed shiny awards. Ellie Bishop, the girl next door, has moved out, people. America, get ready for badass Ellie Bishop, action star!

The meeting winds down with an invitation to Peter's house for a party he's throwing. Another thing that has changed since I got back is the amount of time I've spent clubbing and going out on the town. Basically, I haven't. At all. Toni has given up trying to get me out. It's simple, really, the thought of going to Love P doesn't do it for me anymore. I miss the dancing, but I don't want the one-night stands. And until I can move on from Robin, I doubt that will change anytime soon.

My driver takes me to Gabe's house. I've already messaged my mother requesting that she join our family meeting via Zoom. She peppered me with questions, but I didn't answer them.

Gabe is in a silk robe when I walk in, and I immediately want to scrub my eyeballs to rid myself of the visual. "Put some fucking clothes on, man."

"Hey, you came to me. I'm having a me day, and I like to do that in my robe."

Gross. I don't even want to know what a *me day*

is in Gabe's world. "Fine," I say, not willing to die on this hill. I have a massive battle ahead of me.

"So what's this about?"

"You'll see. Just waiting on Mother." We go silent because we never have anything to say to each other. Finally, my phone rings. My mother's face fills the screen, and she's immaculate as ever.

"Ellie, care to tell me why you've summoned me? I'm busy." Ah, yes, she must have a Botox appointment or something. Gabe sits opposite me.

"I had an interesting call with Sandra," I start. "Care to tell me why she received papers claiming I'm leaving her as a client?" Gabe doesn't flinch.

"I instructed Gabe to do that," my mother says, and I'm speechless. Who the fuck do they think they are?

"And why did you do that?"

"Because you need a lawyer that won't hesitate to do as instructed. Gabe has told me that this Sandra won't do as he says, and frankly, that's not good enough. You're moving to the family firm. They know how to get things done." An SMS message pops up on the screen. My gaze shoots to Gabe when I read it.

"You're suing Robin Stuart?" What the actual…

The text didn't have details, but that was the headline. "We're suing everyone." He's so calm, I want to scream.

"What happened to you is unforgivable. We're suing everyone related to that godawful show," my mother interjects.

"You mean the one Gabe signed me up for?" I can't help the snide comment. These two are unreal.

"Your brother is not to blame."

I take a steadying breath, and then I see them. I

see Robin's beautiful, reassuring eyes in my mind, and I know I can do what I need to.

"Gabe, you're fired," I say calmly. He starts to laugh, and my mother rolls her eyes.

"For God's sake, Ellie, he is not—"

"Yes, he is. I've already requested the papers be drawn up." I haven't, but they don't know that. "It's done. And, Mother, before you try your overly used and tired guilt trip, save it. I've heard it all. I couldn't give two shits what anyone thinks of me or our family. That's your burden to bear." Her face is blotchy, which only happens when she's seething.

Before she can erupt, I end the call and look over to Gabe. "I hope you have a backup plan," I say and then leave. Gabe is too stunned to say a word. Everything feels lighter. For once, I feel like I can breathe. Finally, I'm in control.

My first job is to get hold of Sandra and tell her I finally cut Gabe loose. I need to make sure that we're prepared for whatever barrage of shit he'll try to throw at me. My mother won't give up so easily, either, so I warn Sandra of her, too. Sandra just laughs. She knows she'll wipe the floor with anyone who tries to come at me. I ask her about the lawsuit that Gabe is trying to push against the studio and Robin. Sandra reassures me she'll take care of it. I just hope to Christ Robin hasn't been told. I'll never get a second chance if she thinks I'm suing her.

When I arrive home, I fill Toni in on the day's events. She's over the moon and instantly runs to the kitchen to grab a bottle of champagne. We toast to the downfall of Gabe and my mother's evil reign of terror over me. After the bottle is gone, Toni begs me, literally down on her knees, to go out with her clubbing. I really don't want to, but Toni has been my rock, and I feel like I owe it to her.

Love P is thumping by the time we arrive. I have a nice buzz going, and I'm excited for the night ahead. All I want to do is dance. As per usual, we're ushered in and given a VIP booth. Toni fills our glasses, and we drink. I can already see several women who are trying to get my attention, but none of them interest me.

The dress I'm wearing is one of my more modest styles. Toni tried to get me to wear hot pants. It was never going to happen. I'm happy to be out celebrating my newfound control, but there will be no woman in my bed tonight unless Toni gets hammered and passes out with me.

We head to the dance floor, and I let myself go completely. Closing my eyes, I visualize Robin dancing with me. If I concentrate hard enough, I can feel her firm body pressed against me. Her delicious arms touching my curves. Jesus, I'm turning myself on. Of course, my mind wanders to the night in the shack. Let me tell you, that one night with Robin Stuart is not enough. Not by a long shot. The all-too-familiar feeling of guilt floods my veins. Tears pool in my eyes as I realize that one night is all I'll get. One night in a shitty little shack, but by God, it was perfect.

Toni dances up behind me, giving me those eyes. The ones that ask if I'm okay. I smile as brightly as I can and continue to dance. It's halfway through Rihanna's *Only Girl (In The World)* that I spot someone familiar. I squint because I can't quite place her. Then I know. It's the girl who was kissing Robin in the hospital. Della.

My heart speeds up, and I move to get a better

look. It's as if I can feel her before I see her. Stopping in my tracks, I gaze at Robin, dancing up close with this Della bitch. No, that's not nice. I'm sure Della is lovely, but just not that close to Robin.

"Who's that?" Toni shouts in my ear, causing me to jump. The club bass might be thumping, but I hear nothing, only the rush of blood in my ears. After weeks of no contact, there she is, the woman who has haunted my nights. "Ellie?"

"It's Robin," I whisper. Watching her dance with Della is hurting me, physically hurting me. I didn't know until it was too late how far gone I was on that woman. I don't care that our relationship was formed in traumatic circumstances or that we only really knew each other for a matter of days. What we went through, what I felt with her, is the deepest and truest thing I have ever known. And I lost it, I lost her.

Chapter Twenty-four

Robin

I thought letting go of Ellie would be easy. Out of sight, out of mind and all that. Turns out, I was wrong, really, really wrong. My brain won't stop flooding my mind with memories of our time together. The bad ones, as well as the good. My heart won't stop aching for her, which is ridiculous. For heaven's sake, we spent a few days together. How can I be missing her this badly?

The moment she walked out of my hospital room, I missed her. The contact card she left sat there taunting me. I still have it tucked in my wallet. My fingers itch on a daily basis to pick it up and dial the number, but I don't. Why? Because I'm too stubborn and because I'm afraid of what will happen if I do.

Considering my time spent in dangerous places throughout my life, I like to think I'm a relatively brave person. That's why it stuns me that I'm being such a coward now. Ellie represents everything I want but never honestly thought I would have. During my service, I kept personal relationships to a minimum. I'd seen loved ones of fellow Marines suffer one too many times. Sometimes it was just the distance and secrecy that became too much, others it was worse. They lost the love of their lives, and all they got was a watered-down version of how they'd died.

Even after I left the Marines, I found it hard to connect properly with a woman. Letting another person in isn't easy. Della came close, but that was never going to develop into something meaningful. And then there was Ellie Bishop. A dramatic diva who swooped in and unravelled me in hours. Yeah, sure she unravelled me in the worst way to begin with, but looking back, I can see that there was always something else going on under the surface between us. No one, and I mean no one, has ever gotten under my skin like her. Then, as we got to know each other, I got to see the real Ellie. I found it so easy to open up to her. How did she do that? Make me feel comfortable? She would say that it was the other way 'round, and it was me who made her feel safe enough to open up, but I think it went both ways.

The two of us have some baggage, her with the family and me with my memories of war, but together, somehow in the middle of the fucking Amazon rainforest, we were able to help each other. I think that's why it upset me so much when I realised she had left after we were saved.

The time we'd spent together had been so intense, I just naturally assumed she would be there. My ego and pride took a battering that day, which is why I flew off the handle at her and got so angry.

It's been over a month since I saw her, and I've been struggling to settle down. I thought I would see Ellie at José's memorial. I kept my promise and got him home. If she turned up, I didn't see her, which made everything ten times more painful.

For the first two weeks, I stayed with Colin and Jill, which was fun for all of two days, then it became too much. I'm used to my own space. I like room to decompress, and that was difficult with my two best friends constantly hovering.

Della came to the rescue and offered me her apartment. She's been offered a job out of state and plans to move for at least a year. It couldn't have happened at a better time for me, to be honest. Now I'm not too far away from Colin and Jill, so I get to see them often enough without it becoming overwhelming. I'm also near the beach, which is my dream come true.

Before coming to L.A., I had saved up enough cash to take a holiday but nothing long term. My days in private security are over. I cannot go back to guarding arsehole celebrities. The thought makes me laugh as it reminds me of the conversation with Ellie where I said that very line to her, and she accused me of meaning people like her—which I did.

Colin has offered to get in touch with his agency. It would certainly be different, but I'm not sure I want to be going on any survival shows again, ever! Once was enough. Colin reckons I would be a shoo-in for consulting on movies and TV shows. It would be good to put all my years of training and service to good use.

So Colin set up a meeting with his agent, Jake Gill, a nice fella. We chatted for a good hour. He told me the kinds of jobs he would put me up for, and I was happy in the end. I'd literally walked through my apartment door when my phone rang, Jake's name scrolling across the screen.

"I just left you," I say, laughing.

"I'm that good," he replies. "I have the perfect job for you, and they're looking to hire someone quickly. As soon as I gave them your name, they wanted a face-to-face."

"Is that normal? Like, this is my first job."

"It's very unusual that they wanted to meet you so fast. But once they got your name, they jumped all over it. It stumped me, but who cares? If you get this gig, I think I might have set a record or something. Fastest time between signing a new client and getting them a job."

"Okay, when and where?"

"Can you do today in, say, two hours?"

"Sure." It's not like I have anything else going on. If I sit down, I'll automatically start thinking about Ellie.

Jake sends over the address. It's in the Hollywood Hills. Should I get dressed up? I'm not the glitz and glamour kind of girl. Ugh, I suppose I should make some sort of effort. I'll put on some nice jeans and a clean tank top.

The ride to the house takes way too long. L.A. traffic really sucks sometimes. My Uber driver, Kai, is really nice. He turns up the music, and we bop along together, taking it in turns to sing out of tune. The house Kai pulls up to is impressive. Not my cup of tea. Like I've said before, all this celebrity status garbage doesn't float my boat at all. I probably shouldn't mention that to the director I'm meeting, huh?

We're met by a man in his mid-sixties, I would guess. He has a smile as wide as the Grand Canyon. Why is he so excited to meet me? Before Kai has fully stopped the car, I'm being yanked out the door by this very flamboyant man.

"Robin, darling, it's so good to meet you." Oh, fucking hell, he's air kissing me.

"Um, hello."

"Come, come," he says, waving me to follow him as he bounces towards the front door. I take a second to look back at Kai, who is giving me the same wide eyes as I'm giving him.

"I'll wait for you," he says. Thank God!

"I shouldn't be too long. Thanks, Kai."

Now my exit plan is in place, I jog after Peter. Jake gave me his name when he sent the address. I probably should have Googled him or something.

The house is as opulent as you would imagine. Everything is stark white. It's a little blinding, if I'm honest. The entryway is something I would expect to greet me in a fancy hotel. Oh, look, he has a giant chandelier!

I follow the sound of music down the hall to the kitchen, which is huge and open plan. I can see into the back garden from where I'm standing. Most of the back of the house is all glass. It offers a superb view of L.A. Got to hand it to this Peter fella, he has good taste. In location, not in décor.

"Robin," he calls me from the patio. There's a table covered in fruit and a bottle of champagne. Peter is standing by it, looking really pleased with himself. "Please have a seat. Drink?"

"Thank you."

"Have whatever you want from the table." I nod and then wait. "So did Jake give you the details of my film?"

"Nope, honestly, I only signed up with him earlier this morning, so we were both a little shocked to receive the job offer."

"I was the surprised one." Peter smiles widely. "I couldn't believe it when your name was sent to me. We've been struggling to find the right person for the job."

"And you think I'm the perfect person for the

role?"

"Oh, yes, without a doubt."

"All right, so what exactly will I be required to do? You should know I have no previous experience consulting on movies."

"No problem," he says, waving his hand like he's trying to bat away what I said. "You are uniquely qualified for this."

"Um, okay."

"So the movie is an action/adventure. It's the story of a woman who gets lost in the jungle when her plane crashes..." What? Did I hear him correctly? "She's stranded with nothing but her wits and the pilot. There's going to be danger, gun battles, exotic animals. It's going to be sensational."

I like his enthusiasm, but I'd like to circle back to the plot. Sounds kind of familiar. "The story..."

"Yes, now do you understand why you're the only one I want consulting on this? You lived it." Okay, not sure how I feel about this now.

"You know who I am, I mean, aside from the consulting thing."

"Of course I do. Your story was fascinating. I'd already gotten the idea for the movie. When your story broke on the news, I saw the whole thing playing out in front of me. I knew I had to tell that story on the big screen."

What do I say? Is this something I want to be involved in? The original version of the story was hard enough. Reliving it doesn't seem like a wise idea. "Can I think about it?"

"What's there to think about? You and Ellie have to be on this project." Ellie's name brings everything to a screeching halt. I should have figured out he would approach her.

"Is…has Ellie agreed to star in it?"

"Yes, of course."

Right.

❧❧❧❧

Considering I'm sitting in a movie trailer waiting to get a call to set should tell you how the end of the meeting with Peter went. At the end of the day, the temptation to see and spend time with Ellie overruled the decision-making part of my brain.

After the meeting, I took up Della's offer to party at Love P. Thank God she was visiting. I needed to let off some steam. Although my eyes were playing tricks on me because I could have sworn I saw Ellie. Fuck, I sound nuts. Everything comes back to her.

Even though we're going to be working together, I still haven't plucked up the courage to call her. Running into her on set seemed the easier option. Now I'm not feeling so confident. When I get the call to go to set, we're going to see each other after nearly three months. How will she react? Will she be the diva I met or the same Ellie I got to know? Will she be happy or angry to see me?

"Robin, they're ready for you," Amber, one of the movie's runners, calls through my door.

"On my way." This is the first day of production. I missed the read-throughs and all the prep work. The only person I've been in contact with is Heather Space, the actress playing opposite Ellie. I was pleasantly surprised that Peter intended for both of the main characters to be women. Although, I don't know if the end of the movie will mimic real life.

Time to get this show on the road. Walking to the set makes my nerves feel electrified. My old regiment would be ripping the piss out of me if they could see how nervous I was getting over a woman. Colin got a swift kick up the arse when he tried taking the piss. I doubt he'll do it again.

The set is a giant warehouse with different sound stages set up. Apparently, they're shooting a jungle scene first and need me to advise Heather on a few things. The set is packed. My stomach is roiling as I make my way through the throng of people. A hand on my shoulder catches me off guard. Swinging around, I go to shout at whoever just caused me to nearly die of heart failure but stop short and smile instead. Mic is grinning like an idiot. He hauls me into his body and gives me a crushing hug.

"Holy shit, how are you?" I say into his chest. It's been a few weeks since we last saw each other.

"Great now. Rob, I'm so pleased you agreed to do this project. Cam is gonna shit bricks when he sees you." I love that they still use Mic and Cam.

"Why didn't you tell me that *you* were working on the movie?"

"Wanted it to be a surprise."

"Well, it is that."

"So..." Mic has raised his eyebrows at me. He knows about the fight with Ellie and that we haven't been in touch.

"So?" I don't want to have this conversation right now. I'm nervous enough as it is.

"So have you seen her? Come on, what's going on? Are you being a yellow belly, Sergeant?"

"Hey." I glare and then laugh. "It's going to be super awkward. What if she shouts at me or something?"

"That woman is not going to shout at you. Just see her. She'll be camped out in her trailer until this afternoon when she's needed. Get the awkward shit over and done with in private. Jesus, Robin, grow some balls."

"I love that men use that phrase. Balls are stupidly weak. I'd only have to kick you in the crotch, and you'd be down for the count. Nothing tough about balls, Mic."

"All right, grow some…ovaries? Is that better?"

"Perfect. Right. Well, now we have that sorted, I need to find Heather."

"She's over there." Mic points with his head to a spot over my shoulder. "Once you're done, go and see Ellie. Please."

"Fine," I grumble.

My time with Heather is short. I only had to talk to her a couple of times about her stance when fighting the movie bad guy. Peter told me I could go, but that meant facing Ellie, so I've been hanging around the set. Mic has glared at me several times. I see him make a move towards me. Holding up my hands in defeat, I tell him I'm going.

Ellie's trailer is at the opposite end of the trailer park to mine. Hers is obviously a helluva lot nicer. I stand outside her door staring at the gold star with her name written on it. *You can do this, Robin, get on with it, Marine!*

Waiting is the absolute worst. Why does time stop when you're waiting? It must only be a matter of seconds, but it feels like hours until I hear the click of the lock. I take a step back as the door swings open, and there she is. The woman I cannot get out of my fucking head. And yes, she looks insanely good. Her blond hair is hanging over her shoulders. She's wearing a small amount of makeup, and to my surprise and delight, she's in old cut-off jeans and a tank top. No Gucci or Versace in sight.

"Robin!" Her voice is like velvet. It soothes my ears. *Talk, you idiot!*

"Hi." *Good start, Rob.* "Um…do…do you have a minute?" Why is my voice shaking?

"Of course, come in. Sorry about the mess," she says as she backs up, allowing me to enter. Ellie doesn't seem surprised to see me.

There are a few clothes sprawled about, but I wouldn't call it messy. Messy is ten Marines living together. God, I think I got PTSD from that.

"How are you?" I don't know how to do this.

"Good, good. You?"

"Yeah, good." Silence descends.

"This is awkward, right?" She laughs, and I crack a smile.

"Just a smidge."

"Do you want a beer? I think we need to relax a little." She walks over to her fridge and takes out two craft beers. Popping the top off, she hands one to me, and of course, our fingers brush, and of course, that does indescribable things to my body.

Her eyes are boring into mine, and I can't look away. I know she just felt what I did. "I'm sorry, Ellie, I shouldn't have acted the way I did when you visited me in the hospital."

"I'm sorry I left you." We're still staring at each other. I know we have a major conversation ahead of us, but my heart is crying out to take her in my arms.

I rein in my lust because we *do* need to have

that conversation. Our entire relationship was built on high adrenaline and stress. As much as I've missed her, I think the space between us is good. It's given me time to think about what I want.

"I'm sorry I didn't listen to you. But I'm here now." I want to know she's okay. I want to know she isn't still bending under the weight of her mother and brother.

Ellie puffs out her cheeks and exhales loudly. She gestures to the couch. We sit, and I make sure to leave some distance. "It's true what I said. Everything really was nuts when we got back. I was so overwhelmed, my instinct to let other people take over kicked in. Believe me when I say, I regret not fighting to see you harder. I should never have been apart from you."

"Why did it take you so long to visit me?"

"Because…because I was right back to where I started before. It took my best friend Toni to shout at me repeatedly until I finally snapped. It's going to sound a little far-fetched, but after Toni finished chewing me out, it's like this fog lifted. I was so fucking angry with myself. I couldn't believe I'd let myself get manipulated and controlled by them again. Everything I promised myself in the Amazon was what I wanted. Autonomy, choice, freedom."

"And have you got all those things now?" I really hope she has. Even if we aren't meant to be, I couldn't stand knowing she was being treated that way. By family, no less.

"I do. With some help from my friends, I made some serious changes. It's safe to say that Gabe and my mother no longer have a starring role in my life."

"Are you okay with that? I know they suck, but they are your family."

"They were toxic and emotionally abusive. I have my chosen family now."

"Does that family include me?"

"I know that everything in the rainforest was fraught with stress, anxiety, and danger. I know that having sex in a crappy old shack was the result of an intense situation, but you have to know that I still want more. I want to get to know you. I want to experience what average life is like with you because I really think we have something. You are already a part of my family, as are Mic and Cam."

"But not like a sister, right?" I grin because I'm purposely poking at her.

"No, not like a sister, for God's sake." Her huff makes me grin.

"So should we date?"

"Yes, absolutely. We haven't exactly had the opportunity for romance, have we?"

"You're telling me that fingering me on the floor of a dilapidated shack surrounded by villains wasn't romantic?"

"Oh, no, it was a dream come true." She laughs, rolling her eyes.

"Just so you know, I want more, too. We *do* have something. Yes, it's mainly attitudes towards each other," I wink, "but it's also a feeling that runs deep."

"So let's take it slow, okay?"

Taking it slow doesn't seem to be something my body understands right now. I do want to date her and take our time developing what we have, but right now, I can't deny this physical pull. I want her. I want to feel that connection. That undeniable force that keeps us tethered to each other.

The beer in my hand gets left on the coffee table.

I reach over and take hers, too. She offers no protest, so I scoot closer. Her eyes are so intense I might cry. It's then that I know she's feeling the same as me.

"Are you going to kiss me or what?" she asks. A flare of heat shoots into my knickers. God, I love it when she's feisty.

Without answering her, I pull her into my space. Our lips are millimetres apart. "I've missed you." Then I close the last bit of distance and take her lips greedily. Ellie's tongue pushes into my mouth, and I can't help but moan. My hand goes into her luscious hair, and I pull her in closer. My free hand works the button on her cutoffs.

"Impatient." She gasps as I suck on her neck. Yes, I'm impatient. I haven't touched her in months. After pulling us up to our feet, I snap open her shorts, causing them to fall to the floor. Swivelling us around, I lift her up onto the counter. "Take my panties off," she commands.

"Well, if you insist." Her barely there underwear falls to the floor. I don't know what I want to do to her first.

"Look at me, Robin," she says through a shaky breath. I meet her beautiful blue eyes, and I'm captivated. "I want you inside me. I want you looking into my eyes as I come." Jesus H. Christ, this woman. She draws my face in and kisses me so sensually, I'm ruining my underwear and am almost ready to climax. My fingers glide up her thigh. Her skin is so soft, I could spend hours feeling her body, memorising every inch with my fingertips. As soon as I touch her pussy, I know she's soaking wet. With my hand coated in her excitement, I push into her with two fingers. She's ready for me. A soft moan escapes her lips, causing a tingle to run up my spine.

"I've missed you, too."

Ellie reaches down and unclasps my jeans. The zipper slides down easily, and suddenly, my senses are overwhelmed as she begins stroking my clit. I thrust into her a little harder, adding a third finger. Our breaths are heavy as we bring each other closer to the edge of oblivion. Ellie presses down as I push in hard, and we fall. Our moans are synchronised, and it's wonderful.

"Don't leave me again." I sob as I'm floating down from one of the most powerful orgasms I have ever had. All the emotion I've been pushing down suddenly becomes too heavy to handle in the light of what we've just done. I can't go back to Ellie being absent from my life. I need her like I need air. It's fast, and it's crazy, but it's true.

"I'm not going anywhere," she whispers in my ear. I feel a drop of liquid on my shoulder. Leaning back, I see tears spilling from her perfect eyes.

Whatever comes next, I know we'll face it together. It will be frustrating and maddening at times, but it will be ours. She will be mine, and I will be hers.

Epilogue

Ellie

"No, I can't do it."

"What do you mean?"

"Toni, I can't. I think I'm going to throw up!"

"Are you being serious right now?" Toni is standing in front of me while I hold my head between my knees, trying to stop myself from hyperventilating.

"What if she says no?"

"She's not going to say no."

"You can't be sure. If I'm not sure, you can't be sure."

"Ellie, you're being dumb. Will you calm the fuck down?"

"It's only been six months. It's way too soon. She's going to think I'm nuts."

"You are ridiculous. She's not going to say no. Jesus, she spends more time here than at her own place. I've seen all the clothes she stores here. Robin is already living with you. This is just a formality."

It's true, we *do* spend most of our time here. I can't exactly keep a low profile at her place, and there isn't enough security. But what if, when I ask her to move in officially, she realizes it's not what she wants?

"I can see you spinning out. Relax. Anyway, I know you think that six months is too soon, but let's be honest. You both fell in love after a week. These past six months have just been a fuck fest. I should know, I've walked in on you enough times."

"You should probably just stop letting yourself into my place." I laugh. Since that day in my movie trailer, Robin and I have been together. I still can't believe that we did that after not seeing each other for nearly three months.

Toni might say it's been a six-month fuck fest, and to a degree, she's right. Robin is delicious, and I'm not going to apologize for finding her irresistible. What T doesn't know is that we've spent this half year really getting to know each other.

Surprisingly after our time in the trailer, we slowed things right down and didn't sleep together again until the fifth date. I think we were both so concerned that our relationship was born under extraordinary circumstances that we wanted to make sure it was real before we took things to the next level.

On date ten, I flew us to Florida, so I could meet her mom and dad. I love them dearly, and my heart felt so light watching them interact with Robin. They behaved as loving parents should toward their child. It was heartwarming, and they welcomed me with open arms. Just like Robin, neither her mom nor dad care about my celebrity status. They took the time to get to know me, and it made me fall in love with Robin even more.

Robin hasn't met my mother, and it's not going to happen anytime soon. After I fired Gabe, she disowned me. Hilarious, really, because after all those years of her yelling at me to make sure I protected the family image, it was her who destroyed it. Not that I care. It was always fake anyway. We were never that happy family she tried to sell to her friends, not after

Dad died.

It's been months since I spoke to her. When she screamed and shouted at me for firing Gabe, I simply walked away. I'm guessing it hit her hard that she wouldn't be able to get any more money out of me and she was stuck with an adult son who couldn't look after himself.

A friend of a friend told me that my mom had a breakdown at her country club when one of her irritating fake friends asked her about the rumors pertaining to Gabe's dismissal and his use of hookers.

Like I said, in the end, she was the one to destroy the family optics. I hope she finds it in herself to get some help. Life isn't meant to be that miserable.

As for Gabe, he had to move back to New York and in with my mom. He spent so much time acting like an asshole to everyone he worked with, thinking he'd always have me to cling to that he alienated himself to the point where he couldn't get a single client.

He's also on an ankle monitor because Sandra went after him full bore when I got back. She'd been working for weeks to accrue enough evidence of his stupidity to get him arrested. Gabe went through three different lawyers throughout the court proceedings because Sandra ripped each one to shreds. Sadly, because our justice system is fucked, Gabe avoided prison for fraud. He did, however, get eighteen months on house arrest. The judge put him on an ankle monitor and issued a large fine, one Gabe went bankrupt to pay.

Once again, I don't care. I've taken the time to work on myself. I have excellent friends who love and support me, and I have Robin. Speaking of whom, she'll be arriving soon, and I'm sweating through my top. Why am I so nervous? Toni's right, she's totally going to say yes to moving in with me. Right?

"She's here. El, take a breath. You're sweating, and it's gross." Toni stands and heads to the door. I hear her chat with Robin for a second before she calls to me to say she's leaving. Robin walks around the corner, and all my anxiety melts away at the sight of her.

"Hey, babe," she says, all low and sexy. A shiver runs up my spine.

"Move in with me," I blurt. My eyes go wide because I cannot believe I just yelled it out like that. I wanted it to be more romantic. *Ellie, you idiot.*

"Okay. Do you want me to cook tonight?" Hang on, did she just say *okay* like it was no big deal? "What? Why are you looking at me like that?"

"I just asked you to move in with me, Robin, and you say *okay,* like I told you I want to have takeout tonight."

"Sorry, babe. I didn't think. Well, I'm practically already living here, that's all. I'm sorry if you think I'm making light of it. I promise I'm not. I can't wait to live here full time."

That's a better reaction. See, Robin is made for me. She knows how to put up with my diva side. Yes, unfortunately, it's still there. I can't help it sometimes, but Robin is always the person to snap me out of it.

"So want to break in a few items of furniture?" She grins, waggling her eyebrows at me.

"Rob, we've screwed on every surface in the house." I laugh.

"Not as a couple living together."

"Good point. Take your pants off."

Robin

There's something to be said about living with your girlfriend. My vagina has never been so sore. TMI? Probably, but hell, Ellie hasn't left me alone for the past eight weeks. That's how long we've been living in her house. Sorry, *our* house. Wow, it's weird saying that.

It's wonderful that I get to come home to her, though. After our film wrapped a couple of weeks ago, time together has been hard to come by. Ellie has already started another action film, which she was born to do. Why her dick brother stopped her from starring in them is a mystery. Yeah, Ellie is great at playing the girl next door, but she's sublime in action flicks.

As for me, Peter asked me to consult on another one of his films, so the two of us have been working nonstop, and our hours don't always align. But that's okay because no matter what time I get home, I know I'm climbing into bed with Ellie. If we miss each other in the morning, we make sure to leave breakfast out for the other. It's things like that which make the time apart bearable.

Today is my birthday, and for once, I'm pumped to be celebrating it. Colin, Jill, and little Robin! Yep, you heard me, baby Robin will be over shortly, as will Della. It's still hilarious to watch Ellie try to rein in her jealous side when Della's around. It doesn't help that Della winds her up on purpose. Weirdly, though, they're quite good friends. I don't get it, but whatever, as long as it works for them.

Ellie set up the party, so I'm expecting it to be a

little extravagant. It's something I'm getting used to. I've also been banned from an entire section of the house for a week. God knows what Ellie has planned, but I can't wait to find out. This is the first time in a really long time I'm full-on celebrating my birthday. Usually, I just do drinks and dancing with Colin, Jill, and Della. This year, though, my folks are flying out. Ellie even contacted a few of my buddies from my old unit. I cannot wait to see them all.

Waking up to Ellie going down on me was a wonderful birthday gift. My life is pretty awesome, not gonna lie! The one thing I can rely on is Ellie being unpredictable. Sometimes we make love so tenderly, it's cringeworthy. I'm talking full-on romantic novel style. Other times, sex is like that time in the shack. Fast, frantic, and full of passion. Our relationship dynamic is no different than when we met. I know we can drive each other nuts, but our feelings, our love are true and steadfast.

Since we got back from the Amazon and reconnected, I've seen such a change in Ellie. Maybe it was finally getting rid of Gabe and her mother, or maybe it was the experience in the rainforest that did it, but she has been trying so hard to rediscover who she is.

Ellie now cooks for herself, she cleans the house—not all of it because it's fucking huge—but our room and the areas we frequent the most. We still have Jenny the cleaner, but it was important for El to do things for herself. Her words, not mine. We go to the gym together, and she has taken up kickboxing. She has been honest and open with the people she works with about her health issues, and I can see how freeing she finds that. Her face glows now.

Like I said before, not everything is different. Ellie is still fiery, and we still infuriate each other at times, but it's hot, and we always make up in the best way. Most of those times, it's when we're both a little overworked or haven't seen each other for a long time. After a day or two wrapped up in each other, things settle.

"Babe, breakfast." Ellie has become a pancake master, and I'm all for it. I walk into our kitchen to see a stack the size of me waiting on the breakfast bar.

"Jesus, El, they look amazing, but also like there's enough to feed an army."

"I want you to have plenty of energy. Today is going to be awesome."

I tuck into my food. Hell's bells, they taste good. Ellie joins me, and together we sit silently eating. Our free hands are joined us usual. As soon as we're finished, she slides an envelope towards me. "Happy birthday, baby." Her kiss is soft and leaves me wanting so much more.

"El, you didn't need to get anything else. You've given me too much already."

"Nonsense. Anyway, this is kind of for us both." That has my interest piqued. Of course, my mind goes straight to the gutter. I open the envelope and stare at its contents. There are two first-class tickets to Nepal. I look at them and then at her.

When we started dating, we spent a lot of time talking and getting to know each other. I told her about my brother's wish to trek the Himalayas when he was a teen. I told her I wanted to do it in his honour. I hoped one day I could do it and raise some money for veterans of the British Forces.

"El..."

"Everything is set up. We leave in two months." I honestly don't know what to say. This is the kindest, most thoughtful thing anyone has ever done. "Is it okay?" she asks, and I get that my silence is causing her to panic.

"I love you, Ellie Bishop." Dropping the envelope on the bar, I reach for her beautiful face and draw her in. I pour all my love into that kiss until we're interrupted by Toni breezing in, as per usual.

"Oh, fuck, don't tell me you're doing it again."

"No, T." Ellie laughs. "I just gave Robin her birthday present."

"Which one?"

"The Nepal one."

"That's a good one. Happy birthday, Rob." Toni gives me a hard kiss on the lips and then starts making mimosas. I like Toni a lot. "So what time does everything get started?"

"Shit," Ellie hisses, scrambling off the bar stool. "We need to get ready. Guests will be arriving soon." Did I mention that it's an *all-day* birthday party?

Ellie turns into a tyrant as she wrangles me back upstairs and into the shower. She won't even come in with me because she says we haven't got time for sex. I remind her I'm the birthday girl, but she won't budge. Reluctantly, I shower and dress alone.

There are a few people grabbing mimosas when I get downstairs. My parents are due to arrive any minute. I hear Toni squeal when she sees my mum. They bonded over hunky men on the new reality show they're both obsessed with.

"There you are, honey," my mum coos when she finally stops hugging Toni. I roll my eyes but embrace her hard. I've missed her and Dad.

"Good flight?"

"It was first class all the way. I got champagne." I laugh at her excitement. My dad strolls over and cocoons me in his arms. He has become more tactile recently. It's a little odd, but I'm trying to embrace it.

That's how I spend the next few hours. Greeting and hugging people. By the time midnight rolls around, I am buggered. I've never talked or laughed so much in my life. A few of the guests are staying in the house, so once I've said my goodbyes to the people leaving, I try in vain to sneak away. I really want my bed.

My efforts are thwarted by my oh-so-sexy girl-friend. "Not so fast, love," she whispers in my ear. "I still have one more present for you." *Please be sex!* I'm suddenly very awake. Ellie takes my hand and guides me to the section of the house I've been banned from. "Close your eyes."

My heart is thrumming with anticipation. I hear a door creak open, and she pulls me gently forward. The door is closed behind me, and I wait. And wait. Has she left? "Okay, open them."

The first reaction is to laugh out loud. Ellie has had a complete section of the house transformed into a fake rainforest. "Ellie," I laugh, "what is this?"

"Well, honey. I thought we could revisit the place we met, without having to actually go back. I know some awful shit happened there, but at the same time, the best thing in the world happened, too. It's where I found you and fell in love. So to celebrate that part of our adventure together, I figured we could do a little reminiscing."

"Anything in particular you want to reminisce about?"

"There is one part." Ellie stalks towards me. She leans in, her mouth is a hair's breadth from my ear. "I want you to fuck me like you did in that shack. I want us to come under the trees, listening to the birds." I should mention that, as well as the decoration, there are sounds playing around the room. Ellie has done an excellent job making everything look so realistic.

We may have had to put up with snakes, scorpions, and criminals. Ellie may have had to get over the fact that she laddered her favourite pair of tights, but at the end of the day, through all of that, we came away from the Amazon with the love of our lives. Nothing in the world will ever top that.

"Get strapped and fuck me against that tree," she commands.

I'm the luckiest woman alive.

About the Author

Alyson was born and raised in the heart of England. She moved to Paris in 2015 when she met her wife. Together they moved to the west of France where they now live with their two dogs and pet bird.

Alyson discovered her love of writing in her mid thirties. Her debut book, *A Dance Towards Forever* was inspired by her wife and their very own love story. Alyson wrote *Diving Into Her* and *Always Emilie*, which added with her first book created *The French Connection* series. All Amazon Best Sellers.

You can follow Alyson on social media.

facebook.com/alysonrootauthor
Instagram: @alyson.root_author
Twitter: @alyson_root

If You Liked This Book...

Share a review with your friends or post a review on your favorite site like Amazon, Goodreads, Barnes and Noble, or anywhere you purchased the book. Or perhaps share a posting on your social media sites and help spread the word.

Join the Sapphire Newsletter and keep up with all your favorite authors.

Did we mention you get a free book for joining our team?

Other Sapphire Books From Sapphire Authors

Out of the Ashes - ISBN - 978-1-952270-84-0

When unusual seismic activity is detected on Mount St. Helens, volcanologist Nova "Cano" Kane, along with a team from the United States Geological Survey, is sent to investigate. The year is 1980, and there hasn't been a large-scale eruption on the mountain in over one hundred years.

Dr. Allison "Allie" Albright is a prominent professor at the University of Washington where the seismic activity is being tracked. As more scientists pour into Seattle, she braces for the possible return of Cano.

Neither Allie nor Cano has fully recovered from their breakup four years earlier. Both live with the pain and regret of how their relationship ended. Maybe it's best to leave it in the past and focus on the job at hand.

They must battle the limits of predictive science, the shortsightedness of bureaucracy, and the bias of the media, while fighting their complicated feelings for each other. As Mount St. Helens continues to churn, so too does their attraction.
Which will erupt first—the volcano or their feelings for each other?

The Serenity Nearby – ISBN – 978-1-952270-65-9

Veronica Hockmeier's relationship with her girlfriend/ PhD supervisor is on the rocks. A graduate student has died by suicide in her English Department. And her eating disorder has returned with a vengeance. All Veronica wants to do is get out of town for a weekend, and when her paper is accepted at an academic conference on Emily Dickinson, in Dickinson's hometown of Amherst, Massachusetts, Veronica takes this as a good sign.

On the way there, she is greeted with calamity after calamity: an accident on the road, a person from her past, and what appears to be the ghost of a graduate student in her hotel room. When a friendly hotel worker named Bo Wu shows her some kindness, Veronica can't help but fall for the tall woman with a winning smile—even if she does have a creepy collection of items dead patrons have left behind.

When Veronica's passport goes missing and another body turns up at the hotel, she becomes trapped in a nightmare she can't escape from—not without Bo's help.

Dusty Road Home – ISBN – 978-1-952270-72-7

Melanie Crenshaw has fallen off the proverbial map. Notoriously private on a good day, the world-famous mystery author has gone dark to avoid any public blowback or scandal from her latest failed relationship. Seeking quiet and solace, she retreats to her rural hometown, hoping isolation will be just the atmosphere she needs to finish her novel. But going back home is never as easy as it sounds, especially when a nosy reporter starts sniffing around.

Pulitzer-winning investigative journalist Pilar Stein

has seen people at their worst—and has the scars to prove it. After taking time off to heal from a particularly brutal assignment, she's back in the saddle and ready to reclaim her place among the elite of hard-hitting reporters. Unfortunately, her re-entry story—a profile on elusive author Melanie Crenshaw who has suddenly disappeared—seems to lack the teeth necessary to catapult her back to the top of her game.

Appearances are deceiving, of course, and Pilar soon discovers that what she deems a simple fluff piece might well lead to the scoop of a generation…just not the one she expected.

As Melanie fights to maintain her privacy while Pilar takes a backhoe to her past, the two women find themselves torn between their own professional convictions and their growing attraction to each other. And no matter which road they take, it's going to be a bumpy ride.

You Can't Outrun Your Roots – ISBN – 978-1-952270-82-6

What if instead of meeting someone new, you reconnected with someone from your past?

As Southern as fried chicken and peach cobbler, free spirit Gloria Robinson spent her lifetime building a successful permaculture farm on the tired dirt of former cotton fields in South Carolina. Now widowed, Gloria is certain she'll never find someone new, not in this town. She wouldn't even know how to try. Politically, she fears her years of effort for social justice are slipping backward. She's becoming weary, but she's digging in her heels.

Living in Washington D.C., perpetually single, party girl Anna May Walker floats through life disconnected from her roots in the South. Self-focused, she often ponders how she wronged Gloria in high school. When Anna May's father dies, she heads home to lure her mother to move near her in a retirement community.

Avoiding each other in a small town is impossible, particularly when Anna May's boss unwittingly assigns her to write a story about Gloria's farm. After decades apart, will the old sparks be enough to restart a fire between them?

First comes Marriage: Morgantown - Book One - ISBN - 978-1-952270- 80-2

Take one CEO, one pink-haired alien, a secret marriage, vengeful aliens, unexplained deaths, and a bitter sister out for revenge, and two women's lives will never be the same.

As CEO of MartinTech, Brynn Martin is at the top of her professional game. Her personal life is another matter, but she's not in a hurry to break her single status. All that changes on a Tuesday morning when a bombshell is dropped.

At sixteen, Micah Legon fled her abusive family and home world of Vubloxia. Now, at twenty-nine, she's content and settled in her life, running a cleanup business with her siblings. Then one morning, she gets a phone call that changes everything.

A chance encounter six years ago in Las Vegas at a "Meet an Alien" convention comes back to haunt both women. While Micah remembers the day with fondness, Brynn remembers nothing. After meeting again, both women come to an agreement. However, nothing is ever that simple.

Micah makes it her mission to break through Brynn's tough exterior. Brynn makes it her mission to keep Micah at arm's length. Nothing will stop either woman from getting what she wants. The trouble is convincing the other that her plan is the right one.